Kaiden's world has been utterly upended. The former alcoholic turned thrall is now a vampire . . . with undreamed of powers. How is this possible and what does it mean? Can he be mankind's hope to free them from their degrading servitude to their bloodsucking masters? Just what kind of vampire is he, and what are the limits of his abilities?

Kaiden's feelings for his hunter companion, Johann, have grown stronger. He knows Johann has feelings for him as well, and would gladly push their relationship to the next level. But Kaiden doesn't dare, afraid that once he tastes Johann's sweet, beckoning blood, he won't be able to stop himself until it's too late.

As Kaiden and Johann scour the countryside for vampires and for answers to Kaiden's questions, Kaiden is forced to come to some self-realizations which can either make him or break him. Is he any better than the vampiric overlords, or is he doomed to become just like them? Will the blood he needs to defeat them cause him to lose what little humanity he still possesses?

Vampire
Copyright © 2021 Ravon Silvius
ISBN: 978-1-4874-3263-8
Cover art by Martine Jardin

Published by eXtasy Books Inc or
Devine Destinies, an imprint of eXtasy Books Inc

Look for us online at:
www.eXtasybooks.com or www.devinedestinies.com

# Vampire
# Fallen Empire Trilogy Book 2


## By


## Ravon Silvius

# CHAPTER ONE

Wagon wheels creaked in the distance, the steady clopping of hooves growing closer.

My prey heard it too. The vampire stood in darkness. But to my eyes he was obvious — silhouetted in both the pale light of the waning moon and the reflected moonlight from the snow.

I licked my lips. This would be a good hunt. I was so tired of the foul-tasting blood of thralls. A few of the mindless bloodsuckers growled far in the distance, loud to my ears but probably inaudible to the human next to me.

Johann tilted his head, his brown eyes meeting mine. My hunger pulsed in time with his heart. His delicious scent — maleness and pine and soap — made my mouth water.

I gave him a nod and re-focused on the vampire. I could never have Johann's blood, no matter how good he smelled.

I had waited too long to eat. I should have drunk from the thralls we killed earlier, but I hated their taste. A vampire, though . . . I hadn't bitten one of those since Dimresh. A vampire's blood would be sweet, filling, *delicious*.

Almost like human.

I shifted, a movement so slight it didn't disturb the snow beneath us. The weather was so cold that ice would crunch beneath my feet if I wasn't careful. We would attack soon. I didn't have long to wait.

The usual sounds of a winter night were broken by the thralls growling again, louder this time, and then by the frenzied whinny of two horses. Johann tensed next to me, but his

1

heart beat steadily. He knew the plan. We both did.

The constant clop of hooves became a drumbeat on the dirt road, and wood creaked in accompaniment. "Whoa!" someone shouted, and reins snapped. The sounds grew louder, the wagon appearing around the bend, the dark forms of thralls leaping after it. Herding their prey to their master.

I licked my lips. My fangs grew long. I was *so* hungry.

My nostrils flared at the acrid scent of horse-sweat and animal fear that broke through the cold scent of ice and dormant trees. One of the horses bucked and reared in its traces. The driver screamed as the wagon rocked and began to tilt. Small objects fell. They rolled onto the snow.

The vampire made his move, moonlight flashing on silver hair. And I made mine.

"By my blood, bind him to the earth," I said under my breath. I leaped forward, faster than the thralls who were leaping for the blood of the horses. Faster than their vampire master who was moving to bite the wagon driver. Johann moved like molasses next to me as he raised his stakeshooter and aimed it at the thralls.

The vampire was old, with wrinkled skin and silver hair, but he had the same look as every other weak vampire without a true territory any greater than a mere patch of road to call their own. Hunger showed in his open mouth and bared fangs, but also nothingness. A calculating gaze fixated on the human wagon driver that let me know he thought of the defenseless man as nothing more than food.

I wondered who had turned this vampire, and why. But I only wondered for a moment as I slammed into him just as he turned to face me.

Snow and chips of ice sprayed beneath my feet as I skidded to a stop, my sharp fingernails digging into the vampire's arms. Behind us the first twang of Johann's stakeshooter rang out, and a thrall growled as it died.

The vampire's eyes went wide, just like the eyes of the first vampire I had ever attacked, the whites showing even whiter with the reflection of the moonlight off the snow. "What are you doing here?" he asked, even as sharp claws raked against the skin of my wrists, the vampire struggling to free himself.

I held on tighter, ignoring the lines of pain he was drawing along my arms. Behind me, the thralls growled as one. Two more shots rang out.

"Where is the other vampire den?" I growled, ignoring his question. Johann had said to talk to him, to question him. There were two vampires hunting here in the area. But hunger roared in my ears and my nostrils flared. This vampire didn't smell like rot, like thrall. He would taste *so* good.

He curled his upper lip. "Adrian's den is farther. But this is *my* patch of road. You can't—"

I sank my fangs into him before he could finish his threat. Blood filled my mouth. His two remaining thralls screamed. They were silenced by Johann's shots while I drank.

I probably could have questioned him more. No, I *definitely* should have. But his blood tasted so good, and I was so hungry. I drank greedily. The scratches on my arms healed within seconds as the vampire in my grip weakened. The taste wasn't as good as I had hoped—this vampire was no Dimresh. And he wasn't human. His blood didn't hold a candle to the taste of Johann's blood in my dreams and fantasies. But his fluid went down smooth, the taste filling and rich. So much better than thrall.

There was no sign of his death, no heart to stop beating. He simply ceased struggling.

We weren't alive, after all.

I enjoyed the luscious taste, the vampire blood like fine wine, until a dry voice shot through my enjoyment. "That seems like a treat for you, Kaiden," Johann said from behind me.

I lifted my head from the vampire's neck and licked the last of the blood off my lips. I had drained him nearly dry, and I had not wasted a single drop. "Vampire blood tastes good," I said. "Better than thrall." Thrall's blood was disgusting, flavored with rot and filth, but I wouldn't tell Johann that. Thrall's blood was all I had. This was the first vampire we'd seen since Dimresh.

I blinked as I swallowed the last mouthful. We had made a plan. And now our only source of information was . . . well, I supposed dead was the best word for him.

"Did he give any good information?" Johann asked. "Where's the other vampire den?"

With my stomach full, I doubly regretted not trying to question the vampire more. "It's owned by Adrian," I said. "And he said that this patch of the road was his."

"That's all?"

"That's all. I . . . bit him after that."

Johann frowned, and my stomach twisted. I was supposed to be a hunter, like Johann. I could resist human blood — I had to. But when faced with something available that would taste good, after weeks of what would be the equivalent of drinking rotten milk for a human . . .

I didn't want to be like them. "I'll do better next time," I promised. "My . . . my hunger got the better of me."

"That's all right." Johann sighed, and I hated that he sounded disappointed. Disappointed in me. "At least we know the name now. Adrian. I suppose he must claim some other stretch of road near here. We can scout farther ahead and look for any signs of his territory. Next time, though, maybe fill up on thrall first, eh Kaiden?"

I stifled a grimace. The thought of drinking more foul thrall blood after tasting that was sickening.

No. At least it would keep me alive. Well, as alive as I could be. And I couldn't bite a human. I couldn't risk turning anyone into a thrall. What I had been.

"Don't worry. You're doing well, Kaiden," Johann said. I didn't believe him.

"Oy!" A voice called out of the dark. "Hunters!" The wagon driver leaped down from his seat as he grabbed the reins in an effort to calm the still jittery horses. "Was that it? I led you right to where the others said they saw the bodies. You got him, right?"

"C'mon, Kaiden," Johann said. I frowned, but followed. This was part of my training too, interacting with the people I helped protect from vampires like me. I had lived in a village once, though I barely remembered my life from before. But to be normal, to fit in among humans . . . that would be nice. Matilda would approve. At least, I thought she would. I wished I remembered more of her lessons . . . more of her.

The man smiled when he saw Johann, and clapped him on the shoulder as he drew near. The driver was old, a wiry man with white hair. "Name's Aldrose," he said. "Peter said you two could handle vampires, but when he told me the plan I thought he was crazy. Drive up an unused dangerous part of the merchant road going right past a known vampire den? Alone? My friends always said I was too impulsive for my own good. But there you were." His gaze slipped past Johann, to me. "Is that him?"

"That's him," Johann said. He turned, his gaze urging me on. I felt like a sullen child all of a sudden, someone urged to be social even though they were shy. "Greetings," I said, making sure my fangs didn't show.

"I'll be," Aldrose said. "You're really one of them?"

"If you mean a vampire, yes," I said. "If you mean like them in other ways . . . then no."

"I've seen a lot on the road," Aldrose said, "but never vampires hunting other vampires. 'Cept for the legend outta Brusque, but that's just a story."

5

Johann perked up. "You've heard the legend of Lucien?"
Excitement kindled in my chest too.

"Only bits and pieces from the road. We merchants talk a lot. But yes. It's the old story of the vampire who killed his maker and then died of hunger instead of eating humans."

I frowned. He hadn't died from hunger, at least not in the version Johann told.

"Well, Kaiden here isn't going to die from hunger." As Johann spoke, small tufts of snow began to fall. "He's helping us keep the roads safe."

I stepped forward and couldn't help but notice the tension that entered the merchant as I did so, the way his heart rate picked up. "Do you travel to Penthorn?" I asked.

"Not usually," he said. "Too dangerous there. Not even I'm crazy enough to enter a village where a vampire eats someone every week."

"Not anymore," I said. "Dimresh—that was the vampire there—is dead. You should bring goods there. People will need them."

"I imagine so," Aldrose said, nodding. "Tell you what, Mr. Vampire. After the meet tomorrow afternoon, I'll head back and bring goods to Penthorn. I, uh, can't exactly reward you much any other way." He gave a nervous laugh.

"The meet?" Johann said. "Up in Three Oaks? Isn't it early in the year for that?"

"You know it, aye?" Aldrose said. "Didn't think a hunter would. But it's not in Three Oaks any longer. We change the location and date every year for the past ten years or so. To avoid too many people in one place, tempting the bloodsuckers. Uh, no offense to those present."

I just shrugged. I couldn't blame them. Frankly, the very idea of a lot of humans in one place was appetizing, and I hated that the thought had crossed my mind. I didn't even need human blood. I just . . . wanted it. That would be better than even vampire.

"I wasn't always a hunter," Johann said. "I grew up on the road for part of the year, and I have fond memories of the annual meet." A hint of wistfulness entered his voice, which made me wonder. I knew he missed his parents, but it had never occurred to me that he might miss that sort of life.

"A merchant's son, were you?" Aldrose said. He bowed his head. "Lose your parents to vampires?"

"To Lasren," Johann said, and his jaw clenched on the name. I hated the name too, and hated how the very mention caused Johann to tense in a combination of anger and sadness.

"Not surprising, that one," Aldrose said. "Latest news is he's claimed two cities now, Brusque and Wollasque, which was his original. His territory has no thralls, or so I hear. He has vampire guards instead. Not a place anyone sane enters at night. I mean these days, of course," he added hurriedly. "Back in the day, it was safe. I still remember the lights." He sighed, his breath pluming in the cold air. "Then again, even the stretches of road this far from the capital are becoming less and less safe."

"We intend to change that," Johann said. "Little by little."

"I'll leave you to that. But for now, we'd best get back. I agreed to be the bait for your little vampire killing expedition, but I'd like to be safe back at the barracks the rest of the night so I can leave in the morning." He patted one of the horses on the nose. "I'm sure these two would like to rest too after that scare."

Johann nodded, then met my eyes. "What do you think, Kaiden? I know it wouldn't mean much hunting for you."

"It's fine." I didn't need rest, but humans did. And Johann was still recovering from his injuries from fighting Dimresh. He hid it well, but his breaths were pulled shallow at times.

"Excellent!" Aldrose moved to his wagon and fished a bottle out of the bag on the seat. "Just a little thanks for protecting me. Here." He tossed the bottle to Johann, and even through the stopper and the cold of the winter air, I could smell the fiery brandy. "From the brewery near Hopton. Best they have. Enjoy it when we get back for a job well done."

Johann nodded to Aldrose. "Thank you."

Once I would have enjoyed it too. But that old pleasure, and once obsession, was lost to me now. Even with the way drink had once ruled and ruined my life, I would gladly take that over the hunger for blood.

Aldrose hopped back into his wagon, slapping the reins to get the horses moving. Johann joined him.

I stepped out of the way of the horses, their nostrils flared and ears pinned back as they passed me.

"C'mon, Kaiden," Johann said. "Keep alert. I know you got your meal, but we can keep an eye out for any thralls on the way back."

I nodded. I didn't need to worry about the past and what I had lost. I had a future here. Once I proved to myself I could kill vampires effectively, and control my hunger, I could do better. Protecting merchants and roads was one thing. But I wanted more, for both me and Johann.

# Chapter Two

I stayed downwind of the tempting scent of Johann, ranging ahead of the wagon. Their conversation carried over the usual cracking branches and faint rustles of the winter forest.

"So tell me about . . . him," Aldrose said. "He's really a vampire?"

"He is," Johann said. "He was a thrall, once."

"A thrall? You mean those mindless ones, the ones with the black eyes?"

"Yes. Well . . . not quite. He was always different. Special."

My jaw tensed. I both loved and hated it when he spoke that way.

Aldrose must have picked up on it too. "You sound oddly fond of a vampire. For a hunter, I mean."

When Johann cleared his throat, I could picture in my mind's eye the pleasing image of his blush. "I mean special as in intelligent. And now he's one of our best hunters. I mean, he has to be—no one else can compare. It would have taken an entire squad of us to kill that vampire without him. Now we can patrol farther and protect longer stretches of the road. And we can bring the fight to the vampires like that one— whatever his name was. Kaiden is still learning, but I trust he'll get even better with time."

Fondness entered his voice again. He was bad at hiding it. I paused from my spot behind the trunk of a leaf-bare tree, longing for what I couldn't have.

I had been a vampire for a month now. A thrall two months before that. For the vampires who had lived centuries, I must seem little more than a foolish amateur. Today I had killed one, in a fit of hunger, when I should have questioned him. The only way I could learn was by talking to one, wasn't it? Hunters didn't know much about vampires, only how to kill them.

Part of me ached to learn if I could ever be with Johann. I knew I couldn't have him. He knew he couldn't have me. The risk was too great. Even full as I was, the thought of being with Johann, of being in his embrace and pinning him to the forest floor . . . was so tempting. But the fantasy, or dream, whatever form it took, always ended the same way.

Me with my fangs in his neck.

I curled my fingernails, sharpened to claws, around the bark of the tree I stood next to, leaving a gouge. I couldn't have Johann. I didn't need him that way. Dreams were all those would ever be. I had the blood of thralls, and sometimes vampires. That would have to be enough. If I bit a human . . . I didn't know if I could ever go back.

Our path back to the barracks was clear, no hungry thralls accosting the wagon on the way. The sounds and scents of humanity met my senses, and some of my tension left me. The barracks were growing familiar.

"Kaiden," Johann said as I jogged next to the wagon, re-joining them just before we would pass by the first sentry. "See anything else out there?"

"Nothing," I said.

"I hope that means the road is safer at night," Aldrose said. "Thanks to you guys, of course."

"Johann?" a voice called out. I knew it well.

"Susana," Johann called back. "Returning from the mission. One more vampire down."

"Good. Just an uncountable number more to go." She emerged from her position in the brush, glaring at me as I passed by. "Including you, eventually," she said, low enough that only I would hear her. I didn't respond.

Some in the barracks still hated me, and always would. I understood it. Sometimes I didn't fully understand why Johann had taken the chance on me.

Voices emanated from the barracks, along with the snorts and rustles of horses and the cackling of chickens kept near the mess hall. The three towers of the barracks loomed out of the darkness, hidden by enormous trees until we drew closer. Aldrose whistled in appreciation.

"Like a beacon of hope," he said.

"I'll take you back to the guest rooms," Johann said. "Kaiden, you can stick with me if you'd like to help give our report. I'm sure Lesalie would be interested in what you have to say."

"I'd rather stay out of sight," I said, like I did every night. "Rest well, Johann." He sighed, but nodded.

I did know better than to move like a vampire once I was in the barracks. Hunters were human and slow, but they were trained to spot the quick movements of things like me. I walked slowly toward the center tower, through the heavy doors and down hallways studded with wooden spikes. A fortress to defend against vampires. Johann had explained most of the traps, but I was still careful.

"Is that — oh." A man carrying a tray of food flattened himself against a wall as I passed by. I could feel the weight of his wide-eyed stare on my back, and his tray rattled when he ran. The hunters were used to me, at least some of them. But the cooks and maids, the people who helped the hunters fulfill their tasks, certainly weren't. They knew what I looked like, and they knew to avoid me.

I didn't see anyone else as I climbed the stairs, and I dashed up the last two flights to the small room I now used. It was next to Johann's, and likely had once been a storage room — I couldn't get the scent of mold out of it, and it was so small the bed and bookcase took up most of the space. But it was mine.

A mouse darted away when I opened the door. I let it go. Even if I killed it and risked staining the floor, there would always be more. They were kind of like thralls in that way.

An uncountable number, as Susana had said.

I splashed my hands in the small basin of water I had left next to the bed. The basins were meant to transport water for drinking, but without a need to drink I used it to wash off the residual blood and muck of the night. As a thrall I'd been filthy almost all the time, but now it felt important to be clean. I found myself often smelling nicer than most of the other hunters. Maybe because of Johann.

I had to put him out of my mind. I craved him, with both my mind and body, the way I had once craved strong drink. But I could control it. I had to.

Instead I turned to the books. They had once lined the shelves of Dimresh's castle, but now they were mine. Old books from the fallen realm of Leoren, an empire that had been rife with magic from the goddess Laurel. Now it was magic that only vampires like me could access, and it was twisted and wrong.

I closed my eyes, feeling the magic well inside me, faint but there. I'd found nothing that talked about that part of it. According to the books, priests calling for magic had begged it from Laurel, asking for her aid in prayers and even songs. But I didn't need to ask anyone. Some spells I could use with a thought. For others, I called upon the magic in my own blood.

"By my blood," I whispered. I felt the answer rush through my veins, the magic in my stolen blood ready to respond. Instinct mixed with words I'd learned from ancient volumes, ready to leave my lips. Most prayers were about protection, healing. The magic in me wanted to harm, to dominate.

I relaxed, willing the magic away, not finishing the spell. I didn't want to take a risk. There was no telling what harm I might do.

I wished I had talked to that vampire. There was so much I didn't understand. In some ways, I still felt like a stupid thrall.

I went back to the books, reading where I'd left off the night before. A section on prayers for healing.

After I'd gotten past the section on cleansing water to use in treating wounds, a soft rap came at the door. I couldn't help the smile that flashed over my lips. I knew Johann's knock.

"Come in," I said.

The door swung open. "Reading in the dark, Kaiden?" Johann said with a laugh.

"It's not dark for me." I stood, but before I could pick up the candle on the bookcase to light it on the lantern Johann held, he reached out a hand and put it on my mine. My skin prickled. "Wait," he said. "Let's try and use your magic, remember? See if you can figure out the right words."

Johann was always wanting to try new things. "All right." He breathed a bit better tonight—each night he was improved, his broken ribs mending. I glanced once more over the chapter on healing before flipping the pages back to where Johann had studied them last night. Spells of light.

"Hmm . . . that one." Johann pointed. His scent surrounded me, my body responding to his warmth as it did every night.

"By my blood . . ." The spell was supposed to be "Holy Laurel, grant us warming flame." But I knew that wouldn't work, the magic in me would turn the words. The spell would come out wrong, too strong. I shook my head. "I can't. It's wrong."

"How do you know?" Johann sat on the bed, facing me where I sat on the floor. "I know you've explained it to me, how the magic feels in you. What would happen if you just said the words correctly?"

"Nothing at all. By my blood, grant us warming flame." The candle didn't move. "I know that's wrong. But what feels right" — my body thrummed — "would benefit me and no one else."

"How do you know?"

"I guess . . . I don't know for sure. I just don't want to accidentally —"

"You're afraid." Johann crossed his arms. "Like you're afraid of giving reports, of being seen by others, and talking to them." I frowned. "Like you're afraid of hurting me, even though I've told you that you don't need to be."

"Don't bring that up now," I warned.

"I'm not." Johann sighed. "I just mean that you need to start . . . living a little, you know?" He gave a small laugh, which ended in a slight huff of pain. "But seriously. You're not a thrall anymore, Kaiden. Stop acting like one."

I tightened my lips, hiding the fangs that threatened to show along with my frustration. "I'm *not* a thrall," I said. "And that's precisely why I have to be careful!" I hadn't meant to shout. I clenched my jaw. "You should be careful too."

"Oh?" Johann raised an eyebrow. His complete inability to be cowed by me was both impressive and annoying. "Careful of what? What are you going to do to me, vampire?"

The way he said it sent an unwelcome pleasurable shiver up my spine. I didn't hide my fangs when I spoke this time. "I don't know how my magic works," I said. "I don't know what it will do. I'm stronger than you, faster than you, and I could hurt you by accident. If I lose control —"

"You won't," he said.

"If I *do*, you would suffer a fate worse than death," I finished. "Or even if I don't and I make a mistake with some sort of spell . . . Remember what happened when we fought Dimresh?"

"You mean when you saved my life?" Johann leaned back against the wall with a grin.

"When I hypnotized you into obeying me no matter what and couldn't break the spell!" I snapped.

"Kaiden, think," Johann said. "Do you want to hurt me?"

Fantasies replayed in my mind, of my fangs sinking into his neck as I found blissful release. "No," I said.

"Do you want to control me, dominate me? Set fire to this room, blow up the barracks with your magic?"

"Of course not."

"You were the one who told me magic was about intent. So unless you doubt your intent, what reason do you have to doubt your magic? You're a vampire. We don't know much about they want, but we do know they are masters of their own domains. You can master your magic, but you won't do it by being afraid of it." Johann pointed to the candle. "Now come on, Kaiden. Show me what you can do. Be the curious vampire who tries new things, like the thrall you were before. The one I . . . admire."

Admire. He wouldn't say love.

Of course he wouldn't. I had told him not to tempt me, and he wouldn't . . . at least not on purpose.

I closed my eyes, feeling the magic as part of my being, mixed with the blood I'd stolen from thralls and vampires alike along with my own. "By my blood," I said. I wanted to impress Johann. I wanted to be a master of my own fate, to understand what I was and what I could do.

I hated to admit it, but Johann was right. I couldn't keep being afraid. At least not of this.

"Use fire to . . ." Instinctively words flashed through my mind, recited only in my thoughts. *Burn my enemies. Choke my enemies. Drive foes away.* But I had no enemies here.

"Split the night," I said aloud.

The candle flame leapt up in a gout of fire. Johann leaned

back as the blaze filled the room. No. This wasn't what I wanted.

Then the fire fell, the heat melting most of the wax. Now a half-melted candle burned on my nightstand. The light filled the room, dancing off Johann's brown hair, making his eyes twinkle.

He broke into a grin. "See, Kaiden?"

"That could have been dangerous."

"But it wasn't," Johann pointed out. "And even if it was, it's better to take a small risk and learn then never know, isn't it?" He sat up on the bed, the dancing candlelight casting playful shadows on his muscular, leather-clad thighs. I swallowed. I was learning as a vampire that lust was almost as dangerous, and pervasive, as hunger.

"C'mon, Kaiden," Johann said. I met his eyes. "Now that you feel like being brave, how about you come with me to give the report to Lesalie?"

I blinked. "You haven't yet?"

"It's best you get used to giving reports if you want to keep hunting with us. And she's been asking about you. It's not smart to avoid the master hunter."

"I suppose I'll go with you then."

Johann grinned. But as a vampire, I couldn't quite bring myself to actually agree with him about that last part.

# CHAPTER THREE

"So, vampire. Kaiden," Lesalie quickly amended when Johann winced at the word vampire. "You killed your second vampire tonight, did you?" The master hunter was enthroned in her chair, a portrait of a handsome man behind her — who he was, I had no idea. A stakeshooter graced her hip, and three long stakes rested by her chair, leaning against the wood. I guessed that this had nothing to do with me, she was always this prepared.

"I did." I swallowed, remembering the taste. "The plan we set up worked well." Johann gave me the slightest of encouraging nods. "The thralls were taken care of by Johann, while I attacked the vampire. He was . . . not difficult to kill."

"And you drank his blood?" Lesalie asked, her eyes narrowing.

"I did." I swallowed again, my mouth watering at the memory. He had been so much better than thrall.

"And before that, what did you learn? Johann had told me the night before you would question him, learn more about what vampires want. Did you?"

"I . . . I did learn the name of the one who turned him. Adrian."

"Not surprising. Vampires seem to prey all over stretches of the merchant's road. Or any other well-traveled road, for that matter. People are fools to travel at night, but most have no choice." She sighed. "What else?"

"That was all." Her eyes narrowed. "I drank his blood after that." That had been so much easier to admit to Johann.

17

"You killed instead of questioned him? Why?" Her expression spiked old, faded memories of life, people staring at me with thinly-veiled disgust.

I wasn't a disgusting thrall any longer, but she certainly made me feel like one. I fought not to curl my lip, my anger bubbling. I wasn't truly angry at her. I hated my hunger, the hunger I should be able to control, but which always kept coming back because all I had was filthy thrall to drink when I should be . . .

No, I couldn't even entertain that thought.

Johann kept silent, his hands clasped behind his back, his posture relaxed. He wasn't judging me. I shouldn't care. Lesalie probably wasn't judging me either.

*Disgusting,* the faces in the memories said. *Just avoid him.*

No. I had to make it better. "I'll find Adrian," I blurted. Lesalie's eyebrows raised. "If another vampire is also hunting on the road, he should be killed too, right?"

"Well," Johann said with a chuckle. "We are hunters."

"Do you ask to hunt another vampire because you want to kill it or because you want its blood?" Lesalie asked.

I blinked. She had read my hunger well. I wondered how she'd risen to her rank, and what experiences she had with vampires. "I do enjoy their blood," I admitted. "But that's not the primary reason I want to kill it. I want . . ." I trailed off, working hard to not sound foolish. "I want to prove I'm a good hunter. That I *can* help, even more than most."

Johann smiled. Lesalie just nodded.

"What are your goals, Kaiden?" she asked. "You're a vampire, hunting your own kind. Many hunters have dreams." She leaned back in her chair, gesturing to the portrait above her. "The founder of the fifth order—that's ours, called fifth because it was founded in the beginning of what would have been the fifth century of the fallen Leoren empire's existence. His goal was to return the empire to its former glory. My goal is to ensure safety for the humans who remain. Johann's, I believe yours was . . ."

"To make it safe for merchants and their families to travel again," Johann replied. "If we secure the roads, we can help start trade and exchange of information, and maybe find a way to bring back some of the dying cities and towns."

Their dreams were good ones. But they also seemed impossible. Lesalie met my eyes, and I could read her silent agreement. She knew how insurmountable the hunters' task was. But that didn't stop people from dreaming.

My goals. My dream. What did I want?

What did vampires want?

"I want to know what vampires are," I said. "What makes them . . . us . . . what we are."

And maybe, finally, figure out what I was. As a thrall, I had been unique. As a vampire . . . was I still? Was I like Lucien had been . . . or was I something else?

Lesalie nodded again. "A good goal," she said. "And one you're well-suited for." She grabbed a pen off her desk, scribbled a quick note in tight script that reminded me of the handwriting in the books in my room. "Johann and Kaiden, tomorrow night go to the merchant's road and find this vampire, this Adrian. Question him further this time. We want to learn about vampires, what they want. What true vampires want, not strange ones like you." She gave me a knowing nod. "Don't rely on a decoy, either. The only information we have on this one is what you told me. I'm trusting you."

I swallowed. "Thank you."

"Return when you've learned all you can. Send a message if the plan changes. I expect you to have information when you do come back." She looked up from her notes, staring at me. "Keep your hunger in check, Kaiden. Don't let it sabotage your goals."

"I won't."

"Take the rest of this night, and tomorrow" — her eyes bored into Johann with her last words — "to prepare. I want you to learn as much as you can to help our cause."

Johann nodded, and we both left the Master Hunter's room. Another assignment to find and kill a vampire.

"It's a step up from the patrols we've been doing," I said. "I'll do better this time." I wanted to prove myself, especially to Johann.

"This one will be harder," Johann said. "Last time Aldrose had the information and the location. This time it'll be an old-fashioned hunt." He grinned at me. "You've never done one of those yet."

We passed through a well-lit hallway. Chattering voices, along with the aroma of cooking meat, wound from the door that would lead to the mess hall. "What should I expect?"

"How about we head into the mess and I get a snack and I'll tell you about it?" Johann said.

I swallowed. He may just be hungry, but I was sure he was still testing me, trying to get me used to other people. Dragging me out of my seclusion. I wanted to refuse, but my words replayed in my mind. *I'll do better this time.* This was part of that, part of being a hunter.

I couldn't be afraid.

"All right," I said. Johann practically beamed as he turned down the hall, the voices and laughter from the other side of the door growing deafening to my sensitive ears when he opened it.

I'd never been in the mess hall before when it was this full. A warm room, the stone walls lined with wooden shelving and the center taken up with long wooden tables, filled my vision. Firelight from torches in rows along the walls cast a cheery red glow over the group of five people who sat at one table. The thick scent of savory meat and the tang of wine filled my nose.

This felt so familiar.

*I sat in the back of the room, smiling at a man who had bought me a drink. My clothes were tattered, my hands grimy, but he didn't seem to mind. Laughter rang from the corner where a few people threw dice. At the bar, James met my eyes. He gave me a shake of the head. He didn't like seeing me there every night. Every night I looked a little worse, I knew. A little sicker, a little more desperate.*

"Kaiden?" Johann said. I blinked. The chatter in the room had quieted, no longer matched the raucous alehouse in my flash of memory. The men and women at the table in the center of the room weren't boisterous drunks throwing dice but hunters who glared at me with narrowed eyes. A few I knew—Susana, the woman who had shot me upon seeing me for the first time back when I was a thrall, and Peter, a man who even now reeked of fear at seeing me.

"Sit down, Kaiden," Johann said. He motioned with a nod to a nearby table then slid onto the wooden bench next to me. I no longer faced the table of hunters, but I could still feel their gaze on my back.

"Why did you bring me here?" I asked under my breath.

Before he could answer, a man in plain woolen clothes came up to our table. He smelled strongly of meat and wine scented his breath when he asked "Stew tonight, Johann? And . . ." He raised an eyebrow at me.

He didn't know what I was. Most of the servants had heard of me, I was sure. But I supposed not all of them knew what I looked like. And unless I showed my fangs, he wouldn't know. Drunk as he was, he likely hadn't picked up on the tension in the room.

He may be foolish, for a servant. But I was suddenly grateful.

"Nothing for me, thanks," I said. I was so glad I could hide my fangs.

21

He tilted his head then shrugged. "Bring out a few cups!" Johann called as he left.

"Do the servants usually drink on the job?" I asked. He'd disappeared through a door into what was likely the kitchen, given the strong scent of meat and vegetables that poured into the room when the door swung open.

"He's drunk?" Johann turned to look, then laughed. "That's Ryan. He does favor a drink or two, but he still does his work, so I guess it doesn't matter." Johann turned his smile on me, that radiant look I loved. "But you see? You're not some monster, Kaiden. You *can* fit in and be with people."

I wanted to believe him. The hunters at the next table spoke in hushed tones, but it was still easy for me to pick up on their conversation.

"They think I'm *scouting them out*," I said, repeating their words in low tones to Johann without letting on I was listening. "They're afraid I could lose control at any moment."

Johann's jaw tightened, but he didn't let his smile falter. He turned on the bench instead so that he faced them. "Susana!" His voice reverberated in the small room. "You remember Kaiden, don't you?"

Johann was always one to take risks, even social ones. I swallowed hard and faced the others in the room. One gnawed hungrily at meat on a bone. Susana set down her cup, the liquor inside overlapping the rim.

*"C'mon, Kaiden!" A hand slapped my back heartily, making me laugh as some of my drink sloshed onto the floor. "You can drink that merchant under the table, can't you? Show him!"*

I blinked the memory away. That was a different life. And I couldn't have drink anymore to loosen my inhibitions. I needed to hold onto every ounce of control I possessed.

"Of course we know him," Susana said, her voice flat. The man next to her put down the bone he was gnawing on. "Why are you here, *vampire*?" The single word pounded in my ears. The rest of the noise in the room seemed to quiet, as though the word itself held some sort of power. "You don't eat or drink. Not what we do."

"Johann invited me," I said. I clung to the assurance the statement brought me. Johann had invited me. As long as that was true, I belonged.

"We did well on the assignment tonight," Johann said, barreling through the awkwardness. "The merchant mentioned you, Peter. He said you said we could handle vampires, and we certainly did." Johann leaned back, resting one ankle on his knee. His heart beating faster than usual gave away that he wasn't totally relaxed, but the others wouldn't be able to hear that. "We have another assignment to hunt down a vampire tomorrow night, so I figured we'd take it easy tonight while we can." He reached into one of the many pockets of his heavy coat and produced the bottle of brandy the merchant had given him. He waggled the bottle in the air. "Anyone else care to join us? This'll be loads better than the slop-wine we usually get around here."

"Is that . . . from that place near Hopton?" The man who'd been gnawing on a steak bone leaned forward. "That's good stuff." He gave me one last appraising look, then huffed. "Fine, I'll join you. It's been a while since I had brandy from my old hometown."

"I figured you would like it, Reni," Johann said. Johann glanced at me, gave me a quick wink.

"You're all fools," Susana hissed as both Reni and Peter stood. "Especially you, Johann." She raised her voice as the door to the kitchen swung open, Ryan holding a steaming platter. "You know what vampires can do!" She pointed right at me, and I clenched my jaw. "Bad enough when he was a thrall. But he's a vampire now. He could be manipulating you. *Hyp*notizing you! That's what they do! You think you'll be safe, but then they leave you drained in a ditch for your family and friends to find!"

The room fell silent. Ryan had paused by the door, the food in his hand sizzling on the platter. Susana's heart beat hard.

I couldn't be angry. I wondered who she had found drained. Everyone here had a history with things like me, and none of it was good.

"A vampire killed people I cared about too," I said. "I didn't choose this."

"He wants to help," Johann added. "He—"

Susana slapped him hard across the face. I leapt up, snarling, my fangs pricking my lower lip. How dare she touch him!

Susana drew back, her gaze flicking between me and Johann. Johann put a hand to his face, his neck flushed in anger. Around us, Reni, Peter, and the other man had tensed. None of them carried weapons. I was the biggest threat here, and I closed my mouth. Control. I needed control.

"I'm not hypnotized, Susana," Johann said. "There was no reason for that. And it wouldn't have worked even if I was."

"Slap *me* if you want to be violent next time," I said, a growl I couldn't hold back entering my voice. "Johann didn't do anything to you."

"And what would you do to me if I did?" Susana asked. "What would make you dangerous, vampire? Anger? Hunger? Or is it just when you decide you want to take something? Johann has his stories and ideas, but I have mine too. Vampires are cursed to have no humanity." She spat the last. "You may have killed Dimresh, but you'll be just like him. As soon as you show what you really are, I'll be ready."

She left the room, followed by two of the men. I had a feeling the hunters would begin wearing their weapons even in the mess hall from now on.

"Sit down, Kaiden," Johann said. He rubbed his face. "C'mon. You too, Peter, Reni."

I sat first, barely aware of the other two men when they took their places across from Johann and me. Ryan approached with Johann's meal, but this time he practically threw it at him and ran away.

Vampires are cursed to have no humanity.

*The curse will kill you like the rest.* The memory of Dimresh's words echoed, too close to the words Susana had used.

"A toast," Johann said. I looked up, the scent of brandy stinging my nostrils. A pleasant, familiar smell, one I found strangely soothing. "To those brave enough to eat with Kaiden the harmless vampire." He lifted the uncapped bottle and poured it into Peter and Reni's glasses with exaggerated movements, likely hoping to ease the tension in the air.

*This will ease your pain,* someone had told me once. And at one time it had.

"None for you?" Reni asked. Johann set the bottle down with a thud but then tightened his hand around it, raising an eyebrow.

All I could imagine drinking was blood. My faint memories of life told me I would have jumped at the chance to drink such rare brandy, but now the smell, if pleasing, was like the smell of flowers. Nice, but not something I wanted to eat. That aspect of pleasure, the knowledge of taste and mouthfeel and the burning in my throat and stomach, had been leeched from it. I didn't know how my body would react if I drank, but a deep tightening and a roll of nausea told me not to try.

"No," I said. "No thank you."

Johann eyed an empty glass then shrugged. "So, Reni, Peter," he said. "We'll be heading farther out on the merchant road, likely to be gone for a few nights. Let's relax while we can, eh?"

# CHAPTER FOUR

I stayed while they drank and chatted, the conversation tapering off, growing less restrained over time as they finished the bottle. But there was nothing much I could contribute.

I enjoyed watching Johann, though. He was in his element here, a hunter talking with fellow hunters. He smiled and laughed, gesturing to emphasize a story about an amusing merchant he'd met. He told the story of our attack on the vampire, leaving out my loss of control, making the entire thing sound like an adventure.

"One less vampire that could stumble upon the barracks." Reni crossed his arms. "Thankfully that doesn't happen often."

"You'll be going farther out next time, right?" Peter asked. He was surprisingly soft-spoken. "Do you know precisely how far?"

Johann looked to me, and Peter's gaze flicked to mine and then back down.

"I'm not sure," I said. "Until we find the vampire we're hunting and kill him."

"And take out thralls on the way," Johann added with a nod.

"Once you get to the stretch of road between here and the edge of Brusque, there really aren't many thralls," Reni said. He drew his hands along an invisible line, likely what the road itself would look like on a map. "They don't hunt in such large numbers. Maybe the vampire there keeps them under control."

"Doubtful," I said. "They likely don't hunt on the less-traveled stretches of road because there isn't much prey so far from cities and towns."

Peter blanched, and I slammed my mouth shut.

"So . . . we're the prey?" Reni asked, his voice suddenly dangerous. "Is that how you still see humans like us?"

I ground my back teeth together. I was so tired of this. "No. But if you want to hunt something, you should learn to think like them."

Reni bristled. "Thralls don't think!" His breath smelled like brandy.

"They think about as much as animals do," I said, keeping my voice calm. "And even an animal knows where . . . *humans* do and don't live."

Johann put his hand on my shoulder, his warmth easing tension I hadn't known was there. "Relax, Reni," he said as he gave my shoulder a gentle squeeze. "We're all on the same side here."

"Are you?" Reni asked me. "Vampires never killed each other before you. You're just fine with killing your own kind?"

"Of course," I said, but something about his words didn't sit well for the rest of the night.


Johann stumbled on the stairs. He chuckled when he steadied himself on one of the jutting wooden spikes on the walls. "Sun will be up soon," he said, his voice slurring just slightly. "I'll have to put you to bed."

I followed behind him. It hadn't been long since he'd injured himself fighting Dimresh, and the last thing I wanted was for him to further bash up his bruised ribs by falling down the stairs. So close, his body was incredibly warm, and the tinge of brandy mixed well his own natural, masculine scent.

"I'll be fine, Kaiden," Johann said, regaining his balance and heading up the stairs. "That brandy was strong, but it's not enough to put me under. It's too bad you couldn't enjoy it. Those in Penthorn said you used to love drink."

My stomach twisted. Memories of dark alleys, of lying on the floor of the bar while people stared down at me, flashed through my mind's eye. "I loved it a bit too much, I think."

"Right." Johann's smile faded, and he paused by his door. "Sorry."

"It's in the past," I said. "Another life."

"You've had three of those now," Johann said. He gave me a sage nod when I tilted my head. "Human, thrall, and vampire. I wonder what your next one will be."

*What is your goal?* Lesalie's words echoed, but Johann's idle musing mingled with it. A desire pulsed in my body as my heart once had, the true answer to her question. Something more than knowledge of what I was, and what vampires were.

I didn't want to be something else, something new. I wanted what I once had. I wanted to be human again.

But I couldn't let myself think that. The idea was foolish and impossible. And even if I could be human, that would only make me prey like everyone else here. I was valuable because of what I was.

"Kaiden?" Johann asked. I blinked. "Do you want to come in?" He raised an eyebrow at me. "You seem disant. *Distant,* I mean." He shook his head at his own lapse. "And we don't have long before sunup. We can make some plans for our journey."

He smelled delicious, like pine and alcohol. His blood would combine the loves of both my lives. I really shouldn't. "All right," I said.

His tipsy smile warmed me even as it magnified my

doubts. His room was familiar—I'd seen it often enough as a thrall. Small wooden carvings sat on his bookshelves, framing his books. The spines were faded and worn but not dusty like the ones in my room, the old books from Dimresh's castle that carried the scent of decay no matter how many times I tried to brush it away. His bed was unmade, straw poking from the pallet, and the wool sheets clumped at the end. When he lit a candle, the firelight shone over bits of glass on his work-bench—shards of a broken solar flare.

"I haven't had a chance to clean up since we got back." Johann sat down in the chair by his workbench and peered at the glass. "Although I guess with all the traveling we'll be do-ing it doesn't really matter."

"That's common, isn't it?" I asked. I didn't know where to sit—the only space was on his bed, and I didn't feel comfort-able with that. I stood by the window instead, the moonlight shining through the glass. "Traveling all the time, I mean."

"Of course. It's the life of a hunter. One mission becomes another, and you spend half your life on the road. Kind of like merchants, too." Johann leaned back in his chair so far that the front legs left the ground. His position didn't look very safe, but he balanced somehow. "Although we sleep during the day and work at night, just like vampires." He gave me a grin. "Thinking like our prey."

I smiled back. "Naturally."

He let his chair drop, the front legs hitting the wood with a thump. "Sorry about dragging you into a meal with every-one." He stood, letting his heavy hunter's coat fall from his shoulders. The weight dragged down his shirt, baring his shoulder and a bit of his chest before he took off the coat com-pletely and hung it on a chair. "I just wanted you to get used to people a little more—and have them get used to you, too."

Without the coat he was so . . . I licked my lips. "I under-stand," I said. "And I do think it's a good idea."

"What you said to Lesalie," Johann said, and I blinked. I had to keep up with his changes in topic. "About discovering what vampires are. That's a good idea. I've always been curious too, even though a lot of others say it's a waste of time." He joined me by the window. His warmth and nearness singed my skin.

"Why would it be a waste?"

"Because of things . . . Because of what people like Susana think. Vampires are a lost cause, have no souls, no morality, no . . . humanity." He gestured upward with his fingers, as though a vampire's humanity went up in a puff of dust. "But approaching them that way hasn't gotten us any closer to regaining what we've lost, has it?"

"No." The moonlight shone on him, illuminating the plane of his jaw and the curve of his neck. Strength as well as vulnerability — that was Johann. I put my hands on the windowsill, focusing on the potentially painful wood instead of the man in front of me. "I think . . ." I didn't know how to finish the sentence.

"You have humanity, Kaiden." Johann's tone caused me to meet his eyes. "And it does make me wonder if other vampires do too."

"Would that . . . make you feel differently about killing them?" I asked.

Johann sighed. He rolled his shoulders and looked back out at the night. "I don't think so. I don't know what would. Vampires have killed a lot of people, Kaiden. If they do have humanity, that's almost worse. Sometimes I feel a bit inhuman myself — staying up all night, sleeping the best parts of the day away, and training to kill. But we do what we have to."

I nodded. I thought of Alistair, a man whose name I knew only because his fiancé had shouted it out before he bit her. Two more from my old hometown, lost to Dimresh. "All over

30

the world towns like Penthorn are being preyed on," I said. "The work you do is necessary."

"The work *we* do," Johann said. He put his arm over my shoulder. "I'm so glad to have you around. We hunters usually work alone—I've hunted by myself for years on missions like the one to Penthorn. But having you, a dedicated partner, is nice, even if it's only because most others think you should be watched."

My muscles tightened beneath his touch, even as I relished his warmth and closeness. "You were . . . lonely?"

"Of course." Johann sighed, the rush of his breath washing over me. "Sure, there are other hunters. Peter, Thomas. But there aren't many of us. We can't afford to double up on most hunts, and too often parts of the merchant road go unprotected. Every hunter must be completely self-reliant. We meet people in the towns and villages we visit, of course, but even then we sleep during most of the day, so that we can be awake and alert when we have to be. In winter, like now, we rarely see the sun." He gave me a wry grin. "The longest night of the year is coming. That's hard on us humans."

"I'm sorry."

"It's not your fault." He was stroking my back, his hand moving in pleasing circles that eased the tension there. He was just drunk, I told myself, just tipsy. But my jaw still clenched, my fangs sharp in my mouth. "Like I said, I have you now. You may be a bit uptight, but that's okay."

If I was uptight, it was because I had to be. I met his eyes . . . his warm, dark eyes that smoldered with life and promise. He looked at me the way he did in my fantasies, both vulnerable and strong and so, so willing. So hot . . . so delicious.

*No.* I couldn't do this, I couldn't let this happen. I dug sharp fingernails into the wood of the sill. Splinters fell to the floor as others dug into my skin. I hissed, the pain snuffing out the unwanted desire. Splinters were hardly stakes, but wood *hurt.*

"Oh," Johann said. He grabbed my hand. "Don't know your own strength, Kaiden?"

"I'm fine," I said. "I should go. It will heal once I . . ." I trailed off. Johann was fast as he took two splinters that had cut into my fingers out of my skin, my vampiric healing taking effect as soon as they were gone. There wasn't even any blood, and the pain vanished with their removal.

"I figured you would be more careful around wood," Johann said with a smirk. He put my hand to his lips and kissed my knuckles, as though I were a blushing maiden. "All better."

His lips were so soft. I didn't move, my body frozen. I wished he would kiss my hand again. I wished he would kiss *me*. The moon shone on his face, making him glow, the light almost but not quite reaching me.

He smiled, and I smiled back. I was like a mirror to his vitality, his life, only experiencing things through him. If I didn't have him, I was sure I would have lost what little humanity I had by now. No. I would still be just a thrall.

I couldn't kiss him, couldn't be with him the way I wanted to in my fantasies. He must have seen it in my face.

He let my hand go, and I grieved the loss. "We can't have more?" Johann asked, half a question and half a statement.

Uncertainty warred with sudden tension. We hadn't spoken about that since Penthorn, and now the issue of our relationship, our closeness, was staring me in the face.

I should have left the room earlier, or maybe just not have gone into his room at all. But . . .

"I like being here with you," I said. "Just . . . like this." He gave me a small smile. "But . . . I can't have more. Not . . . not yet."

"If not now, then when?" Johann asked. "Ever?"

I grit my teeth, my body surging with what I wasn't sure was lust or frustration or both. "I don't know."

"Can you explain your feelings to me?" Johann asked. "You're not a thrall anymore. There's no risk of you losing control and biting me." His words hammered at me. He didn't understand the hunger, couldn't understand it. "I can tell you feel for me, Kaiden, with the way you look at me. And I want to give you time to get used to living among humans, and to being a vampire, and . . . damn, I'm likely too drunk for this. I shouldn't have said anything. But I'd like to know." He huffed a breath. "I have stronger feelings for you than just pure admiration. And I know they're real, not stupid vampire magic like Susana says. I felt this way for you as a thrall, and it's only gotten stronger." His gaze bored into mine. "I haven't changed, Kaiden. You have. So please, tell me if there's a possibility or not."

He was so beautiful. It would be so easy to take him right then, to push him down and kiss him, to feel him move beneath my touch and then to take what I wanted. He would tremble beneath my hands and his blood would flow through my fangs, sweeter and richer than the brandy he had tonight.

"I do you want you," I said. I had to speak to keep myself from moving, from making my fantasy reality. "But I want your blood too." He nodded, his mouth flat, as though this was something he'd expected. "I can feel pleasure without blood. I . . . dream of you. But if I was with you, I don't know if I could resist the urge."

"Then let's wait." I could tell from the way he spoke that this was difficult for him too. "Let's fulfill your dream and learn more about vampires. Once we both learn more about you, perhaps we can figure out a way to be together. I'm not going to give up on you before we've barely begun."

I nodded. I hoped that wasn't just the alcohol talking. "Rest well, Johann," I said. My fangs made the words thick.

"You rest well too, Kaiden." He was bad at masking the longing in his voice. "Sweet dreams."

# CHAPTER FIVE

The next night was cold. Johann's breath plumed as he packed the wagon. I caught the scent of hardtack and grain in the wrapped bundles he stowed in the back, heard water slosh.

"And a pillow for you." He tossed it into the light-proof space in the wagon. "I know you say you never need anything, but I always thought vampires liked comfort."

"Maybe ones like Dimresh. I'm used to discomfort." I shifted in place, my muscles tense. The night was beautiful, and so cold that the usual scurrying mice and flitting bats weren't out in large numbers. The quiet would make hunting very easy.

But I had to wait. Humans were so slow.

Finally, though, Johann was ready. He patted the wagon seat next to him. The horse flicked its ears back and stamped when I leapt into place. Johann laughed.

"Try not to give Mint a heart attack, all right?" The horse, who I presumed was Mint, put her ears back, but she began trotting without any further problems.

Johann took a deep breath, then winced when a chill breeze blew.

"Are you well?" I asked. His heart beat strong, at least.

"Just a bit cold. And a bit hungover." He gave a rueful laugh, rubbing his head. "At least if we find any thralls, well, there's your breakfast."

The thought of thrall blood gave me a strange sort of nauseous hunger, especially after the treat from the night before.

But I had to drink that—I couldn't fail like that again. "I'll take care of them," I said. "But don't rely on me. You have to hunt well too." I eyed him, judging how fit he was to fight if it came to that.

"Don't worry. No one's fault but mine, and it won't affect our hunt. Besides, the headache always recedes in an hour or so, and we won't get to where we expect to find the vampire for at least that long."

"You must be uncomfortable, though." I knew I'd been hungover many times in life, but the few memories I did have were of my time at night. Memories of mornings, of the sun beating down on me when I woke, had faded. I supposed vampires didn't have memories of the sun.

"I'm a hunter. I'm used to discomfort." He grinned at me.

The path away from the barracks was familiar. We passed beneath dead-looking trees. The faint glow of the moon through a layer of clouds sent beams of light through skeletal branches. The wagon wheels crunched over brittle twigs and remnants of fallen leaves.

"Not cold at all, eh Kaiden?" Johann pulled his cloak tighter over his shoulders. "We'll be getting more snow to-night."

I tilted my head. "How do you know?"

He tapped his nose. "Just a sense I have. I've traveled enough to know when the air gets this crisp and yet heavy-feeling at the same time, we're going to get snow. Surprised you can't sense it."

Cold, unmoving air to me always meant the absence of scents, livings things busy hiding from the poor environment. "I don't sense it," I said. "But I believe you."

Sure enough, as Mint trotted onward and the lines of dis-comfort vanished from Johann's brow over time, the clouds covering the moon thickened. The night grew darker, and a sharp scent that reminded me both of dust and briskness heralded the arrival of flakes of snow.

"Knew it," Johann said. "Some of the old books say priests of Laurel could predict the weather. I wonder if you can?"

"I wouldn't have the first clue how," I admitted.

"Not curious to try?" Johann asked. "You could see if this will be just flurries or maybe something more. That seems a safe enough thing to attempt."

Safe. Was a vampire's magic ever safe? But I couldn't think of any way a simple prediction spell could go wrong.

"Give it a try," Johann urged. "You need to stop being afraid of what you can do."

I closed my eyes, sensing little but the already familiar scents of the wood of the wagon, Johann's tempting closeness, and the sweat and hay smell of the horse in front of us. Pinpricks of cold met my skin.

How would I predict the weather? Could I?

"Use whatever words come to you with those vampire instincts of yours," Johann added.

"By my blood," I said. I opened my eyes, my vision sharpening. "Show me what my land will be like."

The words came out dull, hollow, and two things happened at once. One, cold whiteness filled my vision, my mind suddenly stretched in a thousand different directions. And two, hunger twisted in my stomach, making me double over and my fangs lengthen. My blood burned in a way I was beginning to learn meant my magic was working, but it burned too hot.

I didn't know what I'd done, or if it had even worked. But I knew with certainty that the spell was too much. There was always a risk!

"Kaiden?" Johann dropped the reins. A warm hand met my shoulder. A hand and wrist full of delicious, filling blood.

I lifted my head. Johann blinked, his heart rate picking up slightly. *No.* I had to control myself. I *had* to!

"That didn't work." I grit my teeth together. My fangs pricked my lower lip. "That . . . that spell was too much for me."

"Are you all right?" Johann asked. "You look . . ." He trailed off. My fingernails had sharpened to claws, my fangs long in my mouth. I knew what he meant.

I was hungry.

But I had to control it. I didn't *need* blood, I just wanted it. And I didn't want Johann's blood. I couldn't.

Whatever drove vampires was magic. And using too much caused me to crave blood. "If they could cast such spells, priests of Laurel must have had a lot of magical ability," I said.

"Are you hurt?"

"No." I willed my claws back to normal, blinking against my craving for blood, longing for a way to repair whatever magical reserve made me what I was. "Just . . . drained. I'd rather not try again."

"That's all right." Johann blinked snowflakes off of his eyelashes, melting water dripping down his neck. I licked my lips. "I suppose that's one spell we don't really need, anyway."

"Right." I wished I hadn't tried. I wasn't like Johann. I didn't like taking risks.

And right now, being near him while so hungry, so drained, was a risk.

"I'm going to hunt," I said. "Stay safe."

"Always," he said. "You too, Kaiden. Hurry back."

His smile sent heat burning through me. I leapt off the wagon into the snow by the side of the road. I wouldn't go far — Johann and the wagon would likely be a beacon for any nearby thralls — but being away from him could give me the chance to scent them on my own and spare him the trouble. And spare myself the frustration that had been building since our talk last night.

My dreams had been too sweet.

I retreated from thoughts of Johann beneath me, my fangs in his neck. I focused on the scents around me, hard to track with the blowing, crisp snow. Something loped nearby. I turned, but it was only a scrawny wolf. Probably trying to decide if the horse was worth going after. One growl from me scared it off. We needed Mint.

The moon rose to its highest point before I spotted my own prey. The thrall was male and weak. All thralls were weak to me now, but this one clearly hadn't fed in a while. Winter was hard hunting, even for thralls.

I didn't even wait for him to scent the oncoming wagon. My leap took me to his throat so fast my feet barely touched the piling snow before my fangs were in his neck.

The blood was sticky and rotten in my mouth. I fought to swallow it without gagging. This was nothing like the vampire's blood from the night before. No, after that treat, thrall blood was even worse than it had been before, thick and laced with the scents of rot and mold.

But this was all I had. I drank deep then let the wretched creature fall as I wiped the back of my mouth with my hand. I gagged again at the foul stench, and used snow instead to clean the rest.

With the blood came the return of my magic, something I was learning to appreciate. That was a certainty, a control, over myself and my strength. I didn't need spells. I just appreciated the power. Even the snowy night seemed lighter and the moon more visible as a faint glow behind the thick clouds. Not a big change, not like the strength from drinking vampire blood, but there.

The night was so beautiful. I wished Johann could see it the same way I did.

The faint light of his lantern appeared in the distance, along with the sound of Mint's plodding hooves. I could still hear

Johann's heart when I listened, a steady, vital thumping. I retraced my steps, heading back toward the wagon, watching him silhouetted in the lantern's glow.

Snowflakes drifted over him, a few melting in his short brown hair and on his skin. His jaw was set, his gaze fixed on the road in front of him. His cloak pulled tight over his broad shoulders, the end of it draped teasingly over his slim hips and muscular thighs.

I licked my lips and then grit my teeth. I had fed. But blood didn't do anything for this sort of hunger. My body surged with Johann's heartbeat.

I couldn't do this. I was watching him, spying on him, the way a hunter would. I couldn't have him. I had told him that last night.

But I could show my feelings for him in other ways. And the best way would be to get the information I wanted. I could fulfill our mission.

"Kaiden," Johann said when I approached again. "Find any food?" He smiled at me, his face lighting up the way it always did when he saw me, his eyes widening, and his heart beating just a bit faster.

Always tempting me. I didn't trust myself to get close, not yet.

"I'm going to scout farther," I said. "Keep being safe."

I ran ahead as he frowned in confusion, his "be safe too, Kaiden" fading into the distance as I picked up speed.

If I had done my job correctly the night before and gotten information from the other vampire, I would know where to go. Instead, I had to search blind. But at least focusing on that would keep me from thinking about Johann.

I kept my senses alert, the world filling my perceptions as I ran. The whirling snow and cold air made scents harder to find. Silence was punctuated intermittently by the rustles of mice moving slowly in tunnels beneath almost completely frozen ground. An owl passed by on wings that were near silent, but it too must not have heard anything, because it kept on going.

I darted between both sides of the road as I ran farther ahead, noting crushed leaves and faded wagon tracks in the snow. Other merchants had passed by not too long ago, but there were none here now. And there certainly weren't any signs of another vampire.

Of course, that was assuming I knew what to look for.

I stopped for a moment, perched on the branches of a tree. I was hunting a vampire, but the first thing any hunter, animal or human alike, needed was to know their prey. And I knew nothing about mine.

Because I had bit the vampire I *should* have questioned. I'd squandered the chance to gain information because I couldn't control myself. And that lack of control just proved that I could never have what I wanted—

My fangs pricked my lower lip, and I tried to relax. There was no sense in thinking that way. I just had to keep searching.

I closed my eyes. *Think logically.* We'd found the vampire last night because we knew where to look, and because we had reports from other traveling merchants. All I had to go on now was a name.

I ground my teeth. What did vampires want? What had my master wanted before I killed him? And what had the vampire I had eaten the night before wanted?

That was the problem. I didn't know. I growled low in frustration, leaping down from the tree. I closed my eyes, Johann's words and his constant pressure echoing in my mind.

"Don't be afraid of your magic," he always said. Using it tonight had been dangerous. But with the thrall's blood, I felt renewed. And if it happened again, I could just find another.

I wanted to do better. I wanted to make Johann proud.

Thinking back over the books I'd taken from Dimresh's castle in Penthorn, the words formed in my mind. Spells and magic of the old empire, now to be used only by vampires like me. Once these had been entreaties to the goddess Laurel by priests. Now . . .

"By my blood . . . guide me to what I will take," I said. Johann's advice was right. I was beginning to learn the forms the magic took, how it felt when a spell worked and my vampire instincts led me to the right words. Sometimes I wondered if I truly needed words. My body thrummed, my own blood burning slightly with a power I still didn't fully understand.

In the distance, a man screamed, so far away a human never would have heard it.

I raced after the sound, no longer caring about being silent. The magic had worked, and I knew what I would find.

In a mere few minutes I'd covered several miles and sent leaves skittering over snow when I stopped. Even as I did, a dark form darted at me.

"Adrian." What I meant to be a question came out as a snarl.

His long claws raked at my face before he leaped back at the sound of his name. His black hair was long and unkempt, his arms and legs bony. He looked young, though I doubted he truly was.

"Who are you?" he growled.

Part of me wished Johann were here. He would know better what to ask, what to say. But the wagon would be too slow. Humans were too slow. And I didn't want Johann hurt.

"Well?" He tilted his head, greasy hair falling to the side. "You don't look like a lord. Speak or get out of my territory."

Speak. I had wanted to find him. This was our mission — my mission. I had to question him, to learn about vampires.

About myself.

"I need help." I immediately wished I hadn't phrased my need like that. But it was too late to take my words back.

His eyes widened slightly, then narrowed. He leaned forward, nostrils flaring. "You smell like humans. But not human blood. And . . . ." He leaned back, upper lip curling. His body tensed. "Who turned you?"

"The one who turned me was killed," I said, speaking carefully. My mind seized on the question. Maybe that was important information, some sort of etiquette. "Who turned you?"

He blinked, some of the tension leaving his shoulders. "Lasren," he hissed, the name like a splash of Johann's burning herbal water. "Lasren chose me. He taught me."

Lasren.

The name of the vampire who had killed Johann's family.

# Chapter Six

"Tell me about Lasren," I demanded. The sound of the name forced me to focus, the memories of my failure and my frustration from before, and even my own goals, fading in the light of something important to Johann. "He claimed two cities. Why?"

"Because he could," Adrian said as though that were the most obvious thing in the world. He shifted his weight, sliding a bare foot over the snow. "Why aren't you leaving? We all share the blood. I've claimed this territory. You being here is pointless. Leave now."

Never. Not when I had him here to answer my questions not only about what it meant to be a vampire, but about Lasren. This was the breakthrough Johann wanted.

"I have questions," I said, and his eyebrow went up. "The vampire who turned me was . . . killed by hunters. I know very little about . . . myself." Lying should be easy, but his sharp eyes scanned me as I spoke, and I doubted he believed what I said.

"You're certainly stupid," he said. But at least he didn't attack me. Or worse, run away. "Your sire was killed and you weren't? How?"

I was missing something here that I should know. "I was . . . too far away."

"You're lying," he said. Fangs flashed from his lips. "But I do believe you know almost nothing about vampires."

"So . . . tell me," I said, and I'm sure my eagerness showed in my voice. "Tell me about us. About Lasren."

"How much of the blood were you given?" he asked.

"I . . ." *My fangs sank into his neck, draining him dry.* "I don't know."

"The more blood the sire shares, the more powerful you are," he said. "The sire determines that. No vampire can be more powerful than their sire, and thus they can't kill him or another vampire. We share the blood, and killing another is like killing ourselves. You'll know if you try it." His glare was still dangerous, but not the look of prey, I realized — more the look of someone annoyed that someone else had wandered into their home.

I swallowed hard. *No vampire can kill another.* I could still taste the blood of the one from last night. He was lying to me, or he was wrong.

Or I was even more different than I had thought.

"So can thralls . . . kill vampires?" I asked.

He laughed, his voice creaky and strange. He must have been turned young, not quite fully adult. "They don't share the blood, so I suppose they could. But they're stupid creatures, and completely controlled by those who make them until they get human blood and become totally mindless. I wouldn't worry." His fangs flashed. "You must be weak, to be afraid of little thralls."

At least his laughing at me meant he didn't see me as a threat.

"I . . . I don't quite know what I can do now. Or what I should do," I said.

"You do what you like," he snapped with a roll of his eyes. His gesture was strangely familiar, an old memory flashing through my brain that I couldn't pin down. "Claim what you want. Drink the blood of those you want. Turn others to serve you. It's not difficult."

Drink the blood of those you want. Like Johann. No. That couldn't be what I wanted. "How do you know what to claim?" I asked. "Who to turn or drink?"

"Find your own space," he said. He tilted his head when I clearly didn't understand. "Find somewhere where there are humans and no other vampires. Kill thralls in your territory if you need to." So vampires did kill thralls, at least ones that weren't their own. "All humans are ours to claim and feed from."

My fangs showed, and he frowned. "All humans are ours?"

"They're food," he said. "My master called them subjects. They belong to us. Any who travel in the territory you claim are yours. And this is mine." He emphasized the word. "So any who enter here are *mine.*"

Johann would be traveling through here soon enough. And he was *not* this scrawny vampire's prey. My nails sharpened to claws, and I struggled to think through a haze of anger. Emotions this strong were still new to me after months of being an emotionless thrall. Johann was mine. But he wasn't. I couldn't have him. So why was this vampire's claim that he would be his so frustrating?

*Focus.* I could deal with anger the way I dealt with hunger. This vampire was full of information, information I had to make sense of.

Territory and blood. Is that all vampires wanted? Or just lowly vampires like this one and the one I had fed from tonight? Adrian was bedraggled and thin, likely not changed much from the teenager he had been in life. A victim of Lasren, as Johann could have been when his family was killed.

I had to ask the right questions. "Why don't you take Lasren's territory?" I asked. "Take it for yourself instead of just this road."

He blinked, his foot slipping on the snow. "Are you crazy?" he spat. "Did you not understand what I said before?

That's impossible."

Because vampires couldn't kill other vampires. But he was wrong. "Lasren lied to you," I said. "Or you're lying to me."

His eyes narrowed. His dead heart didn't beat, but a smell like ash met my nose, like the remnants of a long-burned fire. Magic. Then he leapt at me.

I was fast, but so was he. This wasn't like before, when I had taken the vampire by surprise. Fangs scored my arm. Long, sharp nails raked at my chest. I snapped back at him, swinging a fist out to punch, but he leapt back before I could connect. Blood dripped from my chest, even as the wounds began to heal. I narrowed my eyes. How dare he. I hunted vampires, ate them. Anger swept through me. I would kill him, and I would prove he was wrong.

"Vampires don't kill other vampires." Somehow his voice came from behind me. "Your sire should have taught you that. You should know that, *feel* that. We all share the blood and the binding. You shouldn't be able to kill me. But you . . ." And then his voice wavered, a hint of the scared teenager coming through. "What did you do to Malcolm?"

I wondered if the magic he'd used had meant to bring him here. A vampire he had turned, a request for help to drive me off. I swallowed, caution making me pause instead of leap toward his voice. Malcolm. That might be the one whose blood I'd drunk last night. "I killed him," I said. "I told you you were wrong."

"Why?" His voice wavered.

*Why. A young man dying alone. A teenager, barely out of boyhood, with ragged clothes, his face streaked with tears. A young man, dying, his mother asking why.*

I blinked away the memory, one from another life. But it burst my anger like a bubble.

Adrian was a vampire. But vampires weren't thralls. I knew that, but now it felt true in a way it hadn't before. Vampires had emotions too. I certainly did.

I couldn't feel bad for a vampire. They killed humans. If Johann came past here, Adrian would kill him. I clenched my fist at the thought.

But Adrian had emotions. He was like me. And they had been human too, once. Adrian had, before Lasren had turned him.

Nothing was ever simple.

"Why wouldn't I?" I turned, trying to catch his scent on the breeze. "He killed humans. You kill humans." Leaves rustled, but I didn't turn. No vampire, or even thrall, would be that sloppy. "I won't let you."

"Are you some kind of fool?" His voice seemed to come from two different places at once. "We can eat nothing else."

"You can eat thralls," I said.

"And how are thralls made, fool?" he shot back. "Eating the dregs of another vampire's meal doesn't make you any different."

I grit my teeth together, my fangs lengthening and poking my gums. He wasn't wrong. "Then maybe I'll drink you," I growled.

"Try it," he said. His voice wavered behind his words. His fear, just like his sadness before, gave me pause.

"You talk a lot about making me leave your territory, but where are you?" I called out. "Are you really a slave to what Lasren says, or are you just a coward?"

"You don't understand at all, do you?" Adrian appeared next to me out of the darkness. Claws raked at my face. I stumbled back, blood dripping down my neck. Something hit the back of my head, and lights like the burning sun flashed behind my eyes.

My teeth grit together, my nails sharpening to claws and my fangs pricking my lip. This time when he misted to hit me, I lashed out too. His cry split the night, fading as he jumped away from my second swipe.

"By my blood," I said. "Bind this brat to the earth!"

It took me a moment to find him again. The spell worked on him just as it had on Dimresh when I was a thrall. Now he jumped normally when I spotted him, no more misting into nothingness. I snarled and leapt.

My claws latched onto his arm. In response he bit my shoulder, his fangs sharp and vicious. I held on through the pain, hunger growing as my own blood and energy poured out of me.

I couldn't resist and bit down hard into his neck, taking mouthfuls of his blood.

He cried out again, a sound full of fear and pain.

I closed my eyes, and when I did I saw Lesalie's face, looking at me with disgust. Then other faces, hazy from my time as a human, staring down at me in alleys and on bar floors, their lips curled up and their brows drawn, eyes narrowed.

I clenched my jaw and let him go, , wasted blood spurting from his neck. He fell back, paler even than before. But alive.

"You're disgusting," he said. His expression mirrored the ones in my mind. "How could you . . ."

"You bit me first!" I growled.

"I wouldn't kill!" His voice was weak, his fangs long and sharp, and his fingernails claws. I had weakened him. I could *kill* him. I wanted to. The taste of his blood would be so much better than that of any thrall. "But you . . ." His eyes narrowed. "You won't kill me. You can't." He spoke as though he was trying to convince himself.

"Tell me how to find Lasren," I demanded. I felt strong when I spoke, his blood filling me with power. Magic thrummed, stronger than it had when I bit the thrall. Even the dark winter's night was somehow brighter, the snow glowing with the faint light of stars. "Where is he? How would I kill him?"

"You're insane," he said, his voice weak. "If I tell you, will you let me go?"

"I don't bargain with vampires," I snapped. "That is the one thing my master taught me."

"What do you think you are?" he said. His eyes drooped. He tensed, but didn't move. I could read the hunger in his eyes, in the set of his curled lips . . . hunger driven by his injuries.

Certainty settled in my mind. I would have to kill him. He was a vampire, but he would eat humans. Like Johann.

"Power means you got more of the blood," he said. "I see your master gave you much. More than me." One of his feet scraped the snow as he resettled his weight, preparing to run. "The path to Brusque is the territory of his vampires. He has given it to us. We give it to the ones we make. But Brusque and the humans in it are his."

"So is that all vampires want?" I asked. "Territory? Hunting grounds? Blood?"

"Isn't that what humans want?" he said with a sneer. "Land, farms, and cattle?"

I frowned. No. It was more than that. What had I wanted in life?

"Take my territory and he'll kill you," he said. His gaze flicked away and I knew he lied. "Lasren is powerful, alive since the fall. He'll protect his vampires."

I sneered. No vampire cared about the ones they turned. I knew that from my experience with Dimresh.

"Lasren doesn't care about you," I said. "Did you care about Malcolm?"

His teeth flashed. "You didn't kill him," he said. "You couldn't have!"

He truly believed what he was saying. Vampires were unable to kill other vampires. Except for me.

Was it because I had been a thrall? Why was I so different?

I blinked, and he was gone.

No. *No!*

I couldn't let myself be distracted. He was fast, but so was I, and I was full of his blood.

I fell into the instincts of the hunt, instincts that were sharper than they'd ever been. I had hunted thralls before, but they were slow and weak compared to vampires. I raced over fallen branches and over snow bank. Tree trunks whizzed past and the cold air bit at my skin and roared in my ears. Small traces of him dotted the landscape. A whiff of scent there, a footprint in the snow . . . a twig bent in the wake of his passing. Tiny signs that my senses picked up without my thinking about them.

I was faster, stronger. I had more of the blood. And soon I ran him down, his shape a blotch against the night sky when he darted around a tree.

And then my claws were in his arms.

"I'll give you the territory!" he shouted, shock in his voice. "Why are you —"

Instinct guided my fangs to his throat.

Power sang in my veins as I drank. A strange euphoria filled my body and mind. Like the first rush of energy and dizziness from good ale, a distant memory coming to mind.

The blood mattered. How much of the blood a vampire received from their master mattered. And by killing and drinking vampires . . . was I consuming more and more of the blood he'd talked about, more of the power?

Vampires couldn't kill vampires, but *I* could. I curled my claws into his frail arms. The winter air fizzed on my skin, the stars blazed overhead. I could be unstoppable. No one could oppose me!

A voice came on the breeze, a distant human voice. "Sales aren't worth the risk," someone said. "We shouldn't come so close to Brusque."

Merchants. Like Johann's family.

Johann.

I blinked, the blood suddenly tasteless, my stomach too full. The power was suddenly too much, excitement flowing over into dread.

I was a hunter, like Johann. I had to help the hunters learn about vampires, hunt them more effectively, and help humanity — help that which I wanted to be.

And I wanted to help Johann. The name burned on my lips. Lasren.

He had been turned by Lasren.

This was wrong. I was failing again. What had I been thinking?

Susana's angry words from the night before came rushing back to me. *Vampires are cursed to have no humanity.*

No. I couldn't be like that.

I ripped my fangs away from his neck. Adrian fell weakly onto the snow, blood still trickling. He turned his head, his dark eyes meeting mine.

"You see?" he spat, his fangs gleaming. His skin looked sallow, his hair brittle. "You can't kill me."

I licked the last of the blood from my lips. He didn't know how wrong he was, how close he'd come.

"What will you do if I leave you here?" I demanded.

He pushed himself to his feet, and I narrowed my eyes. Even half-drained, he could move with grace and power. Vampires were truly different than thralls, dangerous no matter what. "I will drink," he said. He tilted his head, and I knew he could hear the merchants nearby.

I grit my teeth. "You won't," I commanded. "You're coming with me."

# CHAPTER SEVEN

The moon had begun to sink by the time I caught Johann's scent. He hadn't gone far—half again as far as we had gone last night when we killed Malcolm.

It felt strange to know the dead vampire's name. A vampire I had killed.

Cool air bit my skin, the snow falling faster in small swirls. Behind me, Adrian followed. He'd given up trying to run after the first time I'd caught him. I didn't doubt he would run again. I had told him nothing, only to follow me. He was obviously learning I was far stronger than he was.

"Kaiden?" Johann called out. I paused, certain we had been silent so far. Of course, Johann was a hunter. Pride in his strength and skills made me smile.

"You want me to feed from him?" Adrian asked.

I snarled, the thought of him feeding from my Johann sending something dark and angry through me. "No!" I snapped my fangs on the word. "Johann," I called out. "We have a prisoner!" Branches snapped behind me. "I'll need your ropes!"

Adrian ran, just as I had predicted. And just like before, he didn't get far.

"You serve hunters?" he shrieked. His fangs snapped toward my neck when I grabbed his arms and wrenched them behind his back. "What are you?" He kicked at me, twisting in my grip.

A horse snorted, and then a crossbow twanged. A wooden stake shot through his leg, his voice cracking on his scream.

I should have brought hunter's tools too.

"Back away, Kaiden," Johann commanded, and I did just in time as the weighted net, bathed in burning herbal water, collapsed over Adrian.

He still struggled, screaming. I turned away from the sight, the hissing burning of the ropes on his skin. He was a vampire, a monster, a thing that would have fed from those merchants earlier or from Johann.

But I was a vampire too. And I knew from experience how much herbal water and stakes could hurt.

"Is this him?" Johann's breath huffed as he dismounted from Mint in an easy jump. The horse snorted and pawed at the snow. Her ears flattened and her eyes rolled at the sight of Adrian.

Adrian lunged against the ropes, snapping his fangs at Johann. In response, Johann fired another stake from his stakeshooter, this one digging into Adrian's skinny arm and pinning him to the ground.

I winced.

"So," Johann said. "Adrian, is it?" Johann's heart beat fast, but steadily. I wasn't sure if he was nervous or if it was just his usual caution.

"You bring me to a *human*?" Adrian hissed, his brown eyes boring into me. "You're not of the blood at all!"

Johann pointed the stakeshooter, this time at Adrian's heart. "Of the blood?" he asked. He stood confidently, shoulders square, the weapon never wavering. This was the hunter I had seen that first time, the commanding, powerful vampire killer he could be. "What do you mean by that?"

"I'll drink you, human," Adrian said. The soaked net dripped onto the ground, the beads of water freezing where they touched snow.

"Talk or die," Johann said. "I don't have all night."

Nor did we, I realized. The moon was low and large in the sky.

"He was turned by Lasren," I said. Adrian's eyes narrowed, his fangs bared.

The stakeshooter wavered, just slightly. Johan's finger twitched on the trigger. "I see." He breathed out once. "Tell me about yourself, Adrian. Tell me about Brusque."

Adrian shut his mouth, his fangs poking his chin.

"Talk!" I commanded.

"Or we could make things hurt more," Johann added. He took a flask from his pocket and popped the lid. The sharp scent of something herbal assailed my nose.

Adrian met my eyes. "You know *we're* supposed to keep *them* as pets, not the other way around. I can teach you what your sire didn't. Just let me drink this man and get my strength back. Let me use the skills I have, and I'll show you what you can truly do." His tone wheedled. He was appealing to me as a peer.

As though I would choose some vampire I had never met over Johann, who had saved my life. My unlife.

I didn't need this brat to show me anything. I drew up my strength, my magic. "By my blood," I said. "I command you to obey!" My magic flared, hunger filling me. That had been a mistake, but it was too late now. "Answer our questions!"

Adrian hissed, but he stopped struggling, the weighted, dripping net setting over his form.

"What do you want?" Johann asked. I wished this could be that easy.

"To get out of here!" Adrian snapped. "To drink you!"

Johann huffed. "Maybe that was the wrong question."

"Tell me when and how you were turned," I asked. "What was your life like before?"

"I was from Wollasque," Adrian answered. "Maybe . . . it's been a long time. Fifty years maybe? Likely more." He drove his fangs into his lip. Blood stained his chin as he spoke, but he kept talking. "I don't remember my life before I was turned. I think I was a . . . baker. An apprentice."

"Fifty years." Johann, whistled. "Before Lasren took Brusque."

Adrian glared at him and said nothing.

"Why are you here and not there?" Johann pressed.

"Wollasque grew dead." Strange way of putting it, but I knew what he meant. Eventually people would have fled, and prey would grow scarce. "We have to follow the prey. Lasren came to Brusque, and I came here. To hunt merchants, or take the dregs from Brusque when they run."

Johann's jaw tightened, his fingers moving over the stakeshooter's trigger. "How many more are on the road toward Brusque?"

"Only one, nearest to Lasren's territory." More blood dripped from his mouth, and I realized he'd bitten his tongue. "I don't know her name. Older than me, much more powerful. She has good hunting grounds. She keeps"—he spat blood—"some humans out of Brusque, and keeps other humans in."

"Why are you fighting so hard not to speak?" I asked.

"Why do you speak to prey like this when he should be your pet?" he snapped. "It's wrong. *We* are above them. The world belongs to *us*, and they are our prey."

"Is that what Lasren told you?" Johann asked.

Adrian's eyes flashed in the growing light. Dawn was coming. "Yes. But it's also what vampires know."

Johann moved his gaze to me. The hunger grew stronger, the magic burning in my blood fizzling out. At that moment Adrian leapt.

Adrian was fast, and I was faster. But neither of us were as fast as Johann's finger on the trigger.

The bolt took the vampire through the heart. His outstretched leap became a heavy fall onto the snow. His mouth was still open, the fangs obvious.

In the end, Adrian was just a corpse.

"Fifty years or more, eh?" Johann said. He touched Adrian . . . no, the body, with his boot. "He didn't look it. Can you still . . . drink him?"

My mouth twisted. "No. Not . . . not like that."

"I hope you got some more information before you brought him," Johann said. He sighed, stepping back from the corpse. "I knew it would be rough, but . . ."

"It's different," I said. "When they can talk and argue and . . . be afraid."

Johann put away his stakeshooter, moving over to put a hand on my shoulder. I leaned toward the touch. "He was afraid?" Johann asked.

"Afraid of me." Johann's hand was so warm on my skin. I hadn't realized how much the cold of the snowy night had seeped into me. "He talked a lot about blood."

Johann raised an eyebrow. "I'd imagine so."

"Not like that. He called it . . . the blood. What a vampire gives another to make them a vampire and not a thrall. How much you get determines how strong you are."

"That's good information." Johann grinned. "I knew this would be useful. Did he say anything else?"

"He said . . . vampires can't kill vampires. Something about this blood prevents it. We all have the same blood, so it's impossible."

Johann's grin faded. "So he was wrong."

"I . . . I guess so."

"Figures." Johann took his hand off my shoulder, breathing on it to get warmth back. "I suppose even vampires can have bad information. Especially weak ones like this."

I didn't think he was weak. Making him obey had been difficult. But I didn't protest.

"So we have something, which is better than nothing." Johann peered into the horizon. I had already noticed the purpling sky. "We wouldn't have been able to take him back anyway, and we certainly couldn't have let him go. Good work, Kaiden."

"Happy to help."

"Not quite as energetic as last night though, eh?" Johann put his hand out. I stared at it for a moment before taking it, relishing the warmth once again. "Not a fan of killing something that talks back?"

"I . . . .suppose not." Uncertainty twisted in my gut. "But they are monsters. I know that." They . . . as though I wasn't one of them.

"That's a good sign." Johann started to walk back toward the wagon where Mint huffed and stamped her hooves against the cold. I followed, my hand still in his. "It just means you haven't lost your humanity. Humans can be murderers too, and I'm sure constables feel just as bad about putting them to death."

"But humans don't see other humans as . . . prey." Adrian had bit his own tongue not to speak to Johann, as though even talking to a human was an insult.

"They see me as prey. I see them as monsters. Well, not all of them." He squeezed my hand. "But I suppose it's good to remember that we all came from the same place in the beginning. Created from Holy Laurel or just born out of nothing, depending on your belief, but all the same. Maybe that blood he talked about is some sort of infection. An organic or magical disease that makes them . . . different."

I frowned. I didn't feel diseased.

Although my back did start to burn, an itchy, uncomfortable sensation, as if to prove his theory. The sky was lightening further, and with it a certainty that I needed to get out of the looming sun, somewhere safe.

"Getting too light for you?" Johann asked.

"Yes." My body began to feel heavy, my eyelids drooping.

"I should rest."

"I'll keep you safe, just like you kept me safe," Johann said. He put another hand on my shoulder. But this time his warmth wasn't enough to combat the already existing burning that the sun promised. I let him touch me anyway, and help me into the small, cramped compartment in the wagon.

"Sleep well, Kaiden," Johann said.

"You too," I said. "I hope."

"The nights are long in winter," Johann said. "I'm as tired as you." He grinned, and then the hatch closed with a click, leaving me in darkness.

Strange to have so much power one moment, and at the first sign of the sun, to feel it drain away.

# CHAPTER EIGHT

Johann had been right about the nights being long—and on the flipside, the days being short. If I dreamed, I didn't remember it. And when I woke, it was once again to the peaceful whispers of the night.

I opened the latch that Johann had attached on the inside, blinking at the glow of the moon on the snow. More had fallen while I slept. Apparently not even the afternoon sun had been enough to melt the first layer.

A pile of blankets was bundled on the wagon, but Johann wasn't there. Wood cracked. Johann's footsteps crunched on snow, drifts of it up to his shins. He carried a thick branch of a tree.

"Seems like you always wake just as the sky gets full dark," Johann said. He yawned. "I timed that well."

"Tired?" I asked.

"The days are only about eight hours or so now—which coincidentally, is about as much sleep as I need. And it's hard to sleep when every other merchant or traveler is going by as fast as they can before night falls." He stretched out his arms and then his neck. "Plus the wagon isn't the most comfortable place to sleep."

I nodded. "The barracks will be more comfortable."

"About that," Johann said. He carried the branch over the wagon, pulling a knife out of his pocket. He began to shave it down—making a stake, I realized. "I don't think we should go back just yet."

"Why not?" I glanced back at the space where Adrian lay,

59

but he was gone.

"I buried him," Johann said. "And yes, we did question him like we were told. But think about it, Kaiden." He stood up, hefting the branch and then going back to carving at it. "Lesalie ordered us to get information, and we got it—but she also said to learn all we can. Well, we learned about Lasren. He's in Brusque still, with just one more vampire between him and us. One vampire who kills those who approach Brusque. We know now that you can fight and kill vampires—easily."

"I . . . I wouldn't say easily."

"But you can do it. We can go take down the other vampire near Brusque. And from there, we can go after Lasren, just like we took down Dimresh. And we can get even more information. Just like Lesalie said."

"Learn all we can," I repeated. "But she also said to come back."

Johann smirked. "I wouldn't have pegged Mr. Powerful-Vampire-Who-Killed-His-Own-Master as being such a stickler for the rules."

"It's not that," I said. "It's the danger."

"Are you worried about yourself, or for me?" Johann raised an eyebrow.

He knew me well. "It seems reckless," I said. "Yes, I'm worried about you. You could be killed."

"I could have been killed helping you go after Dimresh. I could have been killed trying to trap the vampire tonight. I could have been killed hunting thralls any number of times. And I could have been killed trying to talk to a thrall named Kaiden that one night, when I saw that he wanted to survive."

I dropped my gaze. "That doesn't change the fact that I don't want you hurt."

"I'm a hunter, Kaiden. I've been taking risks since I decided to become one." He sighed, moving closer to me, the scent of snow and soap mixing with his usual alluring maleness. He must have washed in near-freezing water somehow, but he was still warm. "I have dreams too—of protecting merchants like my parents once more. With your help, and information from some vampire on the road outside Brusque that we might get, my dream could happen, along with yours. There's no reason to hold back."

He was right. I knew he was right. He was a hunter, and so was I. I wanted to keep him safe. But holding him back from his job would do nothing but ruin the man I cared about.

"Let's do it, then," I said. "I'll keep you safe."

"I don't doubt it," Johann said with a grin. He jumped back into his place on the wagon seat, Mint already hitched to the reins. The horse snorted, flicking her ears in confusion as Johann guided her back toward the merchant road.

I wondered if I should have said something more. Maybe it was the vampire instinct in me, a desire to stay close to my own territory—whatever my territory was. The barracks?

My thoughts scattered when Johann patted the empty space next to him on the wagon seat. I shouldn't ride next to him, so close.

Too close . . .

But I did it anyway, despite my misgivings

"We didn't have time to talk last night," Johann said. "Did you learn anything else from that vampire? Anything you wanted to know about yourself?"

"Not really," I said. "I told you most of it last night."

"And it was wrong," Johann said with a shake of his head. "Vampires being unable to kill other vampires, when you've eaten two already? All the more reason to go farther and get more information. We can send a message back to the barracks if we pass a merchant—which we will. It's the merchant road, after all." He let go of the reins. Mint flicked an ear but continued to plod steadily on. Johann patted my shoulder. I loved that he liked to touch me, but I hoped he didn't try anything beyond these simple, warm touches.

I needed a distraction. "Tell me about the road," I asked. Snow dusted our way, but there were none of the deep drifts that marked the surrounding forest. "I've never left Penthorn before."

"Even as a human?" Johann asked.

I nodded. If I had, I didn't remember. Maybe that was normal. Adrian hadn't remembered much either, from the way he'd sounded.

I could ask other vampires. Maybe even Lasren. Perhaps this plan truly was a good idea.

"Well, the road used to connect all of the cities of the empire," Johann said. "We'll pass by waymarkers — noticeable statues or shrines to Holy Laurel, similar to the one near Penthorn. Some of them used to be inns or churches, meant for the benefit of travelers. Of course, all of them are abandoned now. Or filled with thralls or vampires." He shook his head. "Now merchants have made their own safe spots — easily defended copses of trees, or designated meeting spots. The barracks usually assign a hunter to guard them."

"Will we be passing by one of those?" I asked.

"No. There are none on the way to Brusque. No one travels there anymore."

"Then . . . how does Lasren eat?" I asked.

Johann gave me a side-eyed look. "I assume he feeds from the people who still live there. Just because no one goes there doesn't mean there aren't still people trapped in the city. That gets more common the closer you get to the old capital. More powerful vampires there, more people. The old roads cut off or swarmed by thralls. Only the most skilled merchants get through."

Adrian's words echoed in my mind. *"Land, farms, and cattle."*

I had known things were bad, but they suddenly became

more real. Penthorn was on the outskirts of what had been the old empire, close to thick forests that blanketed the landscape. But where the seat of power of the empire had once been, now was nothing but predators.

Predators like me.

"Have you ever gone this way before?" I asked.

"Toward Brusque? Only a few times since my parents died, and each time . . ." He sighed. "Well, I've never gotten close to Brusque. Hunters know better than to tackle a vampire like him and get themselves killed. Until now, at least." He smiled at me, and some of the weight of the night lifted. "But I've been west toward the old capital, to Wollasque. Mostly as an escort. Wollasque has mines that supply surviving villages and towns with metal. I suppose since Lasren took over Brusque, he mostly ignores Wollasque. Lots of thralls there though, ranging over from the mountains nearby. Wood may kill bloodsuckers, but metal is still necessary."

"I hope not for weapons." I thought of the spears and shields, rusted with age, at Dimresh's old castle.

"People need to eat too. Animals are more likely to die to a metal-tipped arrow than a wooden one. But I see your point. No, not many humans fight each other nowadays. We know who our real enemy is."

People need to eat. Vampires need to eat. I was cheating, in a sense. *Eating the dregs of another vampire's meal.* If there weren't vampires to make thralls, I would have to eat humans too.

"I didn't mean you, Kaiden," Johann quickly added. "You're not our enemy."

I hoped that would always be true. I wondered when Adrian had lost his humanity, thinking of humans as beneath even speaking to. Was it when he had been turned? Or would I be like that in fifty years time, sick of disgusting thrall blood and ready for the fine taste human blood promised?

I licked my lips.

"What's on your mind, Kaiden?" Johann asked. "You're distant." He spoke so lightly, with no trace of fear, his heart beating steadily. He had too much trust for someone who had lost his family to the same vampire whose territory he was entering.

I wasn't ready to talk about my fears, not yet. But I liked hearing Johann speak. "Tell me about the world outside Penthorn," I said. "I'd like to learn more about what I'll see — or people I'll meet." The road stretched ahead of us, no trace of wagon tracks or hoof prints on the snow.

"Meeting someone at night may be a hard ask," Johann said with a wry smile. "Unless you're talking about other vampires. The farther we get from the barracks and the closer to Brusque, the less likely we are to see someone crazy enough to travel this way. No amount of swooning villagers or trade goods would make that worthwhile ."

The image was oddly comforting — Johann with a wagon loaded full of silks like the ones in Dimresh's castle, handing them out to appreciative people who paid him with food and . . . .my fantasy ended there. "What sort of things do people trade?" I asked.

"Most trade the essentials — food, iron, lumber. Sometimes they trade crafts or carvings. I was always fond of those." I remembered the small animals on his bookshelves back at the barracks. "And some still give us money, although I always wonder when people will realize how worthless that is these days. My mother always used to tell me that back in the old days a merchant's life was about living for the rarest trades, getting the best things you could and selling them for so much profit you could build a mansion wherever you wanted."

"That's a nice thought."

"It was just her telling me kid's stories, I know," Johann said. "But I like to think that maybe in the days of the empire it was true."

"Now merchants work for everyone, I suppose," I said. "Instead of making profits for themselves, they keep the last bits of humanity in communication with one another."

"That's exactly right, Kaiden." Johann beamed at me, and his smile warmed me. "I'm a hunter now, and what I do is important. But if I'd stayed a merchant, my work would be just as important."

"If we . . ." I almost said "killed all the vampires," but the very idea felt impossible, so I rephrased my thought. "If there were no vampires, would you like to have the life of a merchant?"

"Absolutely." Johann steered Mint around a slushy puddle. "I love life on the road. Half a year at home, and half a year traveling and seeing the world. Not something a villager like you would understand, of course."

He was teasing me, I realized. I smirked back, careful to keep my fangs from showing. "Some of us prefer baths and warm beds."

"Really now?" He laughed. "That week in a castle spoiled you."

It was nice to chat and laugh like this. I could pretend I wasn't a vampire, that I didn't notice how his jaw moved, how his neck gleamed in the moonlight. I focused on other things.

"I just like being comfortable when I can," I said. "Although the castle was a bit much."

"Vampires must be spoiled for the most part," he said with a snort. "Dimresh, Lasren—why do they have to live in castles? Overkill, isn't it? Who do they think they are?"

"Should they be traveling the countryside as merchants too?" I said. "Claiming more territory?"

"If you could trade land . . ." Johann tilted his head, and I wished he wouldn't, his neck and shoulder exposed to my sight. Commanding Adrian had made me hungry, and time just made that hunger worse. "I don't think that would ever work, even in the time of the empire. I don't know much about farming, but I imagine the land was owned by whoever worked it."

"It's funny how people decide they own things," I said. It was probably the same way a vampire simply decided some place was their territory. And everyone living there food.

"It's human nature, I guess," Johann said. "Very few people are purely . . ." He snapped his fingers. "What's the word? Altruistic."

"You seem to be," I said. "Protecting people. Helping me."

He gave a quiet chuckle. "I enjoy it, though. I love the adventure. The travel. And of course, I like you. Not exactly selfless."

"It's close enough, though." The wagon hit a pothole. The bump brushed his leg against mine. Heat swept through me. I shouldn't be sitting up here, on the wagon seat, with him so close. I should hunt.

But Johann's proximity was so nice, and thrall blood was disgusting. I could go without it for a night, especially after feeding on a bit of vampire blood the night before. I was hungry, but one night wouldn't hurt . . . would it?

"The only truly altruistic person I've ever heard about was in the legends of some of the priests of Laurel. And there were some stories that claimed Lucien was selfless." That name broke my focus on the spreading warmth and tension in my body.

Lucien. The only other thrall who had become a vampire, who had killed his master too.

"Lucien," I said. "Wasn't he from . . ."

"Yes." Johann eye's twinkled in the light of the stars. "I was waiting for you to make that connection. I heard the story of Lucien because Lucien was from Brusque. Lasren may know of it too. Maybe there we could find out more about him. If you're okay with the danger of us traveling there, of course." His eyes twinkled.

The last bit of uncertainty about our self-assigned mission faded away. Maybe our answers really were in Brusque.

# CHAPTER NINE

I shouldn't have gone even one night without blood. Not when I was this close to Johann, and not when we were heading into territory where there were no other travelers. No other travelers meant no one else hunted — and that meant no thralls.

The second night, the hunger wasn't so bad. I didn't think to hunt, the thick snow dampening scents and I unwilling to leave Johann's cheery stories about his training and about the previous day. I loved being near him, listening to his voice, his story about the merchant he'd met who would be delivering the news of our change in plans to the barracks.

The third night our progress stalled, and I had to spend time shoving the wagon through snowdrifts instead of hunting while Johann brushed clinging snow from Mint's hooves.

And on that fourth day I dreamed of Johann. Of my claws gripping his shoulders, drawing blood that dribbled down his back. He tasted rich, just as I had imagined — life and warmth that reminded me of the finest wines from a time when I was still alive, an explosion of flavor that lasted even after I swallowed.

He moaned in the dream when I took him, and moaned again when I bit him. I woke wracked with hunger and my body on fire with lust.

I lay still in my dark enclosure, willing myself to calm down. My fangs pricked my lip. Now it took effort to hide them. I didn't know what was worse — the hunger I couldn't sate or the lust I couldn't satisfy.

*Calm down.* Johann trusted me. I was a vampire now, not a thrall. I craved a lot of things I couldn't have. I could get used to it.

I had to.

Once I had myself under control, I pulled the latch. The thick, fresh scent of snow was gone, and the air didn't feel as cold on my skin. Mint pulled at tufts of brown grass that poked through melted snow. The wagon seat was empty.

Johann's footsteps churned through slush, and I swallowed hard when I saw him. He still wore his tight leather riding pants, but he was bare-chested, his brown hair dripping water over his well-muscled shoulders and down his taut abdomen.

"I was just washing up before we continued on," he said. "The ice has melted on a pond nearby. Cold, but bearable with the sun up to dry off. Well, mostly."

His scent was luscious . . . pine and the last remnants of his masculine sweat mixed with the sharp tang of icy water. The muscles in his back rippled invitingly as he grabbed a cloth from his bag on the wagon, dabbed at the remaining water on his shoulders and ruffled it through his hair.

"Kaiden?" He raised an eyebrow.

I dragged my gaze away. I shouldn't stare so brazenly. "That's a good idea," I said. "I'll wash up too."

I found the pond easily enough, his scent present but faint. There were other scents too—deer, mostly, and the lightest whiff of wolf. I splashed cold water on my already-cold skin, washing away the accumulated dust and grit of travel.

I couldn't wash away the hunger, though, or the heat that burned in me when I thought of Johann. My blue eyes stared back at me from my reflection in the water. When I curled my lip, my fangs showed. Hiding them was difficult. My magic was getting weak.

I'd gone longer than this without food, lasted for a full nine days when I first became a vampire. I could handle this hunger. I was hungry, but it was the eyes of a vampire I saw in my reflection. My blue eyes, not the black eyes of a thrall.

When I returned, Johan had thankfully put a shirt on, though not his heavy coat. "We've got about two more days of travel, I think," he said. "I haven't been this close to Brusque since . . . well, ever since becoming a hunter." I wondered if anything was familiar from his time with his family. "We should keep alert."

"I will." I joined him on the wagon seat, his smile when I did sending a rush through me.

"Hopefully we'll find you a thrall," he said. "You must be hungry. Or we could find that vampire Adrian mentioned."

I hoped we found the vampire. Of course, we'd likely want to question her first. We would need all the information we could get. Especially if Johann truly wanted to enter Brusque.

"I wonder how people will react," Johann said. He drummed his fingers on the wagon seat in excitement and Mint flicked her ears at the noise. "I know that no one's come this way in years. We'd given up on it. No hunter ever returned. Now we know the vampire's guarding the town, and we've long known Lasren is ruling it . . . well, I'm almost afraid to see what the old town is like."

I tried to focus on his words and not on how his shirt didn't fit perfectly and exposed his collarbone and some of his muscular chest. "I thought it was a city?"

"It *was* a city. A lot of places were cities. But with so few people, the population doesn't really support them anymore. Penthorn was a city too." His throat and jaw moved invitingly when he talked. "Pretty much any region that has a castle nearby was once a city. It makes sense why powerful vampires would take over the castle and then prey on the people." He eyed me. "I'm glad you're not like that."

"Me too," I said. I wondered if he'd noticed me staring at

his neck. I looked away, focused on the bare trees that we rolled past. Claw marks were gouged into a few of them. I peered closer, but the marks were the thick gouges from a big cat, nothing more.

That wasn't a good sign, though, that a large cat was brave enough to mark its territory so close to a road. There must be very few people who came this way. If any.

And no people meant no thralls.

The wagon jolted. Johann fell against me, his shoulder hitting mine and his hip brushing my thigh. Very nice.

"C'mon, Mint," Johann huffed. "Warn us, will you?" he added with a laugh. Mint only flicked her tail.

"It's such a shame to see the road like this." Johann peered back over his shoulder. The bump had been a tree branch that had fallen into the road. "I just hope . . . oh, look there."

Where the branch had fallen were other branches, and what at first had resembled a fallen tree became something manmade. Branches curved into a woven arch over a stone carving.

"Laurel," I said.

"A waymarker," Johann said. He pulled back on the reins. Mint's plodding steps stopped. "Mind if I take a look, Kaiden?"

"Go ahead." I followed as he exited the wagon, pushing skeletal branches out of the way as we left the road.

I remembered the small shrine near Penthorn, the small carving that had been made formless by years of rain and ruin. This was larger, the archway stretching over it taller than Johann. He leaned forward to brush snow off the stone.

"I'm always shocked when they're intact," he said. The snow fell away, revealing intricate carvings of leaves that wreathed the statue's shoulders.

"It's impressive," I said. Moonlight gleamed off dark stone, so expertly carved it was almost unreal. Something about it made me unsure if I should draw any nearer or run. The stone holding . . . power . . . reminded me of something.

Could the holy magic still be here? I reached out, my skin prickling with unease. There was something strange about the stone, I knew it. But when I laid my hand upon the surface, it felt like any other stone, just impossibly smooth.

"It's like . . . black glass," I said. "I think it held magic once."

"What do you mean?" Johann moved closer, his face nearly touching the stone. Of course—he couldn't see at night like I could. He brushed the snow back farther, uncovering more of it.

"Hey," he said. "I think . . . .is there something carved here?"

I glanced where he pointed, the words blocky and etched. *The power of the sun will guide you to Laura's rest. Two miles. Follow the statue's glow.*

Johann blinked. "Statue's glow? It's . . . oh!" He reared back, a grin on his face. "Kaiden, do you know what this is made of?"

I blinked. "Stone?"

"Not just any stone. This is the stone we use in our solar flares!" He gestured back to the wagon. "We haven't been able to make this anymore, but now we can. This entire statue is made of just what we need!" He tapped the stone with a fist, the sound dull. "Solid, too. A priest must have used magic to produce this. We could make hundreds more flares with this!"

I didn't know much about solar flares—of the weapons hunters used, it was one of those I couldn't safely employ. A rock like this in a glass lantern that reflected its power when charged by the sun would incinerate any thralls or vampires within a wide radius. No wonder I had been instinctively wary of it.

"Does . . . does it glow? Will it?" I eyed the carving.

"I . . . Aw, don't worry, Kaiden." Johann put a hand on my shoulder. "The stone will only glow when lit by flame, and I'm certainly not going to do that with you around."

I leaned into his touch. "I'm not afraid," I said. "It's just . . . a reminder that my power comes with a powerful weakness."

"Do you miss the sun?" Johann asked.

What a strange question. I wasn't sure how to answer. "I dream of it sometimes."

Johann tilted his head, his neck exposed to my sight. So close. "What kind of dreams? Good ones?"

"I guess so. I see buildings, like Penthorn, except in the light of the sun. Now . . . I think the sun would hurt my eyes."

"You see things clearly right now, right? I can barely see you in the dark under the trees like this, and you're only an arm's length away."

"I can see you very well." *Too well.* The night was as bright as the day to me. I couldn't imagine how searing the sun's light would be. "I can see a mouse scuttling beneath the branches of the archway." The animal froze when Johann turned.

"I'll take your word for it." Johann sighed. "That's amazing, Kaiden. I sometimes forget how different you are."

I frowned. "I sometimes forget that this might be hard for you."

"What do you mean?"

"Staying up all night. Do *you* miss the sun?"

"It's like any other discomfort. I'm used to it. But yeah, I do miss it sometimes. Especially in winter. It's worth it, though."

"What is?"

"Hunting. Making a difference. And lately, being with you." He smiled, reaching out, and I read his intention. I took his hand in mine. "If we can pull this off, we can avenge my parents. We can learn more about Lucien, about vampires, and about you. And maybe from there . . . who knows?"

73

"We could get rid of vampires," I said. "Or even cure them."

"Cure you," Johann said. His breathing changed. He took a step closer to me. His warmth drew me closer to him, his presence a temptation.

"I could see the sun again," I said. Right now, I wasn't thinking of the sun. I wasn't sure what it was, hunger or lust or something else, an emotion that was powerful and new, something I was afraid to name. But something drove me toward him, too close.

"I'd like to see you in the sun," Johann said. "You would be very handsome, I'm sure."

"You're handsome now." I dipped my head, taking in his scent, his warmth. His weight shifted. I read tension in his shoulders when my mouth neared his chin, his neck. His heart beat faster, but he also put his arms on my shoulders, his breathing deep and rhythmic. The sound was soothing.

He was so gorgeous, so warm. To me, he almost glowed in the moonlight, the soft light cascading over his brown hair and pale skin. His eyes sparkled, as they did when he laughed, but now they were half-lidded and so, *so* inviting.

I tilted my head and licked his chin, his skin warm and marred with slight stubble. He gasped at my touch, but didn't pull away.

I wanted this so badly. I wanted *him*. He kept his hands on my shoulders, rubbing them. "Kaiden," he said, his breath a rush against me.

I put my arms around him too, running my hands down his sides, feeling the taut muscles there. His heart pounded in my ears. I licked his chin again. I expected him to lift his head, to kiss me, but he didn't. Instead I licked farther down, moving my tongue over his neck, his pulse fluttering on my tongue.

I could feel him against me, smell his arousal. My body

thrummed with his heartbeat.

"Kaiden," he said, and this time it wasn't so breathy. "Kaiden, w-wait."

I didn't want to wait. I didn't want to stop. I licked his neck, and then his shoulders. The taste of the soaps he'd brought mingled with his taste, which was like his scent, pine and maleness that made me throb.

"Are you sure, Kaiden?" he said.

I was sure. I wanted to be sure. My body burned. My tongue flicked between my fangs when I trailed my tongue up his neck.

I shouldn't be doing this. I was too hungry to risk this. But this was lust, wasn't it? My hunger wasn't overpowering. I could control it. It was just craving, a desire, not a compulsion.

I wanted him so badly. He tilted his head up, meeting my eyes. This close, I knew he could see me. He smiled, his teeth flat and white. Human. His pulse beat in his neck.

I stopped, my body still thrumming with desire. I had started this. He wanted it, I could tell. This would be like my fantasies, my dreams.

But I was hungry. And I wasn't sure if it was my feelings for him that had started this or just hunger. And I still didn't know what would happen if I gave in.

"I'm sorry," I said, and I stepped away. I immediately regretted it, even though I knew it had been the right choice.

"Oh Kaiden," Johann said. Disappointment weighted the sound of my name. "It has been four nights, hasn't it? Is this because you're hungry?"

The words hurt. I wished I could say that wasn't it. "I don't know."

There was so much I didn't know.

"But you are hungry." He sighed, running a hand through his hair. With a few breaths, his heart slowed. He could get himself under control so easily, and I envied him that. "You know, if you bit me . . . ."

"Don't," I warned him. I didn't want the temptation. But I didn't want to leave him. Everything I wanted was right there in front of me.

I turned, feeling the weight of his eyes on my back. I was a vampire now, but I still couldn't have what I wanted. This felt wrong. Some part of me, a new instinct, screamed at me to take what was mine.

"Kaiden," Johann said, and I turned back. He had drawn his stakeshooter.

"Bind him to the earth," a woman's voice whispered. I whirled and Johann fired.

The bolt flew into the darkness. Then something hit me, so hard that bones in my back and shoulders cracked, the force throwing me against the statue of Laurel. I shook from the pain as I tried to get to my feet, reminding me of a time when my hands had shaken as I scrabbled for drink as a human. I tried to turn to mist as the woman moved in front of me, but that didn't work.

Of course not. She'd used the same trick I had on Adrian.

She hit me hard across the mouth. My jaw cracked.

"If you won't eat this human, I will." The woman's fangs emerged from her lips.

# CHAPTER TEN

Y*ounger than me, but more powerful. She has good hunting grounds. Just outside Lasren's territory.* Adrian's words echoed in my mind. I'd been stupid to let myself get distracted when we were so close. Even stupider to enter another vampire's territory when I was so hungry and weak.

And now I was hungrier. My body began to heal, my broken jaw setting itself with a crack and my shoulders and back settling into alignment. That took energy, driven by the blood I hadn't had in too many nights, and my healing was slower than it should have been.

But the vampire wasn't paying any more attention to me.

Her back to me, her long hair cascaded over her shoulders in brown waves as she took a step toward Johann. She moved like the women of the night back at Penthorn had, the exaggerated sway of her hips and the careful placement of her leg showing off what I guessed might be considered beauty. I grit my teeth, my fangs poking my lip.

"A hunter," she purred. "By blood, bind—"

Johann threw something at the vampire. Her incantation turned into a snarl of revulsion as water splashed her front and began to hiss against her skin. Johann didn't wait. He fired his stakeshooter again, this time directly at her.

She misted into nothingness. The bolt hit the stone above where I lay and bounced off, landing next to me.

I had to get up. This was a vampire without a castle, a wanderer outside Brusque. She should be nothing compared to Dimresh. I couldn't let Johann fight alone.

"Your tricks won't work on me, monster," Johann said, his voice loud and taunting. "Show yourself!"

That had to be a bluff. She could hypnotize him with just words, couldn't she? I had done that to him before. I couldn't let her. I would keep Johann safe.

Anger sharpened my vision, driving away the pain and exhaustion of hunger. Johann was mine.

She reappeared behind Johann, and this time I attacked first. I flashed past Johann, his movements slow as he whipped his head to follow my path. I slammed into the vampire, driving my claws into her shoulders as she hit the ground. I snarled, biting down for the kill.

She misted again, my claws digging into my own palms and my teeth snapping shut on nothingness. Then a high-heeled shoe slammed into the back of my head. Pain and then sudden numbness in my legs let me know she'd cracked my skull. I didn't dare move. I had to heal. All I could see was the dirt I lay in, the pain making it impossible to move my head.

"Kaiden!" Johann shouted from somewhere, fear in his voice.

"This is my territory, little vampire," she snarled from above. "I protect it for my Lord. Get away from Brusque."

She wasn't like Adrian. He hadn't wanted to fight, had been easy to predict. This one . . . I had to think. I had to protect Johann.

"By my blood, bind her to the earth!" I shouted into the dirt. Pain answered my magic, but the pain let me know my spell had worked.

"I thought vampires couldn't kill other vampires," Johann's voice rang out from somewhere behind me. "Isn't it me you want?"

I fought to move, to do anything, and then the numbness blossomed into more pain. I was healing. I could move. I had to defend Johann.

I rolled over, the world spinning, blood dripping down the back of my shirt. With that came hunger. I would kill her and drink her blood. I *had* to.

Johann pointed his stakeshooter into the trees. "Come and get me, vampire," he called.

"By blood," she said, her voice sonorous. Johann whirled. He fired at the branches where she was perched, but his shot whistled harmlessly just beneath her feet, past the gaps where leaves would be in spring. "I call darkness on my enemies, and silence."

Nothing happened. But Johann suddenly changed his stance, his gaze distant, cocking his head. She had blinded him.

"To your left, Johann, in the branches!" I called, but his shot flew wide again. I stumbled to my feet, ignoring more blood that dripped from my head and the grinding sound of bone knitting together. I wouldn't be caught off-guard again.

"You are annoying me, little vampire," she said in a barely audible whisper. "This human is my prey. I thought I made that clear." Johann fired at the trees again, but she'd already jumped down, as silent as a light breeze, close to Johann. Too close.

I had to attack her. I had prevented her from misting, but she was strong, uninjured, while I was starving and still healing and didn't know what other magic I could use. I snarled, springing at the vampire. I had to defend Johann. He was mine!

She kicked out as I leapt at her. My ribs cracked, and the force carried me back toward the wagon, my body skidding on slush. I groaned in pain.

"Idiot newblood," the vampire muttered.

"Kaiden!" Johann shouted. He'd hefted his stake now, his gaze still unfocused. "Think like a hunter!"

Of course. I wasn't a mindless thrall. I was a vampire. But

I was also a hunter, and it had been stupid not to fight like one. There were weapons in the wagon. Stakeshooters, stakes, and . . . solar flares.

Johann had said the stone would glow when lit. And the very first spell he'd tried to teach me had been light.

"By my blood," I said. The vampire's head turned toward me, her eyes narrowing. She tensed, probably prepared to kick me if I sprang at her again.

Instead I leaped away, fleeing from her and from the statue, even as I kept my focus on the branches surrounding the stone. I was taking a gamble. I braced myself for the pain even as I ducked behind the wagon, letting the magic flow into me, allowing my new vampire instincts to shape the words. Somehow, as I spoke, I knew it wasn't the words that mattered, but the will. "Bring fire to my enemies!"

Orange light bloomed and then seared the clearing. Even behind the wagon, with my eyes screwed shut, it burned. I screamed, and my cry mingled with a higher-pitched scream from the vampire.

I was reminded of the first time I'd met Johann, when his solar flare had incinerated the other thralls. The glow had been like the sun coming over the horizon. This was closer, my body on fire.

I had made a mistake. I would die.

*An old man in robes stood by a carving of Laurel, running his hands over it. A tree was emblazoned on the back of his robes, green on white. This statue was different, larger, seated in front of a building of white stone, steps leading to enormous pillars.*

*He placed his palms on the statue of Laurel, muttering something I couldn't hear. I heard nothing, the scene silent. But the light was different.*

It was daytime, the sky blue and clouds white instead of a sky of black and clouds of gray. The statue beneath the man's hands glowed once and he turned, looking at me with a smile. He mouthed something, and I leaned forward. But the light was too bright and I couldn't make out his words. Then he bowed.

The scene vanished. All I could feel was pain, and all I could taste was ash. Liquid dripped down my cheeks — I wasn't sure if it was tears or blood. I struggled to open my eyes. I thought I did, but was met with only more darkness.

Something moved my head. More pain bloomed in my neck and on the skin of my cheek. Whatever it was kept moving me. Something snuffled, the sound bursting through the silence of what must have been damage to my ears.

I was healing. I wasn't dead.

Whatever was nuzzling my head and snuffling in my ear whinnied. Mint.

"Kaiden!" Johann shouted. I struggled to move, but the burning sensation on every inch of my skin told me not to. I sagged into the cold wetness of the melted snow on the ground. "Kaiden, Kaiden, where — Kaiden!"

His footsteps hammered onto the slush, and then there were hands on my face, on my shoulder. It should have hurt, but his closeness was soothing instead, the thrumming warmth and life of his touch enough for me to open my mouth.

"Are you all right?" I rasped.

"Oh, Kaiden," Johann said. His heart beat frantically in my ears, almost as fast as when Dimresh had cast a fear spell on him. "Hold on. I'll help you."

His footsteps vanished, replaced by the duller sounds of his boots thudding onto the wagon. I could still hear his heart, the steady drumming. Focusing on it helped ease the pain that danced in sparks over my body.

Hunger twisted in my stomach along with the pain, that more than anything else letting me know just how much damage had been done.

The skin on my arms sent agony through me when I tried to push myself up. I gave up, flopping down into the slush. Mint breathed steadily overhead and bats darted far above me. There was no sign of the vampire.

At least my idea had worked. But I wasn't sure I could recover from this. I still couldn't see.

Something weighed me down. I let it wash over me, an emotion I was familiar with but one that took on new meaning when I was as weak as I was now. A new, dread-like kind of fear.

I didn't want to die. I didn't want to depend on others. I had to heal. I had to be able to protect Johann. I was a vampire. I had fought to become one. And yet I was still lying here, helpless. I needed blood. But as I was, I couldn't even hunt a thrall.

Johann returned, his presence a warmth and prickling along my skin. I always knew when he was close, his scent and the sound of his heart familiar. But with it came a new scent, one that made my mouth water, my stomach growl, and my mind reel.

"Here," Johann said.

"No," I snapped, my fangs sharp. "Don't."

"It's in a cup. Drink it, Kaiden. You need it."

"No." I wanted to run, from Johann and from the craving that roared in my mind. "Please don't."

"The other vampire was incinerated. There are no thralls here, and we have a night and a day to travel before we'll be in Brusque. I'm not letting you suffer. Drink it, Kaiden! There's no risk!"

The scent of his blood came closer, mixed with the metallic scent of the cup. His offering sloshed thickly. He must have bled a lot. I could imagine blood dripping from his skin into the cup, even as my mouth watered.

I wanted to say no, to shove it away. If the deep weakness and pain hadn't been there . . . if Johann hadn't put it in front of me . . . if the scent hadn't been so overpowering, I was sure I could have resisted the temptation.

But instead I drank.

# CHAPTER ELEVEN

This is what I had missed. This is what I had always, always needed. Like the first sip of alcohol to ease the shakes, but deeper, more pleasurable, a luscious wine mixed with the finest stew in the way it filled me with strength. And the taste was all richness, washing through my mouth and satisfying a craving I had lived with my entire existence as a vampire, and before as a thrall. Better than the first drink of water on a hot day, better than the first meal after days of starvation or sickness. No—nothing, even in what little of my human life I could remember, had tasted as good.

For a few seconds, there was no regret at all. That's what scared me most.

Light flooded my eyes as his blood healed me, strength welling in my muscles. Power centered in my chest, and for a moment I felt what must be magic, keeping me alive. Using the blood of humans. Strength greater than what I got from a thrall, greater even than what I got from a vampire.

Johann's blood was pleasure and power.

"Kaiden?"

I had drained the cup dry, licking what remnants I could. Johann's warm brown eyes met mine, and I had to clench my teeth against a desire I still remembered well from my time as a human, when I had reached the end of my cups.

*I want more.*

I couldn't look at him. Not like this. I leapt to my feet, the pain having vanished as the thick, delicious blood had gone down my throat. It was magic, it was power, and it was agonizingly wonderful. It was everything I wanted, all of my fantasies proven true.

The fantasies I couldn't have.

"Kaiden?" Johann reached for me, putting his hand on my shoulder.

"Why did you do that?" I snapped.

"Kaiden, you can't turn me if you don't kill me — and especially not if you don't even bite me. I'm fine!"

"I'm not!" I shouted. I whirled to face him, the gorgeous man I wanted in every way, but the one I wanted most the way I could never have. I hated what I was. Hated my hunger, these filthy fangs that I wanted to use to sink into Johann's neck and take the rest of what was *mine*.

No. He wasn't mine. I couldn't think that, like a vampire.

"Kaiden, tell me what's wrong." Johann had tensed, his heart thudding more quickly. I hated to see the confident smile leave his face. "We're partners. Tell me what's wrong."

I didn't want to. But I had to, if only to keep him from making stupid mistakes like that again. Maybe if I could put it into words, make him understand, I could understand it more myself.

"Your blood is" — I felt vulgar to say it as I ground out the words — "delicious. Like the finest of wines. Better than vampire. Pure and . . ." My mouth watered and I swallowed. "You gave me the thing I craved most, and now the craving is worse. And . . ." I thought of Adrian, the wretched vampire so confused as to how I could treat a meal like an equal. "Now that I've tasted it, I can understand them better."

"Who?" Johann asked.

"The vampires!" I shouted. "How they can drink you. The power your blood gives." His pulse pounded in his neck. I could smell the wound on his upper arm where he'd cut himself, the blood pulsing close to the surface. "It's so good, Johann. It's like you were meant to be food."

Johann frowned, his heart picking up, but he didn't step back. Instead he reached for me again.

I closed my eyes against a surge of hunger, of what wasn't even hunger but craving, like the craving I had used to feel for wine but ten times worse. His hand was warm on my cheek. I gave a small moan.

"Do you want to drink my blood?" he asked.

"Yes."

"Do you need to?"

I opened my eyes. He stared at me, his brown eyes boring into mine, a confident vampire hunter despite the way his heart beat. He may feel fear, or nervousness, but he stared at me despite that, and I knew he was brave.

"No," I said. I swallowed hard. "The pain is gone."

"Do you want to kill me?"

"No." I didn't need to think about that one.

"I'm sorry for making you suffer," Johann said. He took his hand away. "But Kaiden, the stone glowing like a flare incinerated the other vampire. I thought you were dead, and the thought terrified me. I want you healthy and unhurt. I gave you what you needed. I trust you, and I don't regret it."

I didn't know what to say. "You don't understand," I said. "The desire will only get worse."

"Then give in to it." Johann threw up his hands. "You were licking me earlier. I thought we had a chance. I've already told you I would be happy to sleep with you. Would that help?" Hope entered his voice.

"No." *Maybe.* "It's too risky."

"Kaiden, I've taken risks my entire life." Johann ran a hand through his hair, exhaling in annoyance. "Why can't you trust yourself?"

"Because I barely understand what I am!" My voice made a sleeping bird in a crook of a tree startle and flutter its wings. "I can't be sure I won't bite you." *And then lose myself and kill you.*

"Fine." Johann took a deep breath. "Figuring out what you can do was the point of this anyway — or one of the points." He smiled, but I could see frustration in the set of his jaw. "At least I know I can't be hypnotized — at least not by a vampire with her level of power."

"You can throw off hypnosis?"

"I did it before with yours, remember?" This time his smile was more genuine. "Could be a trick we can use again if there's a fear aura around Lasren's castle. The guard's gone — we can go there now."

Right. There was potentially a lot of prepare for.

"C'mon, Kaiden. We have the rest of tonight and tomorrow to travel. I hope to see Brusque before tomorrow night."

"You'll travel all day too?"

"I'm used to discomfort. You should get used to it too." He smirked and I looked away. I knew what he meant, but it was clear he didn't understand.

My hunger wasn't the same.

"If we're going into the town . . . I should hunt beforehand." I didn't want to be hungry, not even a little.

"We haven't seen any sign of thralls in nights," Johann said with a raised eyebrow.

"I'm fast. I can be back before sunup. Will you be safe?"

"I'm a hunter, Kaiden. Don't worry about me." He jumped into the wagon seat. "Should I worry about you?"

I wasn't sure what he meant. "I'll be fine." I paused for a moment, eyeing him, his taut muscles and strong arms.

Then I darted into the trees.

I had thought vampire blood was powerful and filling. But that was nothing compared to human. Drinking even the small amount I had made me stronger, faster. His blood thrummed in me, giving me power I didn't understand. In minutes, I was miles away.

The human blood also made me feel more human. I

paused, alone in a copse of dormant trees, branches blocking the moon. Something in the distance, a wolf by the smell of it, trotted through slush, but I ignored it. The taste of Johann filled my mouth, and the thought of him filled my mind.

*Give in to it.* At least alone I could. I thought of Johann, of his taste and scent and his obvious feelings for me, evident in his voice when he said *happy to sleep with you.* Sleep with me? More like fuck me. Every fantasy I had come true.

*"Give in to it, Kaiden," Johann whispered from below me. I had him pinned down, my fingernails digging bloody furrows into his arms. "Give in to it."*

*I answered him by lowering my head and lapping the blood from his wounds. He moaned in response, grinding himself against me. I let him, molding myself against him, our legs tangled together. We lay on hard ground. There was no softness at all when I pressed him down, just the tightness of his muscles and the heat of his body.*

*He kissed me then, the heat of his mouth amplifying the taste of his blood. His tongue dragged over my fangs, and he gasped as I licked his tongue with mine to get more of the taste.*

*He put his arm around me, pulled me into him and spread his legs.*

*I throbbed at his tightness and heat, my body overwhelmed. We moved together, his breath whooshing over me, his heart pounding. Not enough. Never enough.*

*"Give in to it, Kaiden." The taste of his blood was already in my mouth. I bared my fangs and he tilted his chin up, like he had when I'd licked him, only now I wanted more. I wanted all of him.*

*I drove my fangs into his neck, the taste even better than before.*

It came on me fast this time, my body shuddering, and I moaned. My fingernails drug into the bark of the tree I had leaned against. I was salivating. I swallowed hard, the taste in my fantasy, my release, everything made stronger by the remnants of his blood still in my mouth.

I kept my eyes closed, relishing what I could. When the pleasure faded, I stood, re-lacing my breeches and scenting the quiet winter air.

I was still alone. I wondered if other vampires felt this way after a meal, after any sort of pleasure. Wretched and alone. Or maybe it was just me. I hadn't given in to anything, not fully.

But at least I had Johann to go back to. Fantasies were safe. If I truly gave in, drank as much of his blood as I craved in reality, I would have nothing in the end.

I began to run again, heading back toward the more populated parts of the merchant road. I ran as fast as I could—I wouldn't have much time to hunt and return before sunup. But at least I could avoid the awkwardness of tonight. And thrall blood would work well to get the last of the luscious taste out of my mouth.

Then Johann and I could hunt again, together, and I could keep resisting the temptation. I had to do better.

# CHAPTER TWELVE

*An enormous building loomed above me, glass windows sparkled in the sunlight. Colors gleamed from the glass, coruscating reds and purples and blues decorating the sun-drenched square. Pillars of stone supported the marble building. An archway led inside where the shapes in the windows cast colorful shadows on the polished floors. There was Laurel, and a Laurel tree, and leaves, and men in robes and women in dresses . . .*

I opened my eyes to darkness once again and the sound of Mint's heavy hoof-falls. I had made it back last night with almost no time to spare before sunup.

The dream had let me see the sun again, and now the night looked so different from the day. Moonlight glowed, and the things that were illuminated needed to be studied to see detail, everything creeping and soft and beautiful. Sunlight seared, so bright one couldn't look away, demanding attention, bouncing between panes of glass and setting off shining patterns. The building in my dream . . . why did it seem familiar?

"We're close, Kaiden," Johann called from the wagon seat. "Are you well?"

He smiled at me when I started walking next to the wagon, but I read tension in his shoulders, wariness in the way he sat. I understood. Last night had been strange, and we hadn't had a chance to talk when I returned.

Probably the light from the statue nearly blinding me had made me dream of the sun. At least I hadn't dreamed of Johann, or the taste of him. The thrall I'd found the night before had gotten rid of that flavor.

Still didn't change how handsome Johann looked. Although I could tell he was exhausted.

"You didn't sleep?"

"Is it obvious?" He sighed. "I dozed midday for about two hours, enough time to give Mint a break. We should arrive by morning if we keep traveling all night. I might ask you to take the reins later tonight. If you think you can."

"Of course."

"Have you ever driven a wagon before?"

I considered the question for a moment. Nothing about wagons or horses was familiar, not even shades from my life. "I don't think so."

"No worries. It's not difficult—I learned as a child." He smiled, his gaze distant. "It's strange to think I'm traveling the same bit of road now I did when I was young. The first hunter to get this far since . . . well, since Lasren took over."

I wanted to sit beside him, to be close to his warmth and help him bask in his memories, all of the things I lacked. Instead I kept walking, my feet sometimes sinking into the puddles of water formed when Mint's hooves sank into the muddy road. "Was it much different then?"

"This"—he swung his arm out to indicate the vines and branches that reached into the road, the muddy patches and slicks of ice—"was maintained better back then. The dirt was packed smooth, both by road workers from Brusque and by the wheels of many wagons and carts. If it weren't for Mint's surefootedness, we would have certainly never come this far now. And that's just with a mostly empty wagon, not a cart laden with goods."

"What was it like?" I asked. "To live in Brusque. What should I expect?"

The smile that came over his face made me happy too, a resonance with him that I held onto, even as I stepped over another icy patch of road. "Brusque was thriving when I was young. My parents traveled with me spring through summer, so I was often away, but we always stayed six months in winter. This time of year" — he gestured to the trees — "as we got closer, we would have seen lanterns lit, torchlights through the trees. It would be visible for miles, calling the merchants in. People would gather in the square to listen to the evening news from the crier. Or they'd head to pubs or shows put on by traveling groups."

I couldn't imagine that. Well, the pubs I could — those were the only memories I had left, the laughter and lights and scents that all revolved around ale and wine. But people moving about so freely at night? Seeing shows and hearing news in groups after dark? "How?"

"Remember, Kaiden. Who ruled Brusque before Lasren?"

I had to think. "Lucien. But he . . ."

"Yes. He died a long time ago, so long ago that he was only a story, even to us. We didn't have a vampire lord near Brusque when I was young. It was a safe place. A safe city."

A safe city. "Do any of those still exist now?"

Johann's smile faded, the memories in his eyes clouding over. "Wollasque is ruled by Lasren too. He's not often there, but from what I've heard the city's overrun by lesser vampires and thralls. Brusque, as far as I know, was the last one."

The pain in his eyes broke through my reluctance, my sense of risk. I leapt lightly onto the wagon, sitting next to him in the spot I'd occupied the past few nights. This felt right.

"So . . ." I struggled to put into words what I was slowly realizing. Penthorn had always been a city in the long shadow of Dimresh. My sparse memories were filled with patches and ale, sickness and hardship. I had no recollection of sunny, carefree days. I wondered if the dream I had the night before was a memory I had lost. "Brusque must have been beautiful. And painful to lose."

"Exactly, Kaiden." Johann put his hand in mine. "When I was young, my life was good. Sure, we knew of the vampires. We knew they prowled the roads, and anyone, including my parents, who traveled the roads was at risk. The road north of here is overrun with thralls from Telmet. You took your life in your hands to go up and get metal from the mines near there. But coming back onto this road, seeing the old temples in Brusque, was a sign you were home and safe. At least, it used to be. Now I'm afraid of what I'll find."

I nodded. "But you've always dreamed of freeing the city, haven't you?"

Johann sighed. "Of course. I've always wanted to. But it seemed impossible. First, I was training. Most of us take longer to be ready to face the bloodsuckers than you do." He nudged me, his touch a friendly shove, but it felt like a tease, and I quelled my desires and fought to focus. This was important. "And then I began to research Lasren, and I learned how hopeless even attempting to enter the castle would have been."

"The fear aura."

He nodded. "But that's only part of it. Lasren is said to hunt outside of his castle, so people thought they had a chance. Hunters tried to go after him before, back when he ruled Wollasque. There are records from fifty or so years ago, three separate attempts. But no hunter has been able to kill him, even outside of his castle. And when he came to Brusque, setting that vampire as guard, one who not even hunters could kill, wiping out merchants . . ." He trailed off, and I could read what he left unsaid in the slump of his shoulders, mixed with his exhaustion—merchants like his family.

I gritted my teeth in anger, my fangs sharp in my mouth. "I'll keep you safe," I said. "I'll kill him for you." This was a different feeling than wanting to kill Dimresh. Then I had wanted to protect Penthorn, but a lot of that was for myself, to prove I could be more than a thrall, to prove myself to Matilda, after she had died because I had failed her. Now that I was a vampire, and fighting just for Johann, killing vampires felt both less personal and much, much more so.

Johann was *mine*.

"Relax, Kaiden." Johann squeezed my hand in his. "That's *our* goal. But first, let's get safely to Brusque. Could you handle another vampire like the one you fought last night?"

Talk of last night chased away the anger, replaced with curling shame. "I could. She wasn't stronger or faster than I was. She was just more experienced. And I was . . . weak with hunger and distracted." That hurt to admit.

"I'm sorry, Kaiden." Johann took his hand away, and I let him do it, even as the loss felt somehow more painful than my injuries last night. "I'm not going to give up on you—on *us*. But I'll be more patient. And though I don't regret it, I'm sorry that giving you my blood hurt you in some way." He huffed, pulling on the reins to lead Mint around another patch of ice. "I shouldn't just tell you to give in to things and say you can just resist when I'm bad at controlling my own behavior around you. I was distracted too. We defeated Dimresh—we can't let ourselves be taken by surprise by some wandering vampire."

"I won't be next time," I said. "I'll . . ." I almost said "be good" the way I'd used to as a thrall, but that felt wrong now, a relic from another life. "I'll work harder to understand my magic and use it effectively. I'll need it in Brusque, I'm sure."

"We'll have time to get our bearings while we're in Brusque," Johann said. "And there are temples there. Maybe we can learn something. Just like our original mission, eh?" Johann yawned, and once again Mint was pulling away from the road. I couldn't tell who was more tired, Johann or Mint. Johann's heart thudded slow.

"If you want, you can sleep," I said. "I can take the reins."

"You won't be tempted by me sleeping here next to you?" Johann said with a wry grin.

I had to smile back, hiding my fangs this time. "Not going to sleep in the lightless storage unit like me?"

"I want to be nearby if something happens. I can be alert if I have to be. And besides — I trust you. I always will."

I swallowed hard. I felt desire at his words, at the opportunities they promised, but his trust also made me feel something else — an emotion that had been dull as a thrall but grew stronger every day as a vampire.

It made me feel more human.

I let him lie back, closing his eyes with his hands folded over his stomach, while I took the reins. His breathing slowed along with his heartbeat, a lulling cadence of soothing life, as the wagon rolled on through the night.

I wanted nothing more than to protect him. *My* Johann.

Not mine, though. I wondered at my protectiveness, my instinct to claim him. Was that me, or some vampire inclination? I wished I could remember more of my life.

Maybe I felt this way because of the taste of his blood. The thought scared me.

The moon traveled slowly, moving from its peak in the star-filled sky down to just above the tree line, and the sky threatened to turn purple with the approaching dawn. The road grew slightly smoother. Along the path I spotted wooden sticks set upright, a few with rusty metal pieces where lamps must have once been lit. We were drawing close. I should wake Johann and rest myself soon, hiding from the light of day.

As we passed by one of the old lamps, tension filled me. Goose bumps flashed over my skin, my fangs emerged, and my fingernails sharpened into claws that almost sliced through the reins. The sensation was a weight on my back, a prick of cold down my spine that centered in my core, like the beginning of the urge to fight or flee that ended as soon as it started.

Johann slept on soundly, his heart and breathing unchanged.

Dread settled in my stomach. I remembered that night in Dimresh's castle, when I'd been aware of people moving toward me—a knowledge that someone had entered my territory.

I didn't quite know how I was so sure, but I was suddenly positive Lasren knew we were here.

# CHAPTER THIRTEEN

Part of me wanted to turn back, to get out of his territory and have Johann finish the journey during the safety of the day.

No, that was foolish. He already knew we were here. We had no choice but to keep going.

"Johann," I said. "Johann!"

He roused immediately, his eyes opening and sharpening into alertness, his heart leaping into overdrive. I was impressed. He put his hand to his side, where his stakeshooter rested. "What is it?" He blinked at the sky. "It'll be light soon."

"Not that. Lasren. He knows we're here." I twisted the reins in my hand, willing my fingernails back to normal. The first lesson I'd learned from Johann was the importance of fear, and I was feeling it now. "I'm sure of it."

"How?" Johann peered into the distance. I wondered how much of the trees and lanterns that marked the road he could see. "How do you know?"

"I . . . I felt it."

"I believe you." He spoke quickly, and his heart still pounded, but he sounded calm as he loaded his stakeshooter and kept talking. "Other hunters have reported that vampires seem to know when humans are around. That other vampire found us too. So." He took a careful breath, blinking the last of his sleepiness away. "Let's think, Kaiden. His castle is still a good ten miles off, if I'm remembering right. A good distance from the city, and we're not in the city yet. If he knows we're here, and he hasn't fed, we may be at risk. How fast can you run about fifteen miles?"

"Minutes." I eyed the sky. "The sun won't be up by then."

"If he's concerned with keeping Brusque isolated, he may attack us even if he isn't hungry. That's why he killed my parents. And so many other merchants." He gripped his weapon, the skin of his fist white and blotched with red from the pressure. I licked my lips and turned away, toward the road. "But we may be safe. It all depends on him. Stay ready, Kaiden. I'll take the reins. But let's keep going."

The night air had lost its sense of quiet peace, Johann's breathing fast and his heart beating hard. Birds in trees ruffled their feathers, slowly coming to their first signs of alertness. Mint's breath huffed in white clouds. Twigs snapped a good distance away, but it was the slow, stately pattern of a clumsy family of deer hiding from some predator they had to always assume might be near. Bats fluttered above.

There was no sign of a vampire. But I didn't stop listening, scenting, peering down the road and through the branches of winter-dead trees. The stars began to disappear as the moon sank to their level.

A weight began to drag me down, the first bit of the exhaustion that would force me to sleep while the sun was up.

Next to me, Johann's grip on his stakeshooter relaxed. "Morning soon, Kaiden," he said. "I'm sure he knows we're here. But tonight, I think we got lucky."

"Or unlucky," I said. "We could have killed him."

"Good point," Johann said with a chuckle.

"I'll rest, then." I left his side, preparing to enter my lightless compartment. I almost missed the beds at the barracks — and I certainly missed the plush bed at Dimresh's old castle. But I would be asleep soon enough. Comfort didn't really matter. "Stay safe."

"I will, Kaiden. The day is always . . ." He trailed off. "Well, tonight I'll show you Brusque. I think you'll like it."

"Enjoy the day," I said. His smile warmed me as the sun once did.

I woke in the darkness and stayed still for a moment. I wasn't sure what to expect. If I left the wagon, would I terrify someone I didn't know? Would I be alone in a stable with Mint?

Someone knocked on the wood. When I unlatched it, Johann peered down at me.

"C'mon, Kaiden," he said. "The night is young, and I want to show you Brusque, like I said."

I sat up. The wagon had been left outside, behind what smelled like a stable, the scent of Mint and other horses mingling with hay and leather. Strange to see a building again, after nights and nights of traveling through nothing but overgrown, cold forest.

And as Johann led me around the stable to the town, there were more of them.

Penthorn had been a city once, fallen now to the size of a village. It still had plenty of buildings, mostly houses and a few warehouses that had once held grain. But Brusque was entirely different.

The road beneath my feet was cracked and unkempt, paved with stones that had likely once been smooth. Houses were tightly packed, some even two stories, stairs leading up to landings above my head.

"We'll be staying in the abandoned part of town," Johann said. His voice held a spark I didn't hear often, some secret knowledge he was eager to share. "C'mon. It gets better around the Bendy Road."

Bendy Road. Probably because it curved sharply as we walked around the two-story house, with no scents of humans inside. Had the roads in Penthorn names I had forgotten?

A cat zipped past us as we walked, then paused in the darkness of a house, probably assuming I couldn't see it as it scuttled beneath the porch. Its eyes glowed brightly at me. The road curved farther, and the houses gave way to a town square that reminded me of the one in Penthorn, but much larger. The town well sat in the middle of the square, beneath a wooden tower, a large bell hanging from the wood. Brass gleamed in the moonlight.

"This is where the town crier used to give news," Johann said. "And apparently still does. We got announced today."

"We?"

"I told them you were my partner, but not that you're a vampire." Johann faced me. "People were surprised to see me, but told me they would talk to us tonight at the Rose Inn—or what used to be the Rose. They don't get travelers anymore, so now it's apparently used as some sort of hospital."

"You didn't talk to them today?"

"Only enough to get my bearings and our next step. I had to rest, Kaiden. I have to be alert, especially if Lasren knows we're here."

He had a good point.

The streets were quiet, which wasn't surprising after dark, but something about the silence felt wrong. Penthorn had been quiet too, near the houses, though. Maybe when we got closer to where people still lived it would feel more . . . alive.

"Do things look familiar?" I asked.

"They do." Johann gestured to the bell. "There used to be someone who would ring that every hour." We kept walking and passed by shuttered buildings that smelled of dust and rotted wood. "This is where Bendy Street became Hospitality Street. Merchants used to stay in the inns that were all along here. And the houses you see, every other were where the inn-keepers stayed. Seems like all that's gone, though." His voice still held cheer, but was also wistful, I realized. Here were all his memories, but they were as changed as he'd probably expected.

"I'm sure many people are still safe," I said. I didn't scent humans in the houses, though. Just more dust.

"I'm sure they're not safe if they're here," Johann said. "But thanks." He patted my shoulder.

"I'm sorry."

I wondered if he was upset, but he walked on, shoulders squared. "We're here to help them, Kaiden, remember that. Brusque used to be the last hope of mankind, a city that worked almost as it did in the days of the Empire. That was only a decade ago—I'm sure it can be like that again." He pointed. "The temples are old, but still standing."

Over the shapes of the huddled houses, two enormous buildings loomed, white stone arches glittering in the moonlight. Something about them gave me pause.

"C'mon, Kaiden," Johann said. "Let's find out how the people of Brusque are doing." He followed my gaze. "Then maybe we can see the temples."

As we passed by the bell and walked down what Johann had called Hospitality Street, signs of life entered my hearing. The road became cleaner, more well-kept, no tufts of winter-dead grass poking through the cobblestone or packed dead leaves marring the road. I smelled sweat and horse, cooking meat, ash and smoke, and even perfume. And in the distance lights glowed from houses, and finally from a larger building where voices rang out.

"Bourbon Street," Johann said with a smile. "Didn't come here often as a kid." Despite the name, I smelled very little alcohol on the air, and it didn't have the same raucous, care-to-the-wind feeling I'd seen in Penthorn that lived in my hole-filled memories. Nonetheless, laughter rang into the night when the door of one building opened, sending more light spilling into the street.

"It's the traveler!" someone called back into the room. Then, "You shouldn't wander out tonight! He hasn't selected his victim yet!"

That didn't sound promising. Johann raised a hand in acknowledgement and we picked up our pace.

I soon lost track of our location, the twisting roads and countless buildings confusing my sense of direction. In a forest, it was easy to find my way — I could hunt by sound or smell. The merchant road wound in spirals throughout the forest, easy to find and keep as a landmark. But this city, with buildings that blocked our sight and the constant miasma of scents, was very different. If it wasn't for Johann knowing exactly where to go, I felt sure we would be wandering all night.

I did notice the silhouettes of people moving inside their houses. But when they saw us walking outside, many of them closed their shades or turned away.

Soon enough, we arrived at a building with two paintings along the side. The rose was faded, as though someone had tried to scrape off the crimson color. Next to it, a silvery moon had been painted instead. Behind the building was a large plot of rolling land — and it reeked of death. Fresh death.

"I guess they changed the name," Johann said. I wondered if he could even see the cemetery behind the house in the darkness.

He knocked on the wooden door and it swung open. An older woman peered at us. She wore a woolen dress, the fabric buttoned up all the way up to her neck. "You're the hunter?" she said. She glanced at me, her eyes narrowed. "And you're his partner, another hunter?"

I made sure my fangs were hidden. "Yes."

I must have used the wrong tone, because she frowned.

"Greetings, Sasha," Johann said. "We're here to meet with you, like you asked me earlier in the day. May we come in?"

She stood aside, eyeing us both. Her gaze lingered on the plethora of weapons Johann wore. Her face was lined with age, but her hair was still brown with only a few wisps of gray.

Johann had said this was some sort of hospital, but there was no scent of herbs as I expected. Just the usual smell of human, mixed with a wide variety of blood scents, as though many people had bled onto the floor. I swallowed hard. That explained what must be the cemetery behind the building.

"So, two hunters." She moved to sit at a table that had only two chairs. Johann and I stayed standing. "You're here to try and kill Lasren, I imagine?"

"We are."

"No hunter has ever made it this far. Do you have a plan?"

Johann and I exchanged glances. We didn't really have a plan, just a weapon — me.

"I'm guessing not. But at least you came and got past that witch-vampire. If she's still alive, she'll come after you. That is my first warning. And I have one other."

She looked tired, defeated, in a way no one in Penthorn had. My sense of wrongness grew stronger, mingling with the memory of what the man had shouted into the street.

"Lasren has told us he will not take more than he needs. We are his territory." Scorn dripped from her words, but it was a helpless emotion, an admittance of truth. "Once a month, he selects one of us. He feeds on them for a few weeks, slowly draining them. Sometimes they die. Sometimes they don't. None remember what it was like."

I fixed my gaze on her neck, but if there were fang marks there, I couldn't see them through the fabric.

"And do they turn?" Johann asked.

"No. He does not keep thralls."

That wasn't good news for me. But there was something more here. "So . . . explain this to me," I said. Johann met my eye, his mouth turned down. Apparently he understood what was happening already. But I didn't. "He chooses a victim. He drains them over a month's time. Then they return?"

Sasha sighed. "They return every day. We care for them — Well, I care for them." I suddenly understood what *a hospital of sort*s meant. "Strengthening foods, caring for their . . . wounds. They leave at night, hypnotized, wandering out into the darkness, and he takes them back to his castle. When they're too weak, sometimes he lets them go and chooses another. Sometimes they die."

"What happened to the last one?" Johann asked.

Sasha shook her head.

I couldn't wrap my head around what I was hearing. "You let them go every night? To be . . . eaten?"

She squared her shoulders, meeting my eyes. "Any who fight or resist are killed. Hunters have abandoned us. This system works. We agree not to let people leave the town, and he does his best not to thin our numbers beyond what we can sustain."

Adrian's words echoed. "You're kept like cattle," I said.

"Kaiden!" Johann snapped. He turned to Sasha, whose mouth was set in a firm line.

"I understand," he said. "We won't endanger you, or the . . . system you have in place. But we do intend to kill him. So if you have any information you can give to help us, without implicating yourself or risking anyone, we would appreciate it."

She dropped her gaze, her jaw set. "I would not expect much help from anyone here. People are afraid. If he thinks we're helping a hunter, there could be repercussions for us."

"I understand," Johann said again. "I used to live here. I don't want anyone hurt. But anything. Please."

"Layla . . . his last victim, passed yesterday. They're buried . . . here. In the new cemetery." Johann's eyebrows went up. "It's a place of remembrance for the bitten, an honor for their sacrifice. They're cared for here. They die here, sometimes."

Johann nodded. "I understand. Go on."

"If he follows his typical pattern, he'll l select another tomorrow night. Lasren doesn't show himself — the chosen one will be hypnotized and will wander into the darkness. He chooses those who are alone. Either those in the street, or even those asleep in their beds. His choice will probably be a healthy man. He tries not to kill too many in a row, and the women tend to die."

Johann frowned, but he nodded with a slow blink. "Thank you. We'll do the best we can."

We left the hospital — the place where Lasren's victims were cared for, and where most were buried when they died. Sasha didn't wish us luck.

# CHAPTER FOURTEEN

"I suspected as much. I just . . . never truly realized how strange it would be to see my old hometown like this." Johann peered up at the buildings of Brusque, at the flickering lights in the houses that ringed us. Where people lived who would avoid us for fear of what their vampire lord would do to them if they didn't.

"This is common?" I asked. Unease crawled along my spine. Penthorn I knew. I was used to it. Brusque, the territory of another vampire, so controlled the people in it that they accepted their fate . . . I clenched my teeth.

"I wouldn't say common. But it does happen, and used to happen more often in the past. There are old logs of weak vampires who weren't confident in their hunting ability using their strength to intimidate villages so small they didn't have their own inn. Places like that don't even exist anymore. They would kill one person every so often, but forbid anyone else from running. According to records, we could kill those types of vampires fairly easily. Sneak into their lair during the day. But a vampire like Lasren?" He shook his head, his face troubled. "I expected things to be bad here. But not . . . I didn't expect people to have given up."

He put his hands in his pockets, ducking his head against a cold breeze that held the promise of winter snow later that night. I hated to see the frown on his face, the lost look in his eyes. I hated Lasren then for what he had put these people through, for making Johann feel this way.

But this was Johann. His sadness was hidden in moments

and he stood straighter, breathing in as though the air itself could strengthen him. "We can't let tragedy get us down. You taught me that." He smiled at me. "So let's think, Kaiden. We have plenty of options. What do we know about Lasren? And what should our first plan of attack be?"

He spoke almost as if he was testing me. But my decision was obvious. "We attack him tonight," I said. "He already knows we're here. There's no reason to wait, especially if someone will be taken tomorrow."

Johann blinked. "What do you think would have happened if I'd attacked Dimresh immediately the first night I came to Penthorn?"

I knew what point he was making, but this was different. "You have me now. You don't need to spend time preparing."

Johann huffed a laugh. "And if he kills you, and humanity loses its best weapon?"

That last statement cooled my ardor, but the word he used hurt. "I'm not a weapon."

"I'm sorry," Johann said. "I know you're not. But think. What if he kills me?"

That sent a spike of fear through me. "Fine," I said. "What do you suggest then?"

"You're right that we should be prepared to fight at any moment. Like you said, he already knows we're here. But there's a lot that I'm curious about. The old records say some vampires used to use this strategy of . . . well, keeping people like cattle, as you said. But bleeding them for weeks? Hypnotizing and then releasing them? That's new. Why would he do that? How does he have the power to hypnotize someone from so far away?"

"Does it matter?"

"Everything matters. You were able to kill Dimresh because he didn't expect that level of power from a thrall. I was able to protect myself from his fear aura with your hypnosis.

We were able to surprise him. But Lasren will know you're a vampire like he is, with the same abilities, and he'll be wary."

I was a vampire, just like Lasren. I hated being compared to him. But it was true.

"The strategy—and let's be honest, luck—that helped us kill Dimresh won't work here. We have your powers, and that makes killing him possible in the first place. But we still need to think like hunters. And that means understanding our enemy. Our . . . prey, as you would say." He grinned. "You're more than a weapon, Kaiden, like you said. You can help me."

"But if no one will talk to us, how do we do that?"

"Sasha was afraid. But if I've learned anything from my time talking to people in vampire-infested towns, not everyone is as cautious as her. And it's Brusque." His smile slipped slightly as he turned back toward Bourbon street. "If our luck holds, someone may remember me, and may be a bit more helpful."

I followed him for a few steps, listening to his heart beat and his breathing, before asking. "Why would someone remembering you make you sad?"

Johann paused and eyed me. Then he sighed and shook his head. "You're learning me too well, Kaiden."

I wished he would look at me, and not at the dancing lights of lanterns glowing in the nearby houses. I reached out, putting my hand on his shoulder as he did to me so often.

He leaned into my touch, and I relished the connection. This time, though, instead of sinking into the feelings his touch gave me, I hoped to give him some of my . . . not warmth. I had none. But strength, maybe.

"I miss what I lost, Kaiden. I miss my parents, and my old life." His voice was soft. "But compared to people here, I was lucky. I have training, abilities. I'm not defenseless. I have you. Not as a weapon, but as a . . . a friend." He put his hand on mine, his palm warm even as the winter winds blew. "But those here have almost nothing. I snapped at you when you said it, but they *are* kept like cattle. Animals to a bloodsucker." His teeth snapped on the last word. "And I abandoned them years ago. I ran. I should have done more. I should have come here sooner." He looked up, meeting my eyes, and his blazed. "I want nothing more than to agree with you and march into Lasren's castle and let you at his throat. But if we do that, without planning, without preparing, and then we fail, we'll only make things worse. But still. I should have known. I should have . . ."

I pulled him close, into a hug. He gasped slightly, but let me. I could feel his tension, his anger and frustration, in the tremor of his muscles.

I understood. I thought of Matilda, of all of the things I could have done, should have done, to make her happy. Of the life and people in it I truly had abandoned, memories I would never get back. The anger and guilt that clenched my throat when I thought of it. But Johann . . . he was better than me.

"You're wrong," I said. "Surviving, escaping, learning your skills, helping me . . . it was all for this. So you did everything right. You didn't abandon anyone. You've worked toward a goal. That's all. And as soon as you could, you came." Our mission from Lesalie had changed, but now it felt more right than ever.

"I know, Kaiden." He put his arms around me too, his breathing warm on my shoulder. "At least, part of me knows that. But emotions are fickle things." He pulled away, looking into my eyes. "For many reasons, I'm glad I have you."

Desire curled like a flame within me. Emotions were fickle indeed. "I'm glad to help you," I said, hoping my fangs didn't show. "Just tell me how."

He smiled. "Let's go find people, Kaiden. We need to get information as fast as we can. Maybe you'll even make a new friend. Talk to people. Explore the town if they'll show you around, and learn from them. And from there, we can figure out a way to set things right."

I followed him toward the sounds and scents of humanity, of remaining life in a vampire-ruled town. I tamped down my hunger, my desire, as best as I could.

One thing stuck out in my mind, though, from what Sasha had said. Johann wanted to take time, but I had a time limit of my own.

If Lasren didn't make thralls, I had nothing to eat. And the pleasure and power of Johann's blood still called to me.

Johann stood by the door of the same inn where the man had called out to us. The wooden sign above the door was painted with a sort of plant I didn't recognize, and I couldn't tell if it was because I had never seen the plant before or if it was just because the drawing was crude.

He didn't have to knock before someone opened the door, the din of voices making my ears hurt. Humans in large numbers were loud.

A man wearing an apron peered out at us, and a memory flared in my mind. Another man, one from Penthorn, peering down at me the same way. *"Kaiden. Show me you have something to trade with first, and if not go in the back and clean off the mugs before you drink."*

"Vampire hunters." This man's voice was just as flat as the one in my memory. "Never thought I'd see you here."

"May we come in?" Johann asked. Someone bumped the man by the door, another man peering out at us, the two strangers.

"Are you gonna drink?"

"I have money, if that's what you're asking, and some weapons to trade if you don't take money," Johann said.

The man's heart beat fast, but to his credit his fear didn't show on his face or in any tension in his muscles. There was a faint scent of fear, the tinge of acridity that became obvious when someone was nervous or tense. A lot of people inside must feel that way for it to be so obvious even out in the night air.

"How about we buy a round of drinks for everyone?" I said. Johann's eyebrows went up.

The man huffed, then stepped aside. "Fine then, hunters," he said. "Your money is good here—we haven't lost that yet. But don't be convincing anyone to do anything stupid."

"We won't," Johann said.

The scent of humanity—sweat and smoke and meat and blood—was like a punch to my nose. Once it had meant a meal, easy prey. Now it could be, but I had thoughts, emotions, that were more refined than simple hunger. There were nearly two dozen people inside, men and women sitting at tables and throwing dice while another group sat and drank. A few people sat alone. But everyone looked up as we walked in.

Unlike at the barracks, though, this time their gazes were all fixed on Johann. He was the one wearing the heavy leather coat, the one with stakes at his side and a crossbow hanging from his belt. I just looked like any other human.

They had no idea what I was. It was . . . refreshing. And entering a bar, with firelight dancing from the sconces along the walls, felt familiar. The entire experience was almost reassuring. Some part of me, some emotions that seemed to remember things better than my mind could, felt comforted by the scene.

"Johann!"

A man dressed in tattered silk clothes that looked to have patches of wool on the tears jumped up from his dice game. "Johann, is it really you?"

"Who . . . Maravin!" Johann crossed the room and folded

the smaller man, Marvin, in a bear hug. I frowned. "I can't believe . . . how are you?"

Tension in the room faded, other people going back to their chatting or drinking. A woman carrying a try of empty mugs sidestepped Johann and Maravin and went back to work.

"I can't believe it's you!" Maravin took a step back, appraising Johann. "I thought I'd never see you, not after . . . well! And wearing wooden weapons? You truly are a hunter?"

"Yes. I've come back to help. How many others are here?"

"Becca and Mito are still alive, but living on the outskirts. Safer, most likely." I wished I knew who these people were. I wished I knew what he meant by others.

My sense of reassurance, that momentary flash of belonging, faded. I had no memories like these, people who would appear out of another life and hug and accept me. Johann sat at the dice game next to his old friend, putting a hand on his shoulder.

I clenched my teeth. *Johann is mine.*

"Are you really buying drinks for everyone?" someone asked.

A woman nodded at me from the nearest table. It took me a moment to react, to remember what I was doing here. We needed information. We were hunting a vampire. Johann was working too — it was a good thing he knew people here. That would help.

I didn't like that flash of anger. I had emotions as a vampire, but that was the wrong kind.

Johann had wanted me to get used to talking to people at the barracks. There, where everyone knew what I was, it seemed impossible. Here . . . I had to try. This was part of killing Lasren. Of helping Johann. I met his eye, and he gave me a slight nod before turning back to Maravin.

"Yes," I finally answered the woman. I sat down at her

table, getting her scent. No perfume, no sickness. Just human.

She pushed red hair away from her face. "Why don't you have all the weapons he does?" she asked. She raised one hand, a crook of her finger motioning to the barkeeper, the same man who'd met us at the door.

"I . . . prefer not to carry around so much weight," I replied. A foolish response, but she shrugged as though it made sense.

She pushed her hair around with her hand again, the marks on her neck obvious in a flash of firelight. Not fresh.

"Did Lasren give you those?" I asked. I glanced around the room. How many others had marks like them?

Her eyes widened. "Did someone tell you I was one of the bitten?"

Maybe a human wouldn't have been able to notice the marks in this light. "So you are?"

She sighed. "Yes. Two years ago. There are a lot of us."

"And—"

"Before you ask, no, I don't remember any of it." I shut my mouth, letting her continue. "We would share information if we could—telling each other what to expect, how to ensure survival. But no one remembers. I was sitting in my house near Clockmaker street, and the next moment I was sitting outside as the sun came up. Every night for a month was like that. Sasha took care of me during the day—every bitten stays at the hospital with her. Apparently we're hypnotized, simply wander out into the night toward the castle, and then we disappear. Then one night, nothing happened. He was done with me. I was weak for a few days, but then I went back to my life. Whatever happened on those nights . . ." She shrugged again, as she had when I had answered her question about weapons, but her heart thudded hard.

"Be careful, Ruby," the waitress said as she clunked two drinks down on the table. She gave me a narrow-eyed look before she headed over to another table.

"Careful of me?" I asked.

"Careful of speaking." Ruby sighed, taking a swig from her glass. "Everyone knows not to leave. And everyone knows not to fight. Having two hunters stroll into town right after he kills a bitten . . ." Laughter broke out from Johann's table, and I tried to ignore the flare of possessiveness that went through me. "Well, does talking to you count as fighting? You both slept all day, but you're the talk of the town, you know. No hunter has ever come here before."

"What are people saying?" I swirled the liquid in the glass in front of me, wondering if she thought it was odd that I wasn't drinking.

"People remember Johann. They thought he was killed before the takeover. I didn't know him — Brusque was big back then. The smart ones fled while they could. Now it's just whoever's left in the main city and the few farmers by the northern mountains on the edge of town. Without them we'd probably all have starved by now. Lasren still takes them, though. A few have died." She sighed, the marks on her neck exposed again when she looked down at the table. Her breath smelled like alcohol, and I wondered if her blood would have that tinge too.

I swallowed and put the thought out of my mind. I wasn't like Lasren. I was here to help them, just as I had helped Penthorn. I could save Johann's home as he had helped me to save mine.

"What have you tried?" I asked. "You say he would kill you if you tried to fight or run — how does he know?" Even as I asked it, I thought of the sense I had the night before, the knowledge that he knew we were here.

"How? I have no clue. A few have tried to run, mostly families of those who died. They get drained and left on the edge of the city — or just killed. The farthest we can go safely is to the temples." Her gaze went distant, her pupils wide, like a deer facing down a wolf. She took another sip, her heart slowing down. She didn't meet my eyes, but this was different than the memories of people avoiding looking at me out of disgust, and different than the looks of those in the barracks who avoided my eyes out of wariness or fear.

She didn't want to know me, because she was sure I would be dead soon. It turned my stomach to see, to recognize the cringing look of someone who obeyed someone more powerful. I knew that look. I used to have it when I was a thrall who served Dimresh. Mindless hopelessness.

I had to keep her talking, to learn. "The temples?" I said. I had wanted to go there, and now I did even more. "What sort of things are in there?"

"Useless ancient relics, probably. Same as any other leftovers of the empire."

Useless to humans. But maybe not to me. I looked over my shoulder to where Johann was laughing with Maravin, and now other men too, a group of people who probably remembered him. They were talking about racehorses, and about how some people had maybe gotten away by using them to put enough distance between them and the city. Maravin put his hand on Johann's shoulder, and the two leaned in closer, Johann among old friends who could bring him the camaraderie he deserved and reveled in. Real friends. Not weapons.

My eyes narrowed, my fangs threatening to show, and I forced it down. Johann wasn't mine. These humans were no threat. I needed to focus and do my job, while Johann did his. He trusted me.

"Can you take me to the temples?" I asked Ruby.

# CHAPTER FIFTEEN

I expected Ruby to be leery of wandering down the dark streets at night. Dimresh had hunted those who ventured outdoors, preying on the prostitutes who were desperate enough to stay outside and the drunks who were too stupid or careless—the way I had been. But I supposed in a place where the vampire lord could hypnotize even those in their beds, it didn't matter where you were.

"Still no weapons?" she asked once the sounds of the tavern had faded—at least to human ears. A few people had glared at her as we left, but no one had stopped us. Johann, too, had noted us leave, but had given me only a nod that I still didn't quite understand. I had half-hoped he would stop me, or come with me. He knew Brusque too, and would likely know more about the temple than she did.

He'd said he would show me around, but instead he was remembering the life he once had. I missed our quiet journey together, where he was so close to me. But no. I couldn't be selfish.

"No weapons?" she asked again, more loudly, and I pulled my thoughts away from Johann.

"We'll be fine," I said.

"Do you at least have one of those . . . light things hidden away?" she asked.

"Yes." Lying was easier. "The solar flare. Useful for killing thralls."

"I've never seen a thrall," she said. "I've heard they're worse than vampires." Her shoes clacked loudly on the cobblestones, which were more cracked and broken in this area. More of the buildings were run down, too, smelling of dust and mold rather than smoke and human. A cracked wooden sign lay on the ground, only a few letters remaining.

"They're more vicious," I said. "But easier to kill. Predictable."

"Lasren doesn't allow them here," she said. "One of the benefits of having him rule." She snorted, her words dripping sarcasm.

The thought flowed through my mind like a bite of blood in my dreams. Of course Lasren didn't allow thralls. Lucien had been a thrall. And he had killed his master and ruled Brusque before Lasren arrived. Lasren must know the story. He would know that making thralls was a risk.

"Hey?" Ruby looked back over her shoulder at me. "Keep up. Don't tell me he's hypnotized you already, hunter."

"I'm fine." Suddenly I wanted to go back, to talk to Johann about anything more he might know of Lucien.

*No.* I had made a decision. Johann could handle getting information from the townsfolk. Scouring an old temple at night was a job I was suited for.

We walked on, the temple roof looming over the rest of the buildings. Our path was winding and indirect though, a clustered city full of alleys and crisscrossing roads that confused even my sense of direction. More dust and mold met my nose, the wooden buildings here rotted or even collapsed. The great dome of the temple rose above everything in the distance. If I needed to, I could leap above the rooftops. That would be faster, unless I slipped through rotted wood. How embarrassing if I slipped and died on fallen beams.

"This place must have been impressive when it was a city," I said as we passed another enormous building, three floors high with blackened, open windows.

"Brusque was the heart of the old religion," Ruby

answered. "Or so my grandmother said." Her breathing sent wispy condensation into the night air, and I wondered that she hadn't noticed mine didn't. Humans didn't seem to notice much.

"Does anyone still follow the old ways?"

"Here? Of course not. If any of the magic still worked, Brusque would have been the safest city of all. But look at it now." As we walked around another corner, she pointed at a fallen building. "I sometimes wonder if the legends of the empire were really true. If the magic ever worked at all."

We turned another corner, the street zagging to the left and then the right. And then the temple stood before me, enormous, cavernous ruins.

Remnants of glass windows, now broken, sparkled on the ground in the moonlight. Pillars of stone supported the marble where an archway had collapsed. I blinked, my mind flashing to a memory.

Not a memory. A dream.

*. . . the archway would lead inside, where the shapes in the windows cast colorful shadows on the polished floors. The images were lit by the sun through stained glass. There was Laurel, and a Laurel tree, and leaves, and men in robes and women in dresses . . .*

I had dreamed of this. My back teeth grit together, and I floundered for a moment, searching desperately for a memory to make sense of the vision. I must have seen something similar in a book. But I didn't remember the book, or where I had been when I'd seen it before . . . or why I would have remembered this specific place, this specific building.

"See what you need to see?" Ruby asked.

"You've never been inside?"

"If there was anything of value inside, it's long gone. And the path to the temple's wide open." *A sun-drenched courtyard.* She pulled her shawl farther over her shoulders. "I do want to help you. I'm not like some of the others. Lasren killed my mother, and my father died soon after. So I hope you kill him.

But" — another sigh, a gust of vapor from her lips — "I'd like to live to see you do it. So if he does come after you tonight, I'd rather not get in the way."

*Or be seen near you.* I understood. "You've been helpful," I said. "I'm sorry about your parents." Hers was a common tale, it seemed.

"Did you ever lose someone?" Ruby asked. "What made you decide to fight and not run, or hide, like we are?"

The question morphed in my mind. I had other options. I could be the predator, not the prey. Why was I fighting, and not taking territory of my own, living like I wanted?

"Ask Johann," I said.

She tilted her head, a slow smile growing. "You're together?"

I wished that were true. "No."

"If you say so." She shivered against another gust of wind. "I'm going back. And don't worry. I won't let him get too distracted by all his old friends and forget about his pining partner." She turned with a smirk on her lips.

It seemed humans noticed some things, at least.

I waited until she'd turned around the zagging street corners before I continued on toward the temple. The dream I had, the vision of this temple during a sunny day, when the windows had been whole and the stone hadn't fallen to rubble, was a constant weight in my mind. There had been a decorative statue there, where there was now a blasted mark on the stone. Trees had grown in a garden where now there was only dirt that smelled of lichen and grass cropped by some sort of mammal whose faded scent resembled a rat. And without the sunlight and the windows, the winding, colorful shadows of stained decorations in glass didn't sparkle in the courtyard.

My fangs pricked my lips, my fingernails turning to claws. I didn't like this place. The structure was no different than any other old building in Brusque, but its appearance compared against my memories was wrong. I shouldn't know these things. I didn't know how I knew them, and all of it frightened me, made me want to lash out at something that I couldn't fight.

"Laurel?" I said aloud at the entrance where the archway had fallen, but of course there was no response. There were only vampires now, vampires like me. Maybe this memory was part of that, something Dimresh could have explained to me.

But I had killed him, and I had to fight with what I had, learn on my own. I pushed through the fear and jumped lightly over the fallen stone.

Dust plumed at my feet. Moonlight shone through the holes of once-windows, and dusty square outlines on the walls marked where paintings or tapestries once hung. When I closed my eyes I could almost imagine them, woven images of laurel trees illuminated by streaming sunbeams.

As I walked on, though, I had no more dreams or memories of the interior of the building. Stone had fallen into the hallways, but the path to what must have once been an altar was open. There was nothing there, though. No statue, which I had expected, and no trace if it had ever been there.

I wondered if it had been made of the same smooth stone the one in the forest had been made of. If so, it had either been melted down years ago for solar flares, or Lasren had taken it away so it couldn't be.

Whatever the significance of this great hall was gone now. Stairs along the left side spiraled up to a second floor, and rotted wooden doors marked entrances to a room beyond the hall.

I sniffed the air, but identified only dust, mold, wet stone, and rat droppings. Those were familiar scents by now.

I pushed past the anxiety of enclosing myself behind rotted

wood that could hurt me in ways I couldn't heal from, and went through the doors. The air here was still and weirdly quiet, the sounds of the night outside faint when the wooden door closed behind me. Had the wood been whole and the door flush with the stone, I was sure there would be total silence.

It would also be dark. Moonlight leeched through the rotted parts of the wooden door, but only in sharp beams of white glowing light. Even for my eyes, the lighting was dim.

This room had been important once, but I had no idea why. Completely empty, the stone walls were smooth and bare. There was a lack of scent, too, as though there had been nothing in here left to rot or grow moldy or even create dust the way things in the hall had.

The lack of smells was strange. The darkness, the faded sounds . . . all made my skin crawl. Like a blanket had been pulled over the senses I used for hunting. All I had here were my thoughts, and those couldn't help me.

I left the room, banging the wooden door against the stone as I did. A bird cawed outside, some crow disturbed from its sleep. I wished I had brought Johann.

Foolish. I had to control myself better. This was nothing but an old temple to a god who had no power. There was no reason to be afraid. I was here to learn about Brusque, about how I could kill Lasren. Here maybe I could learn what old priests could do, and only because what they once could do was what I could do now. I held the power here.

The winding stairs were broken halfway up. I had to make an incredibly high jump to reach the second floor. Easy for me. More long hallways stretched ahead of me, the scent of dust mixed with that of wetness and mold. Windows in small rooms looked out over the city.

The temple was huge, but so empty. Even if three hundred years had passed, I'd thought there would be something.

Traces of people who'd lived here, a few intact panes of glass, books or scrolls or lost bedding. Anything. Dimresh's castle had contained old weapons and books, tapestries and furniture and linens. But each room here was bare, the stone cold. On this second floor wasn't even a sign of animal life except for a few feathers that marked birds who must fly in and out.

This wasn't what I had expected. The third floor was the same, and so on until the fourth. The stairs here were broken too, crumbled stone. I had to leap again, pulling myself up with my arms, careful to avoid the jagged wood of the broken door that led farther up.

Here was the inside of the great dome I'd seen stretching over the city. One brass bell had fallen to the stone, tarnished and dull, the rafters from where it had hung over my head bare even of the rope that once held it.

The windows here were as empty of panes as the rest, but something told me they'd never held glass. Moonlight streamed into the dome, the sounds and scents of the city flowing here, the opposite of the place behind the altar. Ruby was walking back alone, toward where fires glimmered in houses. Taverns and inns, homes where many stayed awake, all centered around a small part of what was once a sprawling city. Near the darker edges of the city, butting up against a trail that would lead to the mountains, scattered fires burned, the few farmers who were left protecting their flocks from wolves in the night.

So many of the houses, though, were dark and empty. Bigger than Penthorn, so much more dense, but even so Brusque was dying.

And on the west side of the city, past a dark trail where no fires burned at all and trees had grown over what must have once been part of the merchant road, sat Lasren's castle. Long stone walls stretched over the hill it sat upon. The main keep was stone too, unlike Dimresh's mix of stone and wood.

Lasren's stronghold looked almost inviting, a beautiful castle on a hill against the moon, the design simple and elegant. I estimated there might be maybe an hour of travel from the heart of the city to the castle. Much less for a vampire like me.

I wondered what the castles like this one, like Dimresh's, had been used for during the time of the empire. Why were they built? I understood the purpose of the temple, even if it made no sense to me now why the place was so empty. But who had lived in the castles before the vampires came, and why? What had happened to them?

"I didn't expect you here," a soft voice said, and my body suddenly tensed with icy fear. I whirled, cursing myself for letting someone sneak up on me, again, just like the other vampire on the road had.

And this was worse. There was only one vampire who could be here.

"I thought another may have entered my territory," Lasren said, his fangs gleaming. "But I'm sure you can see there isn't enough here for two."

# CHAPTER SIXTEEN

From Johann's stories about how he had lost his parents, I had expected Lasren to look like Dimresh—tall, powerfully built, a vampire lord who had resembled a war-faring man in his prime. Not a soft-faced, waifish young man, so skinny and frail-looking he resembled someone stricken with illness.

That wasn't even the most surprising thing about him, though. He wore robes I'd seen in pictures from books in Dimresh's study and even from books Johann had salvaged. Robes of white and green, with fabric over his shoulders that depicted the Laurel tree. He was dressed like an ancient priest.

"Who are you?" he asked. His voice held no anger or fear, or even aggression, as Adrian's had. Just simple curiosity.

I narrowed my eyes. He'd surprised me, but he hadn't taken advantage of that to attack. With one spring, I could end this tonight. I shifted my weight.

His eyes widened, and he held up a hand. A gust of wind from nowhere took me mid-jump, blowing me back hard against the stone. My body slammed into it, shock jolting through me. I slid down the stone, recovering enough to land on my feet, leaning against the wall. Next to me, the wind whistled through the opening in the stone.

As I leaned against it, the stone molded, forming around my wrists and ankles before I could move. I lunged, but I was held fast. I concentrated, willing myself to mist.

Nothing happened. Just as in the fight with the vampire the

night before, the one that had nearly killed me and Johann.

No. This was impossible. He hadn't said anything. But my will to turn to mist did nothing.

I met Lasren's eyes. A familiar instinct to run, to fight, to snap my wrists and ankles and attack my enemy screamed in my mind, one I fought to suppress. I wasn't a thrall anymore. And if I ever wanted to understand what I could do, I would have to figure out a way to fight back against a vampire who apparently wielded all of the magics of the priests of the old empire. Fighting wasn't the answer here.

I had to keep calm. He could pin me down, he could use magic, but if Adrian was right, he couldn't kill me.

"Not going to answer?" Lasren asked. "I have no intention of hurting you if you're well-behaved." He spoke to me as though he was talking to a child. His soft voice made my skin crawl. I could imagine him speaking like that to the people he drained, hypnotizing them and using them every night until they were nearly dead.

I had to say something. He had no idea I was here to kill him. I wished Johann were here. Then again, if he were here, he would be at greater risk. I had no way to protect him from what Lasren could do. I couldn't even protect myself.

Unless I learned what it was and could do it on my own. The idea was insane. But it was all I had.

My stomach twisted. "I won't hurt you," I said. Lasren tilted his head, the laurel trees on the dangling fabric on his shoulders rustling. "Please let me go. I just . . . got a bit lost. I won't harm anyone in your territory." I tried to make myself sound harmless. I wondered how Johann would react if he knew I was taking his advice on trying to talk to others in order to talk to a dangerous vampire. The very same vampire who had killed his family.

"Good," Lasren said. He frowned then glanced out the window. "There aren't enough here for two of us. And . . . ."

He glared at me then. "How did you get here? Why did Ana let you past?"

Ana. Who was . . . right. The vampire I had killed, who had nearly killed me and Johann. What would he say if I said I had killed her? I still didn't know if Adrian's claim was true or not. Think. I had to think. What would Johann say?

Johann. The answer was obvious. "A hunter killed her," I said. "He's dangerous."

"I did sense a human enter my territory last night," Lasren said. He ran the tip of his tongue over his fangs. "You both entered it. Ah, I see. You're afraid of this hunter, running away from him?"

I kept my expression carefully neutral. I waited, searching him for openings, waiting for the stone, his magic, to let me go. The thought kept repeating in my mind—one leap, one bite, and I could end this.

"He's very skilled," I said. "He could likely kill me if he found me."

"Kill you? One who Laurel blessed with her gifts?" Lasren asked.

Blessed with her gifts? "Laurel?" I blurted. "The dead god?"

"Blasphemy." He shook his head, smoothing the robes he wore. "She is not dead. She is eternal, as we are. Laurel has blessed us. We are chosen to rule for eternity." He bowed his head, as though he were praying. "I give thanks to her every day for the bounty she has given me. Cities full of subjects, food to fill me and help to continue my learning."

My stomach twisted. Lasren wasn't just dangerous. He was insane.

"What is this hunter's name?" Lasren asked. "Tell me and I can get rid of him for you. A gift from me. Then you will leave my territory, yes?"

I swallowed hard. "I don't know it."

"Too bad." Lasren closed his eyes, lifting his head, like a wolf scenting prey. No. This was different. My skin prickled, the same strange not-scent I'd received before from Adrian at the back of my throat. He was using magic. He wasn't a wolf, or any sort of predator I was used to. He was a spider — and all of Brusque was his web.

He controlled wind. He controlled stone. What else could priests of old do at one time that he could do now?

I had to distract him. I had to *kill* him. But I couldn't move. The stone dug into my wrists and ankles, despite the way my muscles strained.

I couldn't panic. I had to think. He was dressed like a priest, but he was no priest. He was a vampire, just like me. An insane vampire.

He hadn't spoken to control the wind or the stone, or to trap me and make me unable to use my ability to turn to mist. Maybe I didn't need to either. Maybe I could do the same things he could.

I focused on the feel of the stone, the grating against my skin as I struggled, the solid mass of it behind me. *Let me go*, I willed it. *By my blood, let me go!*

Nothing happened. No vampiric instinct came to mind. I was fumbling with magic that this vampire had been using and studying for centuries. There was no Johann here to help me. And if I let him do whatever he was going to do, he would find Johann and hypnotize him, the way he did every other person in Brusque. He would kill him.

I had nothing. Lasren had everything. What could I do? Lasren, the man who'd turned two other vampires I had killed.

*Lasren chose me. He taught me.* Adrian's words echoed in my mind.

What had Dimresh done when he faced death and failure at my fangs?

"Lasren," I said. Blue eyes met mine. "I want to make a deal with you."

He blinked. "What sort of deal?"

"I . . . I don't want you to kill the hunter. I want to learn . . . about Laurel. About her gifts. You can teach me, can't you? And when you teach me, I'll kill the hunter. And any other hunters who come here. Teach me, and I can guard your territory, like . . . like Ana used to."

His gaze fixed on me, and at the same time past me, unfocused. "With Ana gone, my territory is unguarded, isn't it? My subjects might try and get away if they knew." His jaw clenched, the bones in his narrow face obvious. "I have never gifted anything to anyone I did not bite. I bite only my absolute favorites, you know. I could just bite someone and have them guard my territory." His gaze sharpened. "I don't need you."

Staring down a vampire would once have made me quail, but not now. "Then kill me," I said. "Or trust me and let me go. I'll protect your territory better than a newly made vampire." That was a risk, one of the foolish, wild risks Johann would take with his fragile human life. But at least I would finally learn if Adrian's words were true. "Laurel has gifted me with great strength. My master gave me a lot of the blood, but he didn't teach me. I would be happy to learn from you."

Lasren's upper lip curled. "Gifts come with prices," he said. "You should know that." He sounded young then, like a whining child, a tone I knew from the murky memories of my time as a human. "Blood cannot kill blood. Me hurting you would only make you hungrier and more likely to eat my food." He huffed as if that was the most annoying thing in the world.

"If you teach me, I won't ki . . . I won't eat your subjects," I said. "I promise." Inwardly, I reeled. It was true. Lasren couldn't kill me. Blood mattered. Adrian hadn't been wrong.

But *I* could kill *him*. I had every advantage here. Whatever magic, whatever gifts he talked about, his had a price. Mine didn't. I swallowed, my fangs sharp. I wouldn't need to kill his subjects. I would have his blood. I just needed to convince him to let me go. "I'll kill the hunter who's come here, and make sure none ever come again. I know where there are other hunters. I can kill them too, if you teach me how."

Even saying that felt wrong, like a violation of all Johann had done for me. Lasren stared, and for a moment I thought he'd seen through me, seen how badly I lied.

"I will go back to the castle," Lasren said. "My magic will fade afterward, and you will be free. If you're serious about this, about being chosen by Laurel, come to my castle. I will teach you. But if you take any blood, I will drive you from here." His eyes narrowed and he tapped the bell, a dull sound ringing in my ears. "I know my territory. I monitor it and everyone in it. Any vampire lord does the same. Disobey my orders, try to harm me and take my territory, take any of my food, . . . I will find out. I will trap you outside in the stones of the streets, and we will see what fades first once the sun comes up — my magic or you."

I didn't look away when his blues eyes bored into mine. But I swallowed, hiding my fangs, hiding my bloodlust.

I would have his blood. But first, I needed to learn how to deal with his magic.

And I needed to warn Johann.

# Chapter Seventeen

In a blink, Lasren was gone. But much more time passed before the stone snapped back into its normal shape, freeing my arms and legs.

I turned to mist at the same moment, surprised at how reassured I felt that I could once again do something so unnatural. I didn't have powers like Lasren—or at least, I didn't understand my powers as he did—but what I did know, I wanted to keep.

The city stretched below me, four stories down from the top of the temple. The moon had passed its highest point in the sky, arcing downward toward the horizon, and the air was cold. I traced the path I would take through the jagged, winding streets, so much easier to navigate from the tallest part of the city.

Then I jumped, landing lightly on the street below. The scents of the city filled my nose again, ash and mold, mud and stone, and in the distance, sweat and smoke.

I ran as fast as I could until the scents grew stronger, and then slowed to a pace that was more reasonable, more believable if a human saw me. My mind whirled with uncertainty, emotions I was having trouble putting names to. I wanted to help Johann. I wanted to kill Lasren. I wanted to help these people, living in fear of a vampire lord, people like Ruby who had lost others important to them. As I had lost Matilda.

But I also wanted to learn what I could do. To learn magic, to learn what I was. And to do that, I would have to spend time with, and pretend to ally with, Lasren. The one who had killed Johann's family. A vicious vampire lord. A vampire with the powers of the priests of the old empire.

*A vampire like me.* The thought squirmed in my brain like maggots on a corpse. When I'd said I'd make a deal with him . . . was it because I had been afraid? Or did I really want the knowledge?

What did I want most? What did Lasren want? What did vampires want? It all came back to that.

Johann's scent cut through the confusion in my mind, filling me with warmth that had nothing to do with the warmer air created by the burning torches that sputtered every few feet along the streets. I was back where people lived.

"That's interesting," Johann was saying. "Can you think of any other similarities for those he killed versus those who survived? Or any pattern to the ones he takes?"

"I just don't know." The man he was speaking to was old, his voice reedy and faint as it wound down the block.

"C'mon, Anders," another voice said, one that stood out in my mind. One of the men Johann had called to at the bar — Maravin. "You're the oldest in town. You must remember something. Time of night, locations . . . .anything?"

I turned the corner, drawing surprisingly close until Johann noticed and turned, his hand going to the stakeshooter at his belt. He dropped it immediately when he saw me.

"Kaiden!"

Maravin raised an eyebrow at me. "Damn, man, you're a quiet one." I had to remember to pretend to breathe. "I thought you were off with Ruby exploring the temples."

"I saw what I needed to see." I met Johann's eyes. "We should talk about it now." I flicked my gaze to Maravin.

Johann clapped Maravin on the back. "Do me a favor, friend — get what information you can and meet me back at your house. I appreciate all the help you've given us so far. The hunters could use men like you."

I ground my teeth together.

"Of course," Maravin said. "See you soon." He gave me a narrow-eyed look, one that almost made me bare my fangs. He reminded me too much of Thomas.

"Good night, Anders. Please, tell Maravin all you know." The old man nodded, giving Johann and then me a wave as we walked off. I felt Maravin's eyes on my back until we had turned the corner.

"We've noticed a pattern with the people who Lasren has killed over the years," Johann said, his breath misting in the cold air. We, as if Maravin was his partner and not me. His jacket rustled as he pulled it closer over his shoulders. "Most were descendants, or thought to be descendants, of old priests and priestesses. The records are scarce, though, and—"

"I talked to Lasren."

Johann blinked. "What?" His voice echoed down the empty street. "I thought you went to the temple!" he added, his voice a hiss, but still loud to my ears.

"I did. He was there. At the top of the dome." The structure loomed over the city.

"The top of the . . . of course." Johann's eyes widened. "Of course he would have been looking for us. But how . . ." He shook his head. "Did he see . . . no, you talked to him. What did you say? What did you learn? Can you kill him?"

The words were hard to say. I didn't know how to start. "I think . . . I think he has all the powers of a priest of Laurel. He controlled air, and he bound me in stone. I couldn't get close to him."

Johann put his hand on my arm, trailing down to take my hand in his. "Are you all right?"

His words only furthered my confusion. I was sure he wanted to know everything, to hear about Lasren. But first he was comforting me, touching me, making sure I was safe.

How could I possibly feel any desire to leave him, go learn

from Lasren, when I had this?

"I'm all right," I said.

"You look upset."

"I'm not." The lie felt wrong, and I spat out the words. "I tricked Lasren into teaching me how to use magic. He thinks . . . .he thinks I'll be his ally. I'm supposed to leave, to go to his castle and learn there. He's insane, Johann."

Johann paused, blinking. Then a smile split his features. "That's great, Kaiden!"

*It is?*

"This is perfect." He let me go, turning his attention to the dark shape of Lasren's castle. "You can learn what you can do *and* find a way to kill him before he suspects anything. I never even thought of that angle, but it's brilliant."

"What will you do?" I asked.

"Stay here, of course. I want to support you however I can, but at the moment I can't think of anything I can do with you, since I can't go to the castle." He ran a hand through his hair. "I did learn the fear aura around his castle stretches out into the road — no one can get anywhere close. Except for you. Unless you hypnotize me again."

"No."

"But if you learn how to do it safely, then that's an option, isn't it? And if you learn magic and control, you could even find a way to — "

"Don't," I said. I knew what he was about to say.

His brown eyes bore into mine and his expression softened. "What's wrong, Kaiden? Are you afraid?"

Johann knew me too well. I couldn't resist reaching out, and gratitude filled me when he took my hand. I didn't quite know how to put my thoughts into words. "What if I fail?" What if I let him down? What if I doom the entire city of Brusque?

What if Lasren taught me something about myself I didn't want to know, or did something that made me just like the others?

What if he gave me something I wanted? Something I couldn't resist?

"What if you succeed?" Johann asked, the words punching through my doubts. "This is what you wanted, right, Kaiden? A way to learn about yourself. This will benefit you *and* the Fifth Order. You'll be getting information any hunter would dream of. And with it, you can take down Lasren, and then any other vampire we may need to deal with. I know you're afraid. I was afraid to come here too. But if we didn't do it . . . we'd be just like the people of Brusque. Kept like cattle." Pain entered his voice.

He was right. I knew he was right, even as reluctance still simmered in my mind.

"I'll do it," I said. I squeezed his hand, felt his pulse thrumming through him. I wondered if Johann knew just how much I relied on him, on his strength and trust in me. I wouldn't have that when I was in the castle with Lasren.

"I'll be waiting here for you," Johann said. "If you can, find a way to leave a note or a message at the house where you woke up tonight. If not, it's okay — I trust you. You're my partner, and a good hunter. And . . . please, let me know if you need blood."

I frowned. "I won't do that," I said.

Johann sighed. "Fine, then. But can you at least promise to come back to me if you do need help? Any kind of help?"

"Of course." I wished I could be his partner here, hunt like other humans, spend time in a city with people and be with Johann. But that wasn't what I was.

Johann grinned. "Go on then. Learn all that you can and kill that bloodsucker. I did say maybe you'd make a friend tonight. A vampire counts, eh?"

I loved Johann's smile. I hated to leave.

"I'll kill him for you," I said. I wanted to kiss Johann, to taste him before I left. Instead I turned and began to run toward the castle, my gait silent and swift over the cobblestones. In seconds he was too far for me to scent.

I hoped I wasn't making a mistake.

I had hoped that as a vampire I would be confident and sure of my decisions, not at all like the uncertainty and doubt that had filled me as a thrall. In some ways, I had changed. But in others, I was just the same.

Maybe Lasren really would teach me what I needed to know. What it meant to be vampire.

And at least in the castle, Johann wouldn't tempt me so.

# CHAPTER EIGHTEEN

The sounds of the city faded quickly into the chirps of bats and the scrabbling of mice in ruined houses. Then the sounds of the forest met my ears as I entered the merchant road that led to the castle, which was even more overgrown and pitted than the stretch that had led us into Brusque. I dashed over grass that had grown into mats of twisted blades and snarled vines, and jumped over trees that had toppled into the road. A pile of fallen trunks flashed past my vision, a row of trees hacked with axe marks that had probably been meant as a makeshift wall. I jumped over it effortlessly.

The castle loomed ahead. I caught a whiff of something burning and deep, a not-scent that washed over me like the cold winter air I still didn't feel.

"Impressive," a voice said. I skidded to a stop, leaves and dust swirling around me. "No sickness at all." I had no idea what he'd tried to do. "I suppose you truly are worthy to receive the teachings of Laurel."

Lasren misted into shape beside me. I darted backward, my shoes sliding on the dust of the broken road.

Lasren shook his head. "Surely you know how this is done, at the very least." He held out a hand, which turned into insubstantial mist while the rest of him stayed in place.

I swallowed down something that was very close to fear and a desire to run back to Johann. "I don't."

"Who turned you?"

The question I had been dreading. All I could do was give as little information as possible. Getting caught in an

136

elaborate lie could be disastrous. "Dimresh."

"Ah, him." He waved a hand as if shooing away a mosquito. "No wonder you are so . . ." He trailed off.

The idea that a vampire would avoid finishing their sentence to in order not to insult me was disturbing. More than the clothes that made him seem as priestly as the men and women in books who were always shown bending down, kneeling, and giving advice or gifts to others. I was disturbed by his soft voice, his stance, the way he looked at me as though I were a supplicant, my hand outstretched for food.

In a way, I supposed I was. But only for now.

"Come along then," Lasren said. "Tell me your name, little vampire, and let us begin. This night grows old."

"Kaiden," I said. As soon as I did, he was gone, a flicker of darkness. I followed.

My path took me through the winding merchant road, trees stretching over the pitted path until suddenly the forest ended all at once, as though I'd climbed out of a hole in the ground. Black and jeweled sky met my eyes, the moon shining overhead, though lower now in the sky. And Lasren's castle glowed in the moonlight. Vines crept over the stone walls, small white flowers growing from every twist and curve. Wooden doors stained red and studded with silver were shoved halfway open, allowing me access to the main keep, which I could see was connected to the flanking walls, the entire structure an interconnected monolith. The scent of dust and rust met my nose — the gate must have been open for centuries and never shut.

When I crossed through I froze, a glowing moonlit shape on the courtyard in front of me. A dead, gnarled laurel tree.

In my memory, I knew it. Once this had shimmered on the courtyard every day in Brusque, and in other places. In the square at Penthorn, and in a sun-dappled yard covered in trees, shining when the sun was at its peak.

I blinked, the memory fading. Was it a memory of my life, or something more? I must have seen it in a book. But that excuse was getting harder and harder for me to believe.

"Are you moved by its beauty?" Lasren whispered. His voice made my hackles rise and my fangs sharpen. "It *is* so much prettier in the moonlight, isn't it?"

I needed to know. "Where was it before?" I followed the beam of moonlight to a stone archway mounted above the main keep, where the stained glass was now mounted.

"The temple." My memories were right. "But of course, none have use for it now but me." He put his hand to his chest. "That is the first thing you must learn. Do not fear hunters. They no longer have access to Laurel or her powers. She has forsaken them, and the rest of the humans." Unlike Adrian, no scorn dripped from his voice at the word *humans*. There was no emotion at all, just a cold distance. "She has chosen us to survive, given us subjects to sustain us and those we choose to give the gift. The way Dimresh chose you."

"Di . . ." I cursed inwardly, swallowing the word. "*Do* you know him?"

If Lasren noticed the slip, he gave no sign, his pale eyes unblinking. "I do. He is sloppy in those he chooses. Though not as sloppy as Amira." His left fang showed in a sneer. "He does not believe in Laurel. It's no wonder he let you fend for yourself after you performed whatever task he chose for you."

Performed whatever task. I remembered a man, killing his fiancé as he tried to kill me, an order from his master. The one who had *given him the gift*, as Lasren put it. I fought to hide my own sneer.

But there was my alibi, if I ever needed one. The task I had been made for. At least vampires, or normal vampires, seemed to be created with more of a purpose than thralls.

I had to make things sound believable. "After I . . . killed the hunter who was sent for him, he sent me away. He taught me nothing." The memories burned in my mind, of how he'd tried to make me kill Johann, and the lie tasted as foul as thrall blood. "When the hunters sent another for revenge, I ran."

"I imagine Dimresh sent you away so you would lead the other hunter away from him." Lasren shook his head. "He always was a coward, even before Laurel blessed us."

I just nodded. That much was true—Dimresh had been afraid at the end.

Of course, I was afraid now.

"So, newly-made vampire who wishes to protect my territory for me—what will you have me teach you?" Lasren's eyes glittered in the dark. "I'm a fair vampire. And it is, as it always has been, my duty to spread Laurel's teachings to the deserving. Thought never before has one chosen by another come to me. You must be blessed."

He spoke as if he truly believed what he was saying. As if he were a priest from the old books. It was more than possible he was insane, of course. No, I knew without a doubt he was—he treated humans like cattle.

I had to know. "How did you become a vampire?" I asked. "Who turned—"

"No one turned me. I was chosen. One of the originals, like Dimresh. When Laurel's leaves blackened and she withheld her power from all but the few, I was one of them." His eyes shone as he tilted his head to the stars, his gaze distant. "I knew my prayers had been answered when I was given the power I had always deserved."

I swallowed hard, the realization coming over my mind. "You were . . . a priest of the old empire? Alive three centuries ago?"

And Dimresh had been too. Perhaps not a priest, but . . .an original, Lasren had called him. One of the vampires who had caused the fall of the empire?

"Of course," Lasren said. "I am one of the original sires. Do you understand now how lucky you are to have won my interest? One of the blood, chosen by Laurel as we all were, with an understanding of her powers and favor." He spun, hands outstretched, saluting the sky. "It has been a long time since I chose one to teach. None could satisfy me. But you, one who traveled here . . . perhaps . . ." He fixed me with a wild-eyed stare. "Perhaps this is destiny. A message from Laurel. Do you feel you were sent by Laurel to receive my wisdom?"

"Yes," I said. What else could I say?

"Then let us begin," Lasren said. "Explore this, my chosen abode, once a castle and now the only temple of Laurel that still holds power. I have business to attend to the rest of this short night, and the sun nears. Find me at the holiest place within come tomorrow night. Make sure you understand enough for us to begin."

I wanted to ask what he meant by that. But then he was gone. A whisper of sound like a rustle of leaves, and then nothing, marking his sudden absence. Only the castle stretched around me.

This was no temple, possessing none of the beauty of the circular buildings in Brusque, the soaring pillars and domes. Its walls were harsh and high, the rusted iron gates once standing stalwart in their defense.

Lasren was mad. But to kill him, I had to learn how. And to learn what I was, what I could do, I had to gain his trust.

I raced down toward the castle, my gait steady and swift. There was no time to waste. Find him at the holiest place within. What was the holiest place of a castle?

I expected it to be like Dimresh's old home, the fallen castle I'd lived in as a thrall. I stopped immediately upon entering the wooden doors, the metal ring smooth in my hand.

Polished metal gleamed in the moonlight. The door swung open on oiled hinges. And inside, plush green carpets were illuminated by candle-heavy chandeliers.

It was like stepping into one of the books I'd seen of the old empire, but shadowed in darkness and not the light that always permeated the pictures.

Gold polished filigree shimmered in the candlelight, the designs evoking laurel leaves that ringed the hall. Instead of stone, the walls were plastered white and green and yellow, the colors forming a mockery of the sun over lush leaves. A fire burned in a hearth above the wall.

I passed beneath a slit that lay between two stone walls, the jagged metal edges of a portcullis above my head. That, at least, was still rusted in place.

The room inside reminded me of the cheer of the barracks of the Fifth, where people laughed and chatted. But instead of efficiency and function, here it was all opulence such that put even Dimresh to shame. And none of it had fallen to disrepair. There was barely a scent of dust.

I headed up smooth polished steps, the wood so shiny beneath my feet I had to check to make sure it wasn't some sort of brown iron. More chandeliers burned above my head.

I stopped at the first portrait that the dancing candle flames illuminated, my fangs sharpening — Dimresh.

My old master stared at me, his visage blurred slightly by the painter's hand. But I knew him, the same blond hair tied back, the same ice-blue eyes. He looked just the same as he had in my memory.

The same way he'd looked for nearly four centuries . . . before I killed him.

My mouth watered at the memory of the taste of his blood, and I turned away.

A picture of Lasren met my eyes, the same weak chin and features. He wore the robes of Laurel, just as he had tonight.

There were more portraits, but I knew none of the rest. Men and women, dressed in finery. As the hall stretched on, though, a few were different. Every so often, a space would be blank, the wall bare but with the faintest outline that marked a painting had been there.

And at the end of the hall, a single painting hung, larger than the rest, the blond man it depicted wearing a jeweled crown and holding a diamond-encrusted staff. Next to him stood a woman in gold and green robes, a crown in her hands.

The man in the picture looked more regal, and more beautiful, than even Dimresh, his eyes pale blue as he stared into the distance. The artist had taken time with the portrait, and with the background, the laurel tree rendered in fine detail.

Somehow I knew who he was.

The once Emperor Leoren.

Staring at the pictures, at the beginning of the hall where Dimresh and Lasren's paintings were, and then here, at the Emperor, all of Lasren's words began to make a terrible sort of sense, mixing with the words of the vampires I had killed. Maybe part of it was the strange memories I had, the visions, coalescing into knowledge.

The chosen. The importance of blood, of power.

I realized it then.

The vampires hadn't risen from the night and killed those who had once ruled.

Those who had ruled still did. The empire had never truly fallen.

It had been turned.

# CHAPTER NINETEEN

My mind raced the rest of that night before I succumbed to the sleep of the sun. It kept racing the next night when I woke in the space I had chosen. The stone walls of a tiny room surrounded me and shielded me from the light, a basement room that bore the scent of earth and ash and the marks of what had once been a cooking fire. I'd found it the night before, one of the few rooms in the castle not filled to the brim with rugs and plush chairs and lined with polished vases and instruments and bookcases. And paintings.

But it was those paintings that lined the hallways, along with more that had been taken down, that preoccupied me. Did they show every one of the remaining lords and ladies of Leoren—now vampire lords and ladies, rulers of the night?

Could Lasren be wrong? He was clearly insane. Maybe he'd collected the paintings of people he admired or salvaged from other castles. He had taken Brusque before—taken it from Lucien, a thrall turned vampire. And it was clear from the rooms filled with things—candelabras and paintings and tables and armoires that served no purpose—that he hoarded fineries. Maybe his words about those chosen were just deluded ramblings.

But maybe not.

I wished I knew who the ancient lords and ladies of Leoren were, but that had never been relevant. That shouldn't *be* relevant. They should all be centuries dead, killed by vampires. They shouldn't have *become* them.

And yet at the end of the hall my once master had been

painted, looking like one of the illustrations in the books of the old empire. He had owned books from the old empire.

This made so much sense. I wanted to tell Johann, to discuss everything with him. I ached for his company.

But not now. Of course, I didn't have to wonder about these things. I was a vampire too, and one Lasren believed wanted to learn from him. I could just ask Lasren himself.

I headed back up the spiraling basement steps then stopped. A faint floral scent met my nose, mixed with something else.

Human.

The floral scent emanated from upstairs. I followed the winding staircase, my steps making no sound. The fragrance grew stronger as I climbed.

It came from the stairs themselves, my feet slipping on dampness.

A woman knelt on the stairs, a cloth rag in her hand as she swabbed the steps. Cleaning.

I froze. I didn't know her, but she had to be from Brusque. She smelled like the city, like sweat and human mixed with ash from their fires and the mingled scents of the pines that grew nearby. She didn't notice me, her head bowed as she scrubbed.

The state of the castle made more sense now. Lasren used the humans of Brusque for more than just blood.

Thinking of blood made my mouth water. I had to put that idea out of my mind.

"Hello," I said.

Her head jerked up, and she blinked at me. Her eyes were unfocused, half-lidded.

Of course. Hypnotized.

When I didn't say anything more, she dipped her head back down and continued cleaning. Whatever compulsion Lasren used was strong. The business he'd attended to last night . . . he must have meant her.

Bleeding the humans and making them work made a cold, logical sort of sense, and yet also infuriated me.

I relaxed my jaw with effort. I was here to learn. Later, when I knew enough, I would kill him.

He'd said to find him in the holiest place. I had to figure that out first. The faster I learned, the quicker I would fulfill Johann's — and my — mission.

My explorations of the castle hadn't revealed much to me other than that Lasren enjoyed beautiful things, and he liked to hoard them. It wasn't a temple in the same way the temples at the centure of Brusque were, with their wide, inviting spaces.

But not all of it was wide and inviting. I remembered one tiny room, the silent space, beyond the altar of the temple. Would Lasren keep an altar here?

Dimresh certainly had no indications of religion in his castle. Only Lasren seemed obsessed with Laurel. I wondered which was the odd one, Lasren or Dimresh.

There was an easy way to ask. "You," I spoke to the woman who was still polishing the stairs.

She lifted her head again. I hated the submission I saw there, the blank acceptance.

"Do you know if there is an altar here in this castle?" I asked. "A place where . . ." I had to think. "There may be a carving of a tree?"

The woman stared, and I almost gave up before she spoke. "Lasren told me not to go below."

Below. Where I had just come from? There was nothing there except empty rooms.

Or maybe there was more to the castle. I wish I had some sort of clue, or that Lasren had told me something more useful than just "the holiest place." What did holy mean to a man who kept and killed people as though they were his belongings?

Or maybe this was his first lesson. I had magic too, after all. If Johann was here, he would encourage me to use it.

Fear spiked through me, a tension in my neck and shoulders that made me grit my teeth. I didn't know what would happen if I made a mistake. But at least here, in a castle owned by a vampire, if I messed up I wouldn't hurt Johann.

I did move away from the woman cleaning the stairs before I focused, though. Whatever the magic was, however it shaped my words, I decided to let it happen, letting my words form my will.

"By my blood, show me where . . . show me the location of the one I will kill."

I froze, hoping Lasren hadn't heard just how my will had shaped my words.

Then in my mind's eye, an image shimmered. Like the images from before, the memories or visions filled with the sun's light, but this time with what must be reality.

Lasren sat before a carved Laurel tree. He was in total darkness, yet I could still see him in a non-visual way, a sense of location filling my head. The scents of earth filled my nose, and I was drawn downward and outside.

I blinked, and it was gone. But now I knew where I needed to go.

I headed outside, leaving the woman behind, and ignored the pang of hunger that using the magic had caused. The moon was new in the sky, and the air was filled with the scent of cold, that absence of life and stillness that meant more snow was coming. A bat dashed past overhead, and somewhere an owl hooted.

I followed the curving path of the stone walls, and entered what must have once been a dungeon.

No, not a dungeon. Stone walls merged with wood, and I paused. The wood had no scent, not even the acrid scent of death that a fallen tree would have. The surface was impossibly smooth, as well.

I followed the sloping path downward, beneath the castle. The faint light of the moon faded until it didn't penetrate the pathway.

I hadn't moved far in the pitch-dark when my other senses — scent and hearing and something else, something I didn't have when I was alive — told me Lasren was here.

"Good work," he said. "All chosen are drawn here, or will be in time."

I wondered if he would be suspicious if I asked what this place was.

"So many don't understand this room's significance," he said. I was glad I hadn't asked. "The root of the world, the place where great trees, the precursors to Laurel, once grew. It's a wonderful gift. You would be lucky to see it in bloom one day."

None of that made sense to me. "I would be . . . glad to see it," I said.

"First you must prove yourself worthy. You were not among the original chosen, after all." His voice wound through the dark. "What do you know of Laurel?"

I had to be careful. "I've seen her temples and remains of old statues."

"That is not Laurel." Scorn dripped from his voice. "The real Laurel is the power she gave us now. Only we are worthy of worshipping her. That is why we have the magic, and the others do not. It's bound in our blood, in our instinct. You have felt that, yes?"

"Yes." Enough times, the words had twisted in my mouth, fitting what I wanted even if I hadn't known I wanted it. Was he right, and that was the influence of Laurel?

"Good. She calls to you, then. She does not call to all of those not originally chosen. They would not be worth my time. But you may be. And I will teach you what you can do. Laurel has shown me visions. You are worthy."

I swallowed down nervousness. "I'm glad," I said. "What can I do?"

"Anything you want," Lasren said, his voice sonorous and promising everything. "But knowledge must come with control. You don't want to end up like some of the foolish chosen—killed due to their own arrogance."

"Killed how?"

"By humans," Lasren hissed. "That was part of the pact, of the agreement with Laurel. The chosen will not kill one another. But the ones not in the pact, the unworthy, still resist us. So we must be controlled, so that we may control them."

There was so much I didn't understand, and I didn't know if it was because what he was telling me was wrong, delusions in his insanity, or if I was somehow different. I risked the question. "Are there any like us who are . . . outside the pact? Who are dangerous?"

"Not anymore," Lasren said.

He must have known Lucien. I had to learn more.

"Come," Lasren said. "In here, you will learn the basics of Laurel's power. Control of earth, of flame, and water. If you do well, tomorrow I will give you a gift."

I wanted to learn about Lucien, but now wasn't the time. I had to win Lasren's trust first. And of course, find a way to kill him.

"Sit," Lasren said. "Hold out your hand. You do not need words—only weak vampires rely on shouting, and I sense you are not weak. Speak the words only in your mind. *Laurel, bring forth dark flame.*"

I held out my hand, doing what he asked. I didn't expect this to work. My blood wasn't chosen. I didn't believe in Laurel. And the words weren't what I had been using until now. My blood was the power, not Laurel.

But when I thought the words, flame leapt into my hand, throwing orange light around the small room but not burning my skin. The fire's glow flickered over smooth earthen walls, winding, desiccated roots spiraling all around me.

"You see?" Lasren said. His face was obscured by leaping shadows. "Trust in Laurel. She has protected us for centuries now."

I stared at the flame in my hand.

Lasren was insane, I knew that. But the evidence was staring me in the face, and I'd seen it on the walls, the faces of the once-nobles of Leoren.

Were the histories wrong, and Laurel had been the dark god of vampires the entire time?

# Chapter Twenty

I had no clue what I had been able to do before. But Lasren's lessons that night showed me the promise of what I was capable of now.

I had every intention of going down to the city and meeting with Johann. But the lessons ran long as the night passed — how to summon fire and darkness, how to meld stone to my will, how to twist the gnarled branches and roots of long-dead trees to shapes that I wished.

"Excellent," Lasren said as I willed an ancient, desiccated vine back into its place along the dirt wall. "The further from life it is, the easier it is. This is the power Laurel has given us."

He'd said it many times throughout the lessons — Laurel's gift to us was the power over death. Fire, darkness, stone, ancient plants . . . and of course, the most obvious.

Vampires couldn't die, couldn't age. "If you wished it, you could live to see everything around you perish," Lasren said, his voice a hiss. "And then you would control everything."

This was madness. But it felt so true. And the power felt so right. I hated to admit it, but the more I had used it, the more it seemed to become part of me. I didn't even need words anymore once I touched the feeling of each spell. As the magic worked, it was like a rightness, a jutting edge sliding into place.

I grasped the feeling in my mind, a pleasurable shiver going through my body, and I let fire dance in my hand again.

"You are talented," Lasren said. "It makes me happy to see this. Perhaps Laurel chooses anew."

I had to focus. "You control more than just dead nature," I said. "What of the humans? How do you make them do your bidding?"

Lasren's eyes glittered dangerously. "That is harder," he said. "And I do hope you aren't thinking of disturbing my food."

"No," I said quickly. "I just . . . want to learn."

"I have taught you much already, and eventually you will grow hungry," he said. "The magic requires blood. I understand. You have done well so far. I will teach you more tomorrow. You have earned your gift."

I swallowed. I didn't know if I would want his gift. "Thank you," I said.

"The moon sets and the sun will rise soon. Keep practicing. This is a seat of power—it will help you."

"Thank you," I said again, but he was already gone.

I would practice. There was so much I could do now, and the knowledge felt good. I called more power, relishing as the flames leapt higher.

Firelight seared the walls, casting the entire earthen space in light.

A seat of power. The flames in my hand danced over the desiccated roots and then more. Bones littered the floor, unquestionably human. Some of the bones were charred, and others had been crushed into what looked like dust. Somehow, I sensed they were older than even the centuries since Lasren had been turned.

A seat of power for power over death. Was this truly what Laurel stood for?

Was this what I was now?

I let the energy fade, shuddering as it left me. No. I couldn't let power make me into Lasren.

Into a vampire.

*You may have killed Dimresh, but you'll be just like him. As soon as you show what you really are, I'll be ready.*

The words echoed, and suddenly I ached to see Johann. I wanted to feel human again, to talk to him and know I wasn't like Lasren, a vampire surrounded by death and mind-controlled humans he fed from.

But the sun would be up soon. I was fast, but I couldn't take such a risk. Especially not if Lasren was watching me.

But there was something else I could do. I had found Lasren. I could find Johann.

I didn't even need words anymore. I closed my eyes, searching for the power, the will over my surroundings. I didn't need Laurel's name, either. Lasren believed in her. I believed in my own strength. I hadn't been chosen by a twisted god, even if she was real, a god of vampires.

*Johann, where are you? Show me. Show me the location of the one I want.*

My body thrummed with the idea of *want*, and then I saw him, an image in my mind's eye.

He was shirtless, alone in a wooden room, seated on a bed. I licked my lips, a flash of want, of need, sharpening the image in my mind's eye. This felt like hunting, but hunting with magic, and for something I craved in more ways than one. The room was sparse, something that looked like mold growing from the walls. It was the old house where we'd stayed, where I had woken, the abandoned house old and decrepit and safe from prying eyes.

But Johann was beautiful, glowing with moonlight that shone through a cracked window. The pale light danced over his flat stomach and the dusky trail of sparse hair that led downward. His hair was slicked back and wet, and a bead of moisture ran down his chest. He must have just washed.

Johann wiped his damp skin with a towel, the muscles in his shoulders and arms rippling. I wanted to feel them on me, feel his warmth, his human strength, nothing compared to mine but so natural, so . . . alive. I craved it. I craved *him*.

Then he turned his head, and for a moment I thought he

had somehow seen me, or sensed me. He paused, then stood. I grew dizzy as the image wavered, Johann moving toward something.

A door. A wooden door which swung open to reveal another man. Maravin. Johann's friend.

The two men spoke, but it wasn't their mouths I focused on. I couldn't hear them, the magic not that potent, and my will didn't bring their words to my ears. It was Maravin's gaze that caught my attention.

The other man's gaze roved over Johann as the same way mine just had. Taking in his beauty, his strength, his nostrils lightly flaring as he caught his scent. But Maravin was human, his attraction all too obvious, and his desire blatant. He didn't want Johann's blood. He just wanted Johann.

My Johann.

The two men kept talking, Maravin gesturing first to the walls, and then to the side, out the door. Johann shook his head then shrugged.

Maravin touched his shoulder, lightly, a smile on his lips. A smile that teased and promised. Johann didn't see it, but I did.

More gesturing out the door. Johann sighed, his shoulders drooping, and then ran a hand through his hair. He glanced back at the room, the room where he'd been waiting for me, but then finally nodded. He grabbed his coat from the door.

The sky as they left was purpling. Maravin put his hand on Johann's shoulder, his victorious smile searing the image in my mind.

The image vanished as the first tinges of sun-tiredness hit me, along with a rush of rage.

How dare he? How dare Maravin take *my* Johann?

My fingers curled into claws, and my fangs lengthened, the sharp points pricking my lower lip. Anger rushed into the void the magic left. *How dare he?* How dare that . . . *human!*

Anger boiled in my body, mingling with the rush of adrenaline and power that using magic had given me. I wanted to call magic again, to see Johann, to claim him. The desire was stronger now that I knew I could.

As soon as it had rushed upon me, the urge began to fade, twisting with the pull of the rising sun. I needed rest. I needed to calm down. The magic wouldn't come to me, the power in my blood weakening as the fatigue rose.

It didn't matter if Johann spent the day with Maravin. It *shouldn't* matter. I tried to push it out of my mind as I headed back toward the castle, hiding from the purpling sky.

Johann cared for me. I knew that.

But I'd pushed him away. I had told him again and again how we wouldn't work, *couldn't* work.

He had waited all night for me.

And I had ignored him, hadn't sent him a message, hadn't seen him.

Johann trusted me.

But Maravin was human, and could offer him everything I couldn't.

My teeth grit together, my claws scoring against stone as I swung the door closed and headed down the hall to the tiny, lightless room where I would spend the day.

I was a vampire, with power and magic, and most of all, emotion, emotion far stronger than anything I felt as a thrall. But even in my human life, I couldn't remember being this angry.

For all I knew, Johann was with Maravin right now, tangled with him in the light of day, while I slept in the dark.

# CHAPTER TWENTY-ONE

*In my dream, I walked down a sunlit hallway, my feet loud on pol-*
*ished walkways. My path took me through the stone hall that*
*transformed into green, intermingled boughs growing over my head*
*into a natural tunnel. My path sloped downward, then grew darker.*

*Someone walked behind me, their footsteps quiet, padding along*
*in bare feet. "Just a bit farther," they whispered, their voice reedy*
*with age. "You will see."*

*The sunlight faded behind me, and soon I couldn't see at all.*

*"Kaiden," Johann's voice came from behind me. I whirled and the*
*light ahead blinded.*

*The dream wavered, and then Maravin was there. Pulling Johann*
*away, his hand on his shoulder, Johann taking his hand in his.*

*I snarled, the sound echoing.*

I woke to darkness. But this time it was just the darkness of
Lasren's castle.

Maravin. How dare he.

I focused, the magic welling in my mind. I had to see!

My power swelled, and flashes of images formed in my
mind's eye. A dark room, but not dark to my eyes, where a
snuffed candle dripped wax onto a desk. Ants crawled down
the side, holes marking where they traveled. Maravin slept on
the bed, shirtless.

And alone.

I focused. I wanted to see Johann. Where was he?

"Spying on my humans?" Lasren's voice said, and my focus broke.

I blinked in darkness, but I could sense Lasren here,

standing in my small room. No—I couldn't think like that. This was his room, his territory, as this all was.

"I was just . . ." I didn't know what to say. "I haven't touched them."

"I understand," Lasren said. "You are weaker than I am. It's only natural that use of magic makes you hungry, despite my lessons on how not to waste your power."

I was hungry, but not so hungry that I couldn't control myself. This was a different sort of hunger that drove me to find Johann. But I couldn't tell Lasren that. I was supposed to be helping Johann, figuring out what I could do and how to kill vampires more effectively. Not obsessing over some human.

I could do my job. I could be good.

Even if Johann might be with Maravin instead. Using the time I was away to—

No. I had to focus.

"Does using magic make you hungry also?" I asked.

"That is the price we must pay," Lasren said. He waved a hand and a flame appeared, illuminating him and the stone wall behind him. "Though it's no price at all, really. We have power over all, and over those we feed from. You asked me last night how to control them—it's difficult. Not all can do it, not even all of the original chosen. You must be a chosen of Laurel. Then it will be natural to you. We will see . . . later."

I shivered at his words. Domination had come naturally to me, even as a thrall, when I had controlled Johann. I just didn't want that to be that way.

"What will happen if I don't eat?" I asked.

"You will grow weaker. Hungrier." Lasren stroked his chin. "But Laurel would not let one of her chosen die."

I waited for him to actually answer the question, but that was all he said. Suspicion of his gift, and what that would mean, began to grow in my mind, along with an unwanted surge of savory anticipation.

I had to be good. I had to focus. "Thralls are hungry all the time, right?" I asked. "What purpose do they serve?"

Lasren's eyes narrowed. "Thralls are twisted things. Only foolish vampires make thralls, ones who have not learned to listen to Laurel. There is risk in making them."

Excitement made my words come quickly. "What kind of risk?"

"Thralls are not bound by our blood. They are not chosen. Oh, many claim they can be controlled — and most are. But a tamed beast is still a beast, and dangerous. Humans are useful. Thralls are not."

This was it, it must be. The story of Lucien. "How are thralls dangerous?"

Lasren's jaw twitched. For a moment I remembered another man, a shadow in my mind, his jaw twitching in anger before he struck me and a cup fell from my hand. But the moment passed.

"There is no need to worry about thralls," Lasren said. "Simply take your meals carefully. Control your will — do not let them turn. Do not let them die from loss of blood while your fangs are in their neck. If you do, drain them completely. If you can't and they turn, well, there is an easy fix."

I swallowed. "What is that?"

"Simply decapitate them. Not even a thrall can recover from that."

There had to be more information. "But why do other vampires make thralls, then?" I knew why, of course. But what would Lasren say?

"Because they are foolish," Lasren said. "And do not have the same mastery of Laurel's power that I do, the power over will, the power over their hunger. Come. Learn well from me tonight and I shall reward you as I promised."

Hunger tinged the brief war of anticipation between learning more magic and a desire to search the castle and learn more of what I could on my own. But I knew better than to argue, and so I followed the other vampire back out into the night.

I expected him to take me back to what he called the seat of power, the crypt of bones. Instead he led me to the top of his castle. Crumbling ramparts overlooked the forest and the few distant burning lamps that marked the city of Brusque. Cold wind blew over the castle, ruffling my hair. We stood near a tree branch that had grown over the castle, one that still smelled slightly of the leaves that had fallen for winter.

"Your power is impressive," Lasren said. "But there is more to understanding Laurel's gift than just power. You must achieve understanding. *That* is harder."

"I'm ready to try," I said.

"Good. Understanding and creativity mark a true vampire lord. Knowledge of how something is structured, of how it once worked and once lived. Once you have that, you can exercise control. And you must also learn to identify what you cannot control, and shape it into something you can."

I narrowed my eyes. "What do you mean?"

"You said you were running from a hunter, yes?"

It took me a moment to remember my lies. "Yes."

"What do hunters use against us?"

This I had learned from Johann, and the answers were easy. "Wooden weapons. Herbs. Solar flares. And, I suppose, decapitation, like you said." I swallowed hard, remembering a hunter with a sword severing the head of a thrall in the first battle I'd seen between humans and thralls.

"Wooden weapons and herbs," Lasren said. "Objects once filled with life. There is no life force more powerful than that of a tree, and even dead wood burns with it. Herbs can give life as well as take it. And the sun, of course, provides life to the planet. Do you understand?"

"Life opposes us?"

"No." Lasren shook his head. "Think, Kaiden." The way he said my name reminded me disturbingly of Johann. "Things filled with life are simply in a different stage of being. After all — everything dies eventually. Herbs rot. Trees wither. And the sun sets. Now do you understand?"

I shook my head. "I don't."

"Your will is power, Kaiden. Power to control. Controlling things that are full of life is hard, but not impossible. Watch."

He reached up and grabbed part of the branch that was growing over the ramparts. With a flick of his wrist, he snapped it.

Then he plunged it into his own chest.

My body went cold, shock rooting me in place. I reached out a hand, but no magic came to mind. Nothing came to mind except a sudden, impossible hope that I had succeeded, that Lasren would die and Johann would be so happy —

But then Lasren turned to mist, the branch and a few drops of blood falling to the ground. The branch twisted, and the smell of the leaves that had once adorned it turned to the harsh, acrid scent of rotted wood.

Lasren reappeared, his fangs flashing in the moonlight. The hole in his robes revealed his unblemished chest.

"Anything that contains life contains death," Lasren said. "Will it to die fast enough and it can't hurt you. Then anything can be healed. Although" — he ran his tongue over his fangs — "such magic will make you hungry."

Fear rooted in my gut. Not only fear of the upcoming test — I knew Lasren would have me try it too, use my magic and make me ravenous to learn this trick. I *did* want to learn.

But even more, fear rose at the enormity of my task. Lasren could live through a hunter's most common weapon. He claimed to have power over life and death.

How were we supposed to kill him?

I had to keep focused. But it was Lasren's words I used to

push down my fear, not Johann's lessons. *Everything dies eventually.*

If I could understand things the way Lasren wanted me to, I could figure everything out. That was all I could do right now.

"Teach me," I said. *"Please."*

Lasren's eyes glittered. "I will," he said. "I have plans for you. Now come. We will begin where I taught you yesterday."

He vanished, faster than a shadow disappearing into firelight. I had to follow. Whatever he knew, I needed to know.

I needed to understand.

The bone crypt was just as I remembered. But as I neared, a strong, almost mint-like scent met my nose — one that reminded me of the hospital where Johann had lain after the fight with Dimresh. Herbs. Lasren waved me inside.

Another scent mingled with it — human. The same woman from last night stood in the crypt, her eyes glassy and unseeing. She held a clay bowl in her hands filled with liquid, and the scent emanated from it.

"Once these herbs grew here, in this crypt," Lasren said. "The vines here were once their twining roots. I do not remember their name, or what they were once used for. To ones like us, they bring pain. I have eradicated the plant in all places, but it grows here stubbornly. However it will be useful to you to learn how to understand the interplay of life and death."

Something about what he said didn't sit right with me, but before I could focus on it, about why he couldn't remember and what that might mean, the girl strode toward me.

Glassy-eyed and expressionless, she flicked bits of the water at me, sloshing the bowl.

I leapt away — or tried to. But a vine snarled my leg, and the water hit my pants and soaked through.

I cried out, the sound dull in the crypt. The liquid burned, hissing on my skin as though it boiled. The pain was mind-numbing.

"Understand it," Lasren's voice said in my ear. "Life and death. The link between them. If *it* is dead, it can't hurt *you!*"

My teeth gnashed together. I'd been injured before, had been cut and hacked and survived a blast from the statue that had been like a solar flare. But something about this herb was different, the pain unrelenting and without reason, this herbal water that threatened to eat through the skin of my leg. Why? Why did it hurt so badly?

"Understand it," Lasren said as I shivered with pain. Useless advice. "Force it to conform to Laurel's will. *Understand Laurel's will.*"

Laurel's will. Laurel's will meant nothing. But *my* will mattered. Johann had always said to trust my instincts.

I willed the plant with magic — willed it to stop hurting, to leave me alone. Nothing happened. The pain deepened. The water seeped through my pant leg into the skin and muscle. My foot weakened and I dropped to the floor.

Instinct wasn't working. *Understand it*, Lasren had said. To understand meant to use the right spell, to . . . to . . .

Understand it. Instinct wouldn't work. Instinct was raw and powerful and had gotten me this far. Instinct had driven me as a thrall. But if being a vampire meant understanding, meant control, that could be the key to more than just fighting this pain.

Understand the herb. Understand . . . the link between life and death. Laurel's will? That couldn't be. I couldn't accept that. Laurel wouldn't do this, give vampires power to torture and kill.

But the link between life and death . . . I seized on that. Herbs could heal. But to ones like me, they killed. Herbs eased pain in humans. They brought pain to ones like me.

Those who lived, they helped. Those who were dead . . .

they hurt.

But I wasn't dead, was I?

What was I? What did it mean to be a vampire, and why did herbs hurt me?

The answer felt impossible to grasp, even if I wasn't burning with pain that centered on my leg. But somehow, Lasren had found it.

"I don't know," I gasped. "I . . . don't know what Laurel wants." Why would Laurel want to hurt us, if we were supposed to be chosen? That made no sense.

The pain was spreading, like rot. Nothing made sense. My magic scrambled. I reached out with it, toward Lasren, toward anything. *Help me.*

I closed my eyes, the pain surging to a crescendo. The view of the crypt wavered. I bared my fangs from sudden hunger.

I blinked, and a vision flashed before my eyes.

*Men and women in green robes strode in darkness down a flowered path, their way illuminated by a lantern held by the woman at the front of the procession. Trees grew over their heads, the branches interlacing. One man stumbled into the tunnel the trees formed. His friend grabbed his arm and helped him onward. The path sloped down, the flowers that the firelight revealed and then shadows hid no longer growing as the tunnel of branches became a tunnel of stone and then dirt.*

*The man in the front of the procession filled my vision, the green of his robes and the gold trees on his tabard marking him as a priest of Laurel. He crouched beneath the rocky lip of the cavern and then entered.*

*His firelight bathed charred bones. He spoke a word, one I couldn't hear but yet knew, a prayer to Laurel. The fire in his hands spread to braziers along the walls, revealing marks of ash along the stone and an enormous, unlit pyre in the center.*

*Vines wound around the pyre, pulsing green with heart-shaped leaves. He bent down, plucking the leaves from the vine as the rest of the procession followed.*

*The priest began to speak, his mouth forming words I couldn't hear, couldn't understand. Another priest brought a bowl toward him. He lifted his hand and lifted his head, his mouth open as though he was calling to someone. Praying.*

*Six people brought a box at the end of the procession – an enormous wooden box.*

*A coffin.*

*The priest spoke and the fires flared. Then the cavern was doused in darkness.*

*A tiny light appeared, so bright it burned.*

"Focus, Kaiden." Lasren's voice broke through. I lay on the ground, the pain in my leg all-consuming. But something about the vision made sense.

All of the visions made sense now. This wasn't a residual memory of the books I'd studied, or a fantasy . . . or even a dream.

These were visions of the past. This crypt, this cave, had once been . . .

I didn't know yet what they'd been. But now I understood a little more.

The vines had once been alive, and now surrounded me, dead. They had been what was burning me now.

All I had to do was take out the life. And seeing what it had been made it easier to undo it. To make it what it could become.

Dead.

I didn't need Laurel. I only needed my own will, my own power.

*Wither.*

The pain lessened, but not completely. I extended my focus, on the herb that had soaked into the water and into my skin. I brought it death, death from outside, from everywhere. I brought it death from my memories, from the past that had long since faded and the pain I could barely remember, a pain as I had died.

And then the life didn't hurt.

The hissing noise of my burning skin stopped. My leg, a bloody mess, began to knit together. All that remained of the herbal concoction was just water and dried root, like the ones around me. What was left looked like ash.

"Very good," Lasren said. "Everything dies. Life is a side of reality, but it is pointless and short. Death is final and forever — like us."

I got back to my feet, the truth of his words sitting in my mind. I had felt that truth, and I had used it. It felt... I couldn't put it into words. It was like what a priest would have felt if he had seen Laurel in front of him, but bigger. And darker.

Frightening.

"We will have more lessons like that," Lasren said. His voice was full of excitement. "Power over death is why we are chosen. Since you can do what you just did, it's clear you are chosen as well, even if you were turned later. Your coming here must have been Laurel's will. Your being turned was fate."

Fate. My fate to be a thrall, and then a vampire?

"Now, your gift," Lasren said. "For performing so well. I imagine you need it after that."

I met his eyes as he snapped his fingers. Then the woman stepped between us. She smelled of perfume and thrumming, bloody life.

She bared her neck for me. Thoughts of death and fate and what my strange visions meant faded as hunger rose.

"Drink," Lasren commanded.

# CHAPTER TWENTY-TWO

The woman, eyes unseeing, waited with her neck bared. Lasren waited behind her.

My mouth watered. I hadn't eaten in two days, and using magic, as Lasren had taught me, drained my energy. Made me hungrier. And I needed blood after my magic finished healing the burn the herb had left on my leg.

But all I could see, all I could feel, was the thought of Johann's disappointment.

I had reveled in power that Lasren had taught me, but it hadn't made me like him. I wouldn't let it.

"I . . . .do not want to offend by eating your . . . food," I said.

Lasren waved a hand. "It is freely given."

I swallowed. I could use this as practice. Take just a little blood, learn how to control myself, leave her alive.

Drain the blood of a living person, as she was controlled by a vampire I was supposed to be trying to kill.

My fangs were sharp in my mouth. Pure hunger. It wouldn't be like biting Johann.

Johann. What would he do if I . . .

What would he do if he were here?

I wished I could see him. I wished he were here, helping me. He kept me grounded. Alive.

I couldn't have Johann here, not yet. But it was an excuse.

"I appreciate your gift," I said. I had to choose my words carefully. I wasn't just dealing with a dangerous vampire. I was dealing with a lord of the Empire, and one who had, in his own way, given me more than I ever expected or frankly deserved. "But—"

"But?" Lasren blinked in surprise.

"But I . . . I would prefer two things, if possible," I said. "I do not want to take one of your . . . clearly favored choices, and weaken or kill her." I made a small gesture to the woman, who didn't acknowledge it or take any notice of me as I discussed her fate. My stomach turned. "I prefer the blood of men myself. In addition, I . . . well, is eating not a private thing?"

I feared anger. But instead, Lasren smiled.

"You continue to impress me, Kaiden." I wished he wouldn't use my name. "Of course. I see your hunger isn't as great as I expected. Naturally I would want my gift to be something you favored. I will take her instead."

I hoped I hadn't just consigned her to death.

"Take the rest of the night to continue your practice. Explore the castle. Pray to Laurel and deepen your understanding." His fangs flashed as he smiled.

He took a step toward the woman, his fangs long and sharp. He clearly had no qualms about eating in front of me. He bent down over her neck.

I didn't know if she would die tonight. There was nothing I could do. Nothing I could have done. Or was there?

"One moment," I said.

At least he paused, his hand still on her unresisting shoulder.

Something he'd said still bothered me, and that was an excuse I could use to stave off the woman's fate. Maybe a few extra minutes would give her the strength she needed to survive the loss of what blood he took. If he didn't plan to kill her outright.

"Can you tell me what life was like before the turning?" I asked. "What were you . . . and the empire . . . like before?"

"Before?" Lasren straightened. "Ah, Kaiden." I resisted curling my upper lip at his use of my name. "What a strange question. Do you remember the time before your sire chose you?"

"I don't." That wasn't entirely false. I had only bits and pieces. I wished I remembered all of it. I wished I remembered more of my life with Matilda, and the faces and names of people who had once known me from Penthorn.

"To be chosen is to give up one's fleeting life. That is what life is, after all, what you have just learned. Fleeting. A blink of an eye. Used up and reabsorbed. A waste." Lasren's fingers curled around the woman's chin. "To answer your question, I remember some things. I was a priest of Laurel, but I did not live here in Brusque — I lived in Wollasque. I traveled often — I know that much. I met with nobility — I was always respected. I preached to any who would listen. And once a year here in Brusque, we would conduct . . ." He frowned, then shook his head. "Well, there was a celebration here in wintertime. One of the bi-annual celebrations of . . . something that no longer matters."

Disappointment was almost worse than the previous pain. Lasren didn't remember his life as a human. That, at least, was true of all vampires. The only keys to the ancient empire, and they had forgotten.

But somehow, I could see. Visions of the past, reflected in my memory and in my dreams, of the places I had seen. There had to be clues there as to what it all meant, what had happened to turn the nobility of the old empire into the "chosen."

And there was one other major clue in Brusque that Lasren might know about. But finding out about Lucien would require even more finesse than turning down his gift.

And now wasn't the time. Lasren was already bending back down, going for his prey's neck.

The woman. I wished I knew her name. I didn't want to be

like him, taking blood from a human. I didn't want to feel hunger as I watched.

"I will go . . . explore as you asked." I had been given time to myself. And it was past time to report to Johann.

I turned, dashing up the tunnel and into the night.

The moon shone just above the trees. I had wasted half the night in pain, although the lesson had been worth it.

I paused at the exit of the tunnel, peering down at the gnarled roots and loose dirt. Rocks were strewn outside. Now that I studied it, I could tell what had once looked random was deliberate, the placement of the gray rocks marking the entrance. Moonlight glimmered on imperfections in the stone, shiny flecks of minerals I couldn't name.

No visions came to me. The place was important, a place of power where priests had visited in the time of the empire. I wished I knew why.

Maybe Johann would know. Hunger made my mouth water, but I was used to that. I wanted to be near Johann, that was all. I needed to.

My speed took me through the forest and back toward the twisted, dilapidated buildings of Brusque. This late at night, no one roamed the streets, though the scent of humanity, the woodsmoke and sweat and swirling acridity, met my nose as I came close.

He'd said he would wait for me at the house where we had stayed the first night. He had been there last night. I slowed when I reached it, but I knew what I would find.

His scent was faint and mingled with another's. Maravin. He hadn't returned since last night.

I growled low in my throat, my fangs pricking my lower lip. Maravin. He would be with Maravin, wouldn't he?

Tracking by scent was surprisingly easy. I knew Johann's scent so well, the mixed aroma of pine, maleness, and blood that thrummed just beneath his skin. I swallowed hard as I crept down the streets, ignoring the sounds of the soft breathing of people who slept behind closed doors and latched windows. Rats squeaked behind walls, rooting in garbage, and cats and dogs hissed and snarled and hunted the rats and mice. Compared to Lasren's castle, the city was cacophonously loud. Full of life.

It felt strange to dash through streets of a once-bustling city as though I were once again a wretched thrall. I was a vampire, able to wield immense power that I was finally beginning to understand. If I wanted to, I could have whatever I wanted, *who*ever I wanted. Lasren's words floated in my mind. *Chosen.*

Of course, even if I wanted to use my power, no other humans strode streets in the dark of night, not this late. Even the bar was quiet, the scent of alcohol faint on the air. One man had fallen outside, the source of the scent, collapsed but breathing near a turn on Bourbon street.

I wondered if I had looked like that once.

The thought grounded me. I was a vampire, but I wasn't like Lasren. Becoming a thrall had been a fluke—even Dimresh had said he hadn't chosen me for any real reason. Becoming a vampire was the same, a fluke when Johann had taken pity on me. Maybe Lasren and the other fallen nobles were chosen, but I certainly wasn't.

I couldn't let Lasren's madness spread to me. I needed to find Johann.

His scent led me straight to a small house on a street I hadn't learned the name of. I paused for a moment, uncertain, staring at the house that was supported by a wooden foundation, the ground beneath it nothing but icy mud.

I scented both Johann and Maravin. His friend.

Something crawled in me, an emotion that shouldn't make sense here. Fear.

What if Johann really was with Maravin?

I didn't want to know. I didn't know what I would do if I found that out. My emotions felt tenuous, vacillating between fear, sadness, and something else.

I could do this. I had infiltrated the castle of a mad vampire lord and convinced him to teach me. This was nothing to be afraid of.

I headed up the rickety wooden steps and knocked on the door.

Someone moved inside, and I knew him immediately from the sound of his footsteps. Johann.

"Kaiden!" he exclaimed as he opened the door. His voice dropped. "I'm so glad to see you!"

Instead of inviting me inside, he stepped out onto the wooden stoop and closed the door behind him. "Maravin is asleep," he said. "And he thinks you've been killed. Many do, although I told them you were hunting in the countryside near the farms. They think I'm being foolish, or in denial, but . . . well, sorry. I'm just glad you're back." His eyes shone, and warmth I hadn't felt since seeing Lasren filled me. I had missed Johann so much. His presence was like a beam of sunlight that I could never truly see. "Please, tell me. Have you found a way to kill Lasren?"

He smelled so good, though there was another scent on him, an unfamiliar one. But that faded as he spoke. I loved hearing his voice, his breathing, sensing his closeness. It was intoxicating, and reminded me of how much magic I had used, and how hungry I was.

I had to focus. I was here for a reason. And the easiest way to push past my hunger and fears about Maravin was to talk.

I told Johann everything about Lasren, the moon lowering in the sky as I did. Lasren's frightening powers, his exquisite control of magic, and the magic he had taught me. His apparent immunity to conventional vampire hunter weapons. And of course, the most important fact of all.

"Lasren was a priest of the empire," I said. "And I think . . . I think every vampire lord was once a noble of the empire also."

Johann had been quiet as I spoke, but at my words he sucked in a breath of shock, his eyes going wide. "That can't be," he said.

"I am . . . sure of it." His denial caused me to doubt myself for a moment before I remembered what Lasren had said about what he could remember of the empire, and the paintings on the walls.

"The Fifth Order was taught that the nobles were killed by the vampires, not that . . ." Johann took another deep breath, staring into my eyes. "Why would the nobles who were once stewards of the land, and priests of Laurel, do this?"

A memory came to my mind, unbidden, of Penthorn. "Why would a vampire bite and kill the woman he was betrothed to?"

"Because he was ordered to by the one who bit him. But to think that Lasren was once a priest of Laurel . . ." Johann shook his head, horror written on his features. "Maybe his mind was always twisted."

"Or maybe becoming a vampire twisted it," I said. Johann's eyes met mine. "Maybe . . . he really did lose his soul."

I didn't speak the fear, but Johann must have seen. "You won't end up like him, Kaiden."

"You don't know that," I said. I'd told him of the magic, but not of the way it made me feel, the power it promised. There were no words for it, the mastery of my surroundings and extension of my will that naturally sought to dominate. Dominate the elements, and dominate life. As I stared at him, words rose in my mind, the same ones I'd used before to bind him when fighting Dimresh. More than words, a feeling — *be mine. Obey me.*

I couldn't do it. I didn't want it. But it would be so easy.

More than his blood, he was what I wanted, in every way,

and now I knew how to make that happen. Maravin couldn't have him. I could.

I closed my eyes, digging my nails into my palm, focusing on pain. I was no vampire lord, just a drunk from Penthorn. I couldn't have what I wanted. I didn't want it. I couldn't want it.

"Kaiden," Johann said. I opened my eyes as he touched my shoulder, his hand fiery warm. "Are you all right?"

I swallowed, my fangs long in my mouth when I spoke, my body responding to his touch. "I'm fine."

"You haven't had blood since you got here." His mouth quirked in a smile, but it faded. "I can tell. Are you . . . suffering?"

"No," I said, too quickly. Johann frowned. "Lack of blood just weakens magic. It's not dangerous."

"When we fight Lasren, I imagine you might need that magic," Johann said.

I didn't like where this conversation was going. "Tell me how people here are doing," I said. "Lasren took a woman, but I don't know her name. Have people here spoken of her?"

Johann blinked, his mouth twisting, but he accepted the change of topic. "Yicca," he said. "Daughter of a farmer who keeps chickens. She's not seen often, preferring to stay on the outskirts near the farms. Now she's staying in the hospital, of course. It didn't seem like she was bitten last night, but she found herself standing in the center of town come morning, and she's gone tonight."

"She'll have been bitten tomorrow," I said. My mouth watered at the memory of Lasren biting her, and I hated myself for it. "And when he isn't feeding from her, he's making her clean the castle."

Johann huffed, his jaw tensing. "I suppose it could be worse."

It certainly could. I didn't know Lasren well enough to

know if he treated his conquests the same way Dimresh had, fucking them while biting them. I didn't want to know.

"I want him dead," Johann said. "We need to figure this out as fast as we can. Find a weakness. Or see if he can resist a solar flare the same way he can—"

Something moved inside, and I turned my head. Maravin.

Johann followed my gaze, and when Maravin called out even he could hear it. "Johann?"

"Out here, Maravin," Johann called. "Talking to Kaiden."

"Kaiden?" Heavy footsteps plodded to the door. "Are you imagining things or—oh, it is you!" The door swung open, Maravin looking me over.

My nostrils flared. Now that he was here, I could pick out the subtleties in scents that had escaped me before. Johann's scent was on him, and his on Johann. It was all I could do not to snarl.

# CHAPTER TWENTY-THREE

I fought past a surge of anger to pay attention to the conversation.

"Kaiden's been patrolling the areas near the farms, just as I've said," Johann said. "I told you he wasn't killed. You said yourself Lasren doesn't take two people at once."

"Yeah, but Lasren hates hunters," Maravin said. He stepped out onto the stoop, standing far too close to Johann. "He doesn't take them, he just . . . kills them. You need to be careful. The same reason I told Johann not to stay in that abandoned house all alone."

I didn't believe for a second that was the only reason he had brought Johann to stay here. His reasons were obvious with the way he stood, with the way he breathed, with the way his eyes sharpened when he looked at Johann. *My* Johann. Their scents mingled. It could be nothing, but it could be everything.

I couldn't speak more of what I had learned with Maravin here, not if we wanted to keep the truth of what I was a secret. I wished Johann had stayed in that abandoned house, where we could speak in private and make plans.

An urge rose in me, callous power. I could make Maravin leave, a simple stretch of will. I could render him deaf, so he couldn't hear us. There were so many ways I could get rid of him, and they would all be so easy.

"Maravin, you mentioned there was a statue of Laurel nearby, right?" Johann said. "A hidden one?"

"Yeah," Maravin answered. "Made from that same stuff

you showed me—the stuff in your solar flares. It's small, though, not like the one on the outskirts of town you talked about."

I blinked, focusing through the magic that thrummed in my blood. Maravin was helping us. Helping Johann. I couldn't just remove him. He was Johann's friend, that was all. His attraction to Johann didn't matter. The scents could be misleading.

Dammit, I had to focus. All that mattered was Johann.

"Can you show us?" Johann said. "It could help us make weapons, I think."

"Sure." Maravin clapped Johann on the shoulder, an easy pat, but he didn't take his hand away. "I think it's the last statue that Lasren hasn't dragged off. He gutted the temples, or at least what was left of them. Like I told you—he collects old Empire stuff. Targets descendants of priests and priestesses. No clue why. He's taken other statues like it, but missed this one."

Johann met my eyes and raised his eyebrows. Clearly he had been doing his own research too. I wasn't the only one working here, and I had to remember that. Johann was my partner, not my possession.

I couldn't be like Lasren.

I had to remember to pretend to breathe, to move slowly like a human, as we followed Maravin out into the streets and then to the overgrown forest that ringed this part of the city, one that grew in a patch between the streets and the temples in the distance.

"This was overgrown even before Lasren," Johann said, lifting an overhanging, rotted bough out of his way. "But it seems worse now."

"Everything is," Maravin said. "Though I don't know why this random patch of forest grew here in the first place."

Somehow I did, though no vision came with the

realization. This had been a park once, cultivated trees in the center of the city. Some of the rotted vines on the forest floor looked familiar, like the ones that lined the crypt Lasren had shown me. More curled around our feet as Maravin led us on.

Finally he stopped, knelt down and brushed the rope-like vines out of the way.

"Is it there?" Johann asked.

I saw it immediately. A small carving of Laurel, made from the same dark stone of the one that had almost killed me and had killed another vampire — Ana. She had had a name.

"Here, see?" Maravin pointed it out to Johann's weak human eyes. "A little Laurel. It was a shrine once, I guess."

"You're right." Johann knelt down, brushing more of the vines and leaves out of the way. "It's half-buried here, but I don't think it's fastened to the ground the way some are. Looks as though it was carried. But it's definitely made from the solar stone. I wonder . . ."

I read his uncertainty without him having to speak it. I couldn't imagine how Lasren could survive a blast like the one that had killed Ana. But I hadn't imagined he would have been able to survive a stake through the heart either.

"I never thought it would be important, but we may as well dig it up if it's useful," Maravin said. "I'll keep an eye out for others like it."

"How did you find it in the first place?" Johann asked. His fingers tested the earth, but it was frozen solid.

"Hiking around." Maravin shrugged. "You know how it is. Not much to do in Brusque since the traders stopped coming. Cutting through here's a faster way to get to the remaining farms. Besides" — and he chuckled — "I know you used to love this sort of old stuff. Guess I was looking out for you even before I knew you'd come back."

"If you aren't careful, I'll bring you back with us and make a hunter out of you too," Johann said with a laugh. "You'd certainly liven up the barracks a bit."

"I'll consider it if you really can kill Lasren," Maravin said. "It's damn good to see you alive, you know. And just this past day . . . hearing you talk, it's like we really can win this."

"We will," Johann said. "Humans won't be servile to vampires forever. I just wish more people here in Brusque were like you, Mar."

Mar. An old nickname? Or something new, from their time together last night? I clenched my jaw, and my fingers threatened to curl into claws before I forced myself to relax. Maravin was his old friend, a human, who could give him whatever he wanted. I was just . . . a vampire. Different. I could never know or relate to Johann, to the memories of his life before becoming a hunter, the way Maravin could.

This was infuriating. *Johann was mine.*

"We'll need tools to dig this up," Johann said. "The ground is frozen solid. We don't have time to wait for winter to end."

"I can grab a shovel," Maravin said.

"I'll wait here with Kaiden," Johann said. The use of my named quieted the angry buzz in my ears. "We'll see if we can make any progress."

When Maravin's crashing footfalls grew farther away, Johann motioned me over. "Can you pull this out?"

I had started to focus before he finished speaking, kneeling next to him. I imposed my will on the vines, on the ground, the way Lasren had taught me. The cold made it easier — more of the greenery and seeds that were in the earth were dormant or dead.

Johann's breathing quickened as the earth shifted around him, the vines pulling back. The statue of Laurel toppled over.

I stopped. There was something else, something deeper. I could feel it.

"Did La . . . did you learn that from . . . .?" Johann's hushed whisper sent his warm, sweet breath over my skin.

"Yes."

"We should figure out if solar flares will work," Johann whispered. He leaned close, as if I could have trouble hearing him when he spoke so low. I could hear his heart beating in his chest, an excited pattering. "Have you learned how his hypnosis works, or how to break the fear aura? Maravin says some of the bitten remember fearful dreams, but nothing else, so maybe something about the hypnosis makes them immune to the deadly effects of the fear. Is there a way you could use that to get me into the castle? Have you learned where he stays within the castle?"

The questions hammered at me, and shame burned. That was what I should have been focusing on—making plans to kill Lasren, not reveling in the powers he taught me. Johann and even Maravin had been getting closer to our goal than I had.

"Kaiden?"

*Focus.* "I will keep learning what I can," I said. "It is . . . difficult. Using magic makes me . . . ." I thought of Yicca, of her blood. Of the hunger that even now made my mouth water, of the man in front of me.

"You're hungry, Kaiden. Hungrier than when we came here. I can tell. Using the magic does that?"

I pulled my gaze away from his neck, swallowing. "I'm fine."

"I can give you blood again," Johann said. "You look like you need it. I can get you a cup of it, like before."

"No," I said, my fangs snapping on the word.

"Kaiden, you're suffering. And if you keep learning from Lasren and magic makes you hungry, it's only going to get worse."

"You tempting me is making it worse," I growled.

"Then take blood," Johann said. "You need the strength. I'm worried about you." He reached for me and I stepped away. Dead vines flattened beneath my feet. Minor pain from the burning herbs from before made my leg twinge.

"Kaiden, please," Johann said. "For our plans to work, I need you at your best. And I care about you. I don't want you suffering. Just—"

"You offering me blood is making me suffer," I snapped. "Just stop! I don't want your blood and I don't need it. I can manage this without you!"

Johann huffed, his jaw tensing. I wished I hadn't said that. I didn't want to hurt Johann.

And of course, it wasn't true.

"Fine," Johann said. "What else have you learned, then? Can you at least use hypnosis on me, get me inside safely?"

I grit my teeth. "I haven't learned about the hypnosis yet. Lasren is . . . protective of his humans."

"His humans. Ugh." Johann shook his head. "The world will be so much better without him. Brusque can be the way it was, the way I remember it." He nudged the fallen statue. "I hope you get to see it, Kaiden. I can bring back everything we lost, and show everyone here that they can have hope again. So far the only one who seems to have any hope left is Maravin."

My stomach twisted. The way he talked about him, that admiring tone . . . I had heard it before, but before he had been talking about me. Now . . . I couldn't resist asking. "You're . . . very close with him, then?"

Johann's sudden tension, the increased pace of his heart, was the answer I needed, but not the one I wanted.

It hurt, more than it should, but I couldn't let Johann see that. It was better that way. If Johann wanted to be with Maravin, he should. I couldn't give him what he wanted anyway. Not without hurting him. I was a vampire. Chosen, if I believed Lasren, but I knew better.

Twisted. Dead. My magic controlled death and brought

death. I had been foolish to think I could have Johann, not when he had someone warm and alive, like him, to be with.

"Kaiden . . ."

Emotions could hurt. I had forgotten how much. Or maybe the weakness I felt was just the approaching dawn.

"Did you . . ."

"Nothing happened, Kaiden." Johann huffed. "Nothing is going to happen until this is over. For me, with anyone. You made that clear just now, remember?" His tone hurt more than Lasren's herbs had. "Maravin is an old friend, that's all. I need to focus on saving my city. Okay?"

I could read his frustration. I'd turned him down so many times, had turned down his offer of blood just now, yet expected him to just wait for me when he had a willing human as an option? And now I was distracted from the mission we were supposed to be focusing on. This was Johann's dream, to save his birth city and kill the vampire who had killed his parents. Why couldn't I just . . . be good?

Pain still pulled, deep inside, mixing with anger that I didn't like. "I understand." This was fine. *No.* Johann could be attracted to others, it was only natural. *How dare he.* Maravin was a better choice. Maravin wouldn't drink his blood in the throes of passion and risk killing him. Johann didn't need to offer Maravin his blood in a cup.

*Johann is mine!*

I dug my nails into my palms, the claws scoring deep. The physical pain centered me, even as the injury healed immediately.

I had a job to do. Pain, even emotional pain, had to be ignored.

"I'll learn all I can," I said. My voice sounded flat to my ears. "I'll report back tomorrow, I promise. I'll learn where Lasren sleeps and figure out if a solar flare will work, and about hypnosis."

"We'll get him, Kaiden," Johann said. He smiled, but the

smile didn't seem as bright as I was used to. "We'll get him together."

I nodded, then turned and vanished into the forest. I was sure he would make some excuse to Maravin.

# Chapter Twenty-five

*Two men knelt, digging at the ground. They wore unmarked woolen clothes. As they dug, some of the fabric frayed when it caught on a reaching branch. The small statue of Laurel looked on.*

*One man pushed the vines out of the way, and the one whose clothes were caught reached up and pushed at the branch, sending a few orange leaves falling to the forest floor. Dappled sunlight beamed down onto the hole they had dug.*

*And in the hole lay a skeleton, the bones bleached clean, no trace of life or who it had been once been remaining. The grave was shallow, the edges rough. In the distance, the temple gleamed in the afternoon sun, its windows cracked and the courtyard pitted.*

*One man bowed his hand. The other held up something — a small, gleaming silver object. It was circular and detailed, a pin on the back. A brooch of some sort, laurel leaves etching the edges, and a laurel tree engraved in the center. There was writing on it.*

*When I focused, the dream shattered, just as the man laid the brooch into the hole.*

The dreams were usually visions of the empire. I blinked in darkness, bringing back the details. But that had clearly been after the empire's fall.

There was no question that was the spot where I'd been last night, where Maravin and Johann and I had dug up the statue of Laurel. Confusion and excitement thrummed. Something was there. It felt important, as though I was on the cusp of realizing what these visions meant. I sat up, my muscles tense. If I could just go back out there and find that object, find that skeleton, it would mean the visions truly were real. I could tell Johann. And maybe —

"Kaiden," Lasren hissed. I froze.

He didn't call up light, but I didn't need it. The room I was staying in was pitch dark, but I had sense of him, of his stance near the door, as I was sure he had a sense of me.

"I gave you leave to explore the castle last night. Not the town."

My muscles tensed, and I was acutely aware of my hunger, my weakness, compared to him. I wondered if the woman — Yicca — was still alive.

"I did not feed on your humans." If he had used the magic I had used to spy on Johann and Maravin that first night, he would know about our plans. He would expose my lies. I readied myself to fight, to use the one advantage I had — the fact that I could kill him and he couldn't strike to kill me. I was tired of this, of Lasren. I wanted to be with Johann.

"I know you did not. If you had, I would have rooted you where you stood and you would have been dead this past morning."

The threat washed over me. Once, before I understood how such magics worked, it would have frightened me. Now I wondered if he was telling the truth. Couldn't I merely use my own magic to undo his?

"But I do not approve of you going into town. I can sense your movements in my territory. I sense any chosen who are here. And I forbid you from entering the town without my leave. Do you understand?"

I fought not to snarl, hunger and anger mixing together in a spice of frustration. He was ordering me around as though I was a thrall!

I pushed the anger away. It could have been worse. He could sense my movements, but hadn't spied on me. He hadn't seen me with Johann, or heard what we had discussed. He hadn't seen the statue.

For the first time, Lasren suddenly didn't seem so unbeatable. I would obey him, and continue the charade. I would keep learning.

For now.

I bowed my head, my fangs sharp. "I understand. I was just . . . looking for the hunter. You taught me to resist his weapons, but . . ." I needed to turn this around and get information. "I still fear the solar flare."

"Ah, of course." Lasren nodded. "That is the one weapon the hunters have that we are truly weak to. Light is life. But their weapons are fading. One blast will hurt you, but only two will kill. And they do not have enough." He smiled, his fangs sharp. "They are powerless. And I will teach you how powerless they are. Tell me your taste. I will bring you food tonight. You may eat at your leisure—after you learn the proper magics and respect to Laurel."

I swallowed. I couldn't eat. Not yet. I was hungry, certainly, but I couldn't. I wasn't like Lasren. I needed a thrall, the thick blood foul, but at least then I wouldn't be killing anyone.

"Tell me what you like," Lasren demanded.

What would he say if I asked him to bring me thrall? No, I couldn't. He hated thralls, didn't tolerate them in his territory.

Lasren raised an eyebrow, and I realized I was testing his patience. Before anything else, I had to answer his question. Asking for a human made sense. I had to ask for a man, because if I asked for a woman he would wonder why I hadn't bitten Yicca the night before. It wasn't that I wanted the blood. It was just for the mission.

"Men," I blurted, and regretted it. I would only tempt myself more. "Strong, healthy men."

"Explore the castle as you should have last night," Lasren said. "I will bring you one. From there, you will learn."

No. But before I could stop him, change my mind, he was

gone.

What was I doing? I didn't want a man's blood. I couldn't want it. I had the strength to turn down Johann's blood, so why had I asked for blood from Lasren? I couldn't use my situation, Lasren's attention, as an excuse to take what I craved.

A memory flitted through my mind, snatched words in my voice. "It's not like it will hurt me more than it already has," as I reached for another drink, my head already spinning. There was blood on my hand, but I didn't remember from what.

*No.* I was supposed to be good. I wished Johann were here.

Johann. Thinking of him always helped. He had given me things to do. I had to do them. A solar flare would injure Lasren, but one wasn't enough.

It was a good thing Johann had found that statue.

And if I was supposed to explore the castle, I could at least figure out where Lasren stayed, and where to bring Johann to kill him. I had until he found me my breakfast to do it.

I didn't see Yicca anywhere and hoped that didn't mean Lasren had drained her to death last night. The halls of the castle were dark, the candles in the chandeliers unlit, moonlight shining through glass windows the only illumination. The pale glow spread over the curving banisters and intermittently through the long hallways. The paintings of the once-nobles of the Empire stared down at me.

Dimresh had stayed on the top floor of his castle, but as I climbed higher into the main tower, I got a stronger scent of dust, of age. Rooms where the plaster had been polished to the point that the stone of the castle showed through held collections of objects—fine silks hung on mahogany stands, a golden chest, a fan made of peacock feathers sitting on a desk made of some sort of pale green stone that I didn't recognize. Lasren's castle held items that any merchant would likely kill for.

But there were no plush beds as in Dimresh's castle. Opulence, but no sign of residence. No scent of Lasren.

The room at the top of the tower smelled strange, the herbal scent burning my nose. I wasn't surprised when I opened the door to find the statues.

Statues of Laurel made of every material imaginable, and of every size, took up the space. Some had bits of stone awkwardly attached, as if they'd been ripped from the building or wall they had once decorated. And more than a few were made of the same solar flare material that Johann had so prized.

No wonder he'd said the hunters didn't have enough.

Lasren certainly wouldn't sleep here. Maybe he prayed here to the goddess he loved so much. But the statues did nothing for me.

Seeing them like this felt wrong, but not in a blasphemous way. More as though they were fake. A statue of Laurel outside meant something—a place of safety, a marker, or a memory of the empire. Strewn around the room like this, they were just more objects Lasren had collected. Meaningless. A hoard of resources the humans needed to fight, but nothing more.

I wondered what Matilda would have thought if she could see this. I wanted to remember more of her words, but couldn't. Her death was clear, how I had tried to save her. Her life—like most things from my life—had faded.

I turned away, heading back down the hallway, my feet silent on the plush carpeting. A mouse scurried in the walls to my left, the only other sign of life. The past was gone. I had to focus on the present, on my mission.

Where did Lasren sleep? How could I get Johann inside to kill him? How could *I* kill him? I was ready for this mission to end. There was nothing here but a madman clinging to things from the past that may never have had power in the first place.

My journey took me to the lower floors, just above the stairs that wound down to the dark place where I slept. Nothing. No beds, no scent of Lasren.

I started moving faster, ignoring the detritus Lasren had collected. He had to sleep somewhere. If not a bed, then at least a room, or a pallet.

Unless he slept among the objects he'd collected, he didn't have a bedroom at all. I snarled in frustration, my stomach cramped with hunger. Nothing he did made sense! Nothing in this castle even made sense. The space felt small, the stone too thick. There were objects, but nothing useful. I would at least think Lasren would have books, considering he was a priest. Even Dimresh had books.

My mouth watered, my stomach hollow. I was too hungry to think. I leaned against a stone wall, a fantasy rising unbidden. Johann would help me. He would figure out where Lasren slept, would bring many solar flares and sear the walls, cleaning the castle of Lasren's influence. Lasren didn't belong here. And afterward, when it was safe, Johann would come to me, willing, wrap his arms around me and pull me close. His blood would be so rich—

*No.* I shuddered, willing the hunger and the heat in my body away. No fantasies. I had to keep looking. There had to be something, a clue, anything. I slammed my fist against the stone wall I leaned on, banishing thoughts of Johann's blood from my mind.

The sound thudded like a knock on a door. I blinked.

I hit it again. Then again.

The stone was hollow.

Of course. Lasren had mastery over stone as well as his subjects. What better way to ensure no one could get to him while he slept?

I called up my magic, the burning in my blood. But before I could part the stone, a luscious scent filled my nose. I licked my lips.

"Kaiden," Lasren called from the stairs by the entrance. "I've brought you your meal."

Fear mingled with anticipation. I swallowed hard, but the hunger didn't abate. I wanted this.

*No.*

It was part of the mission.

*No.*

I dashed up the stairs, my movements faster than when I had hunted as a thrall. I wanted blood.

*No.*

Lasren stood, motioning to the dead-eyed human who stood next to him. Then he licked blood from his hand, his fangs sharp.

"He's quite healthy," he said. "Good blood, fine taste. Of course, your lesson comes first."

I grit my teeth, wanting . . . and wishing my want would go away.

My supper was Maravin.

# CHAPTER TWENTY-SIX

I took a step forward. Maravin smelled of the trees near the castle—dormant winter wood, mixed with his natural scent, the ashy scent of the city and sweat and blood that still stained Lasren's fangs. But Johann's scent was mixed in with the rest, albeit faint, and that was what made my mouth water and my fangs sharpen more than even the scent of the blood.

Johann was mine. I could drink Maravin and never have to worry about his attraction to Johann again. Never have to worry about Johann's old friend. Johann would be entirely mine.

I pulled back, my own thoughts like a slap.

Did I think things like this before I'd been a thrall and then a vampire? Or was this part of losing my humanity, as Susana had said?

"Is he suitable?" Lasren said.

"Yes." What else could I say? I couldn't keep putting this off forever. If it wasn't Maravin, it would be someone else. Maybe even Johann. And I still didn't have a plan.

"Before you drink, I should teach you a power every vampire should know. Not all are capable of performing it—only those given the power by Laurel. The *true* chosen. I do not think you'll be able to do it, but I am curious, so I shall teach you. If nothing else, it will educate you on how to identify your betters."

My betters. By that, Lasren meant himself, I was sure, and his words galled. I had shown Dimresh who the better one between us was. Anger stewed, mixed with my anger at

Maravin for tempting my Johann. I could bite him now. He was right there, his gaze unseeing.

Dammit. Focus. I had to focus. I wasn't losing my humanity, not like this.

"The true chosen can control the humans who provide us with blood, as you see here. Control of their faculties, of their fear, and of their minds and memory is the ultimate proof that we, the chosen, are meant to rule for eternity. Any living thing is ours to control."

He didn't move, but as he spoke, Maravin approached me, his steps as even as his heartbeat. All of this reminded me of the first time I'd used my power to hypnotize something, to control it—a dying dog, walking to me and waiting to be killed.

Maravin tilted his head, exposing his neck. He didn't blink. His pulse thudded, the artery in his neck fluttering with every beat.

"Try," Lasren said. "If you cannot, I will let you feed here undisturbed. If you can . . ." He smiled, as though the thought was laughable. "I will give him to you. A gift to recognize one who is truly worthy of Laurel."

I knew I could do it. I had done it even as a thrall. Why Lasren thought this would be so hard, I had no idea. I could take control of Maravin now, show Lasren my power, and take all the blood I wanted.

I swallowed, licking my lips, the magic ready. I wanted this. I wanted to take what was mine. Maravin was right there. He was right here . . . for me.

Focus. *Focus!*

"I'm not sure how," I lied, my words thick. "How do I truly . . . control a human?"

"First, you must ask Laurel for the power," Lasren said. "Ask her to recognize you as among the worthy, one who deserves to rule."

I nodded, closing my eyes as though praying and listened to his nonsense.

"Then, use your will, like you used it before. Mold the human's will to yours. They really are no different than stone or fire or the wind . . . or even animals." He tapped his chin. "Perhaps I should have started you on one of those."

I was tired of listening to him. Maravin was mine.

I met the man's dead eyes, my will blooming in me like a fire in a hearth. But it wasn't fire I controlled. I didn't need Lasren's permission, and I certainly didn't need power from Laurel.

*You are mine,* I said in my mind. And then he was.

Maybe the difference between now and when I'd hypnotized Johann was the difference between being a thrall and being a vampire. Maybe it was the knowledge of my own magic that Lasren had taught me. Or maybe it was just the hunger. But when the magic worked this time, I felt it. Maravin's attention, his body, was mine to use as I wanted, full of possibilities.

And blood. Blood that would grant me immense power, whether I sipped it every night or just drank it all now.

"You did it," Lasren said. The surprise in his voice broke my concentration, but I didn't need to keep concentrating. Maravin was mine now. "I . . . I commend you."

His smug tone was gone, replaced by something I didn't like. Calculation. Respect. And danger.

I had overplayed. I was supposed to be a foolish, young vampire fleeing from a hunter. I *was* a foolish young vampire, nothing but a once-thrall.

What was I doing? I was supposed to be trying to kill Lasren, save humans like Maravin, not salivate over them. Not use them just as Lasren did.

Not lose my humanity.

What would Johann think if he saw me now?

"How . . . .how do I undo it?" I asked, my voice shaking. That wasn't all affectation. I didn't want to control someone like this, not like before. Not like when I'd done this to Johann.

"You must be careful with this power," Lasren said. His tone was heavy, commanding, almost as it had been that first night I'd met him. "It is a marker of a true chosen of Laurel, and rare."

Of course. Only vampire lords could do it. And if all the vampire lords were the once-nobles of the empire . . .

How was I able to? How was I able to hypnotize Johann even as a thrall? Was It because I had drunk Dimresh's blood, had killed the vampire who made me, just as Lucien had in the stories?

Would Lasren think that, and understand the threat I posed?

There were too many questions, so many things I didn't understand. I felt as though the solution was here, in this castle . . . or back at the temples . . . or somewhere in the visions in my dreams. But I was supposed to be focused on killing Lasren, not finding answers.

"Let us test what you can do," Lasren said. "A true chosen of Laurel can manipulate a human's basic instincts. Fear, anger . . . desire. Any human who approaches my castle with ill-intent will perish to fear. Such an aura must be set by killing humans first." Of course. The fear aura was the first thing Johann had taught me about the danger of vampires—vampires like me. "Any human I wish to approach me will be filled with the desire to serve me, in whatever way I wish. I need only think of them, and I can bring them to me."

"Think of them?" That seemed impossible. "You can call one from here?"

"Of course," Lasren said. "This is my territory. All who dwell in it are mine. I picked this one for you because I could sense he was keeping near the hunter you are so afraid of."

Lasren grinned, his fangs sharp. "Soon you will be ready to kill him. I imagine you already are. You likely don't want to kill this one yet, I would think, but if you can construct a place of fear from his bones . . ." His eyes narrowed and his mouth turned down. "I suppose you could make a territory of your own. You are owed one, I suppose, if Laurel has chosen you."

His words echoed. Dimresh had said something similar, when he'd tried to get me to leave him. A territory of my own. Is that what I wanted?

Lasren kept muttering. "Why would she pick a new chosen? Is it because more of us have perished to the hunters? No, that couldn't be."

He didn't know how I had the power either. But if he kept thinking, even in his madness he might figure it out. I didn't know if that would be good for me, help me learn what made me so different, or if it would be very, very bad.

"How do I use them?" I asked, hoping the question would distract him. "How do I control them so . . . well?"

Lasren blinked. "It's simple." Their minds are yours. Think of it as though you are extending *your* mind, *your* will. The power Laurel has given you. Make them think what you want. Make them forget what you do not want them to remember. Or" — and he waved a hand — "if you want to release them, draw it back. They'll return to themselves. And if you did it right, they will not remember anything you do not wish them to."

"And . . . they will be safe? Their minds will be their own?"

Lasren raised an eyebrow. "I suppose. Although I have seen instances where they are not. They give up on fighting my will and become mine permanently, their minds gone even when I withdraw my will. I grant them death then."

Fighting his will. Johann had been right. He had stayed in my control when we had killed Dimresh, so he would be safe. People had to have the strength to end the control and come back to themselves, as Johann had. As most normal people would.

But some in Brusque had given up, it seemed. Not that I could blame them.

Maravin still stared, unseeing, unblinking, while Lasren discussed driving humans to despair and death.

"So, Kaiden. This one is yours. Will you drink him tonight?"

"I . . ." I didn't know what to do, what to say. I wanted to. But I also wanted to end this.

"Am I permitted to . . . keep him here during the day?"

Lasren frowned. "No. Any human here will perish to the fear aura during the day. An aura of fear around your territory can be maintained, burnt into your territory with the bones of those you drink, but strict control like you have now cannot be held while you sleep. And you do not have your own *territory*."

My own territory. The words settled in my mind. Having a territory would feel right, in a strange way. I didn't truly want one. But having a home, a place where I was in control, not answer to Lasren . . .

"Feed from him then return him. I will make sure you return him correctly, and fix your mistake if not. Consider it part of your training." Lasren's fangs flashed in a smile. "Which, I must admit, will end sooner than you think. Laurel must have granted you such powers as a reward for learning from me. She rewards us both. I will find a worthy place for you to rule, and you and I can manage the humans together." His gaze grew distant. "Once you kill the hunter, we can expand beyond Brusque, along the Leoren Road. You can take travelers if you wish, and funnel others toward me to replenish my dwindling stock."

My stomach turned, and my fangs pricked my lower lip. As though I would answer to *him*. Serve *him* in any way.

"I will . . . think on it. For now, I will eat. Alone." I hoped Lasren didn't notice my anger. Maybe I acted this way because of the hunger. I needed blood and I needed a plan. I was tired of Lasren's madness.

But first, I had to deal with Maravin. I willed him toward me, not even needing the words, and headed down to the dark room where I slept.

Maravin silently followed.

# CHAPTER TWENTY-SEVEN

He smelled good. Not as good as Johann, but good. Healthy, rich. His blood would flow well in my mouth and go down smoothly. His blood would give me the power I needed to kill Lasren.

Or it would make me just like Lasren.

*No.* I had complete control over Maravin, enslaving him to my will. I was already like Lasren.

I leaned against the stone wall, the urge to feed battering at me. The craving was a constant swell against logical thought, the need to make plans, find what was behind that hollow stone wall, to figure out where Lasren slept, figure out what I could do to kill him.

Think. If I could just think, I could resist temptation.

I could send Maravin away. Send him back out into the night. And when I slept, the sun would set him free. That would be the best choice, the logical choice.

But I would still be hungry. And no progress would be made.

Think. *Think!*

I wished Johann were here. Think of Johann. Johann could help.

"Tell me," I said, licking my lips as I spoke. "Tell me about . . . about Johann."

"He and I are friends." Maravin's voice was flat, emotionless. "When we were young, I would visit him often when he came back from the merchant road. We would explore the old temples."

The old temples? There was nothing left. Of course, before Lasren, there may have been. "What was in them?"

"Old paintings. Statues of Laurel." All the ones I had seen, no doubt. "Books. Holy scriptures. Johann would try and read them, but they never meant anything to me."

The books had to be here somewhere. Lasren had stolen everything else from the temple, so he must have taken the books too.

There had to be more to this castle than I knew. Hidden rooms, hidden passages. I needed to find them, but I needed to make sure Lasren didn't know what I was doing. And to use magic to undo whatever he'd done to hide them, I needed blood.

Maravin's pulse beat in his neck. The situation always came back to that.

"Tell me," I said. "What sort of plans is Johann making? What has he told you?"

Maravin breathed out, then in, repetitive and deep. "He has told me that Lasren will be killed. That the plan he has in place will give him the best chance possible of winning back Brusque."

I ground my teeth together. Of course. I was the plan. And I had no plan. My teeth clicked, the points of my fangs stinging my gums. Lasren was immune to stakes, immune to herbs, the weapons we'd used against Dimresh. He was weak to solar flares, but I couldn't use those. Only humans could, and one wasn't enough.

I might have strength to fight and kill Lasren myself, if I could just bite the man in front of me . . .

No. Distraction. I needed distraction. "Tell me, Maravin," I said, my fangs sharp. "Tell me the history of this castle. Of Brusque. What was it like, for humans living here, before Lasren?"

"Before, merchants came here for safety. We were a hub of

trade, safe from vampires." His voice was dull, thudding off the blank stone. "I was young. We would explore the temples. Some people even explored this castle, but I didn't. This was where the old vampires lived. I thought they might come back. People said Lucien was harmless, but he was still a vampire."

"What else did people say about Lucien?" I demanded.

"Some said he took blood only from those willing. Others said his bones rested in the castle, protecting it. Others say they were descended from those who shared their blood with him. Some people said that was just a story."

"Is there anyone alive in Brusque who would remember or know more?"

"I don't know," Maravin said. "Lasren killed many of the older people first."

Lucien. He had been the key to me becoming a vampire, more than just a thrall. Somehow, I felt he was the key to what I was. Lasren wasn't my sire, but I was still walking in Lucien's footsteps, plotting to kill a powerful vampire.

Were Lucien and I just oddities, thralls who had gotten lucky? Or was there something else that linked us?

I'd never truly know. Lasren had scraped away any traces of Lucien and had never risked creating another like him. The man was mad, but he was cautious. I could understand his caution, in a way. If I took his territory, I wouldn't want traces of Lasren remaining either.

Taking Lasren's territory. The thought felt right. Everything in it, the castle, the temples, and the people . . . all mine.

The thought entered my mind like a bolt of lightning and I grasped it, the plan, the insane, dangerous plan blooming.

Maravin was mine. He was here, unharmed. Johann could be mine too, but two humans would be killed if they approached alone. Lasren was fast, and his magic was powerful. They'd be strangled by vines or crushed by stone before they could get close.

But what if I could take more of the humans? Lasren's precious humans, his property . . . The bitten had been taken here before. If I could bring enough of them in, and they all had weapons . . . solar flares, made from the statue Johann had found . . . there would be too many for Lasren to take them all. He'd even said that one flare wouldn't be enough. But an army of them . . .

No. They'd be killed. The idea was foolish and wrong. Humans weren't my personal army to be used to take my own territory.

But on the other hand it also might work. Lasren was powerful and smart, if mad. But distract him enough and I could kill him even as I was now, and I wouldn't need blood. Controlling Maravin was so easy. I could supply the humans with weapons, have them approach the castle and hide until I saw the moment to strike. Then it would be mine. All of it, all of Brusque, would be mine.

No. This was wrong. I didn't want the castle as my territory. I just wanted Lasren dead. For Johann.

Maravin stared at me, unblinking.

"Maravin," I said. I could only hope he wouldn't turn the entire town against me, or worse, against Johann. "I'm going to give you a message for Johann. Once I do, you will exit this castle and return to him. Give him the message. And . . ." I paused, trying to think of a better way. I could go to Johann myself, but if Lasren saw me, he wouldn't be pleased. He already didn't trust me. Or, if he did, then he was leery of my power.

Time was running out. I didn't want to antagonize Lasren any further. Not until I was ready. Not until I, and Johann, and anyone who would agree, had a plan. And this was the best way.

"Once you leave, and are clear of the gates, I want you to

remember everything you heard and saw here."

Maravin didn't blink. "I will."

"Then tell Johann to make solar flares. Ask him what he thinks of me hypnotizing anyone who will let me to attack Lasren, to distract him so I can kill him. Tell him to prepare as many flares as he can. I will send him a message when I'm ready."

It was past time to finish this mission. I didn't have the strength to keep doing this.

"Go," I said.

Maravin turned on his heel and left. I waited for Lasren to notice I hadn't bitten him, or to have somehow overheard. I braced myself. Part of me prepared to pounce on Maravin, to take the strength I needed to fight.

But nothing happened. The man's footsteps faded. I could sense him, *my* human, *my* servant, as he left the gates.

He started to run, and then he was gone. Somehow I knew I could find him and take him back if I needed to. But that would make me even hungrier. And I was already hungry.

I sat down on the stone floor, listening to the faint sound of bats squeaking as they darted through the air outside the walls. Lasren would think I was feeding . . . or worse. I would stay here, alone, with nothing to do but wait. Wait until the distraction was ready. Wait until I was ready to fight a priest of Laurel, a vampire who'd been alive for centuries.

Of course, I didn't have to just wait. I closed my eyes. I had seen Johann before when I wanted to. I may not be able to be with him, talk with him. But I could use my power, and *see.*

*Maravin ran, clumsy and slow. I had forgotten how much time and effort it took for humans to run, to avoid the gnarled tree roots that jutted from the ground and push through the reaching winter-bare branches. His breath rushed from him in heavy visible clouds of condensation, a mark of life but also of exhaustion, of growing weakness, and cold.*

*But he kept running, the lights of the city growing closer bit by bit. His heavy footsteps smoothed when he reached the winding roads. He ran past the house Johann and I had once stayed in, and then past the inn where lights burned inside. His pace quickened. He passed by the same drunk man I'd seen the other night, but either didn't see him or didn't care.*

*Part of me wondered if I could reach out and take the drunk's mind too, but I didn't. I could re-take Maravin's, but I didn't. I wanted to see what he would do.*

*He ran around Bendy Road, past it to the house I recognized from the night before. Without pausing, he burst through the door, his mouth opening and closing in what I was sure was a scream, a call for Johann.*

*There he was. Johann wore his usual coat, but this time there were no stakes strapped to his belt and no stakeshooter at his hip. He carried a chisel in his hand and a formless lump of shiny black stone — what had once been the statue of Laurel.*

*I wished I could hear them. Whatever power I was using to see them wouldn't let me, or maybe it was possible and I didn't know how. Pangs of hunger grew worse, but I ignored them. I wanted to see.*

*Maravin's mouth moved and he gestured. Johann said something and Maravin's hand flew to his neck.*

*When he moved it away, Johann peered at it, his mouth a thin line. Then he shook his head, a wry smile moving over his features.*

*Maravin was shouting then, and Johann nodded, only replying sometimes. I wished I knew what they were saying. I was sure my message had been sent. But that was all I was sure of.*

*Maravin wasn't my friend. Fear marked his movements, fear and anger. He pointed at the statue Johann held, and I could guess what he was saying.*

*Kill them both.*

*Johann never wavered, always calm, always strong. As Maravin shouted, then quieted, the discussion less heated, my vision wavered. Maybe I was growing weak from lack of blood. Or maybe . . .*

*I fought to keep watching. The two men were talking now while Johann kept chipping at the statue, his eyes bright. The windows stayed dark.*

*If I kept watching, maybe I would see a glimpse of natural light.*

But of course, the power slipped from me. I lay back against the dark stone wall, wondering if my plan would work. What Maravin would think. What Johann would think.

Most of all, as sleep came over me, I wondered what Johann would look like in the light of the sun.

# CHAPTER TWENTY-EIGHT

I hoped to dream, but I didn't. There was only the yawning emptiness, the weakness, of the growing hunger.

I woke to that hunger, my fangs long in my mouth. The only sound in the room I stayed in was the scuffling of a mouse in the wall as it lapped at water that had leeched from the stones.

I waited. The air smelled clean, fresh, and cold. There was no sign of Lasren.

Good. I had work to do. I was sure Johann would keep his end of the bargain. Johann would sacrifice for me, for Brusque. Maybe others would too. Given enough time, I was sure Johann would convince enough people.

And even if he didn't, it wasn't like I needed anyone's permission.

No. I couldn't think like that. Once I figured out where Lasren stayed, I could send for Johann and he would help me, find those who were willing. He was always so willing.

I swallowed hard, a fantasy rising unbidden.

*Johann would lie beneath me, legs spread and chin tilted up, naked and inviting. His taste and warmth would fill me, and I could have all of him I wanted. He would moan when I took him, and then when I bit him . . . claimed in all ways. Mine.*

I dug my nails into my palms, banishing the lust and hunger. I had a job to do. Johann would make the weapons. I could trust him. I needed to learn where Lasren stayed, where he would be weakest, so we could flush him out.

Answers to all the questions that rattled in my mind would

come later.

Maravin's scent from the night before lingered in the halls I passed throug, and then faded as I headed away from the winding stairs toward the wall I'd found, the one that had rung hollow. Even with my hunger, I had the strength to call up Lasren's teachings and mold the stone away enough for me to see inside.

The scent of dust and earth met my nose. The humans Lasren brought to clean his castle clearly weren't permitted to come here.

No light filled this new passageway, no windows to let in even the radiance of the moon. I navigated by touch and sound and scent. My feet were silent on threadbare carpets, the stone beneath my hand was layered in dirt and grime. The farther I went, the quieter it became, the sounds of bats and bugs and mice — the sounds of the castle I'd grown used to — not reaching here.

The passageway stretched on. I wondered if I had simply found a forgotten part of the castle that not even Lasren knew about. Then my hand brushed something new along the wall.

In the dimness, my keen vampire's eyes spotted a dark square. I focused, bringing my will to a flame that danced in my hand. Lasren had taught me well.

Another painting, this one of a handsome older man who wore spectacles. He was no one I knew, but I was sure this must be another lord of the old empire. Another vampire. The temple of Brusque made up the background. He wore a golden brooch, engraved with a picture of a dove. Strange, but I didn't have time to think on it.

I kept moving, and the firelight that I willed into being revealed more paintings. Some were torn, as though whoever had moved them had done a sloppy job. Others were so faded I could barely tell if they depicted a man or a woman.

These were the missing pictures from the main hall. Why

they were here, I had no idea.

I stopped at another painting, this one clear. Another man, he knelt in a sun-dappled patch of grass. A wispy shape floated above him, but that wasn't what caught my eye.

He wore the same brooch I'd seen in my dream. Only now the words were clear. *Laurel, savior, ruler of our nation.*

Was this the man who was buried there? That couldn't be. I was missing something.

I growled low in my throat. I couldn't allow myself to be distracted. I was here to find Lasren.

I let the flame I held vanish, plunging the passageway into darkness. The paintings became square shapes in pitch-darkness. Not even my keen vampire eyes could see when there was no light at all.

I kept moving, silent and quick down forgotten halls. I fell into a pattern I was used to — the silent steps of a hunter.

The ground began to slope downward. The scent of dirt grew stronger, mingled with other, older scents. Dead roots trailed along my fingers.

The scent of earth and air met my nose. Even without seeing, I sensed I stood at a fork in the passageway. The one to my right, the one I estimated would stretch away from the castle, smelled familiar. Earth and dirt, mud, and even the scent of human. This would lead to the place where Lasren had trained me, that strange crypt beneath the ground. I hadn't seen a tunnel there before that led to the castle, but clearly I still had much to learn about Lasren's territory.

I went left, down the tunnel that quickly became worked stone once again. It sloped back upward, and then down again, finally ending at a blank stone wall.

I put my hand on it, listening. There was something familiar. There should be a door here.

But I didn't need one.

I molded the stone, pushing through. The stone was

thinner than I thought it would be. The width of a door.

The interior was silent and dark, the only opening the door I'd just made. The air smelled strange, and made my skin crawl. I'd traveled so far down the winding passageways that I had no clue where beneath the castle I was — or if I even still was beneath the castle. But I did know one thing.

I wasn't alone.

"Why did you come here?" Lasren's voice seemed to come from all around the room even as I sensed him, an inky form in the blackness ahead of me.

"I—"

"I know why," Lasren continued, cutting me off. "Laurel showed me. She grants me visions, you know, of what will happen. That, more than anything, is what proves I am chosen. That we all were."

I tensed as he spoke. Something was wrong. My instincts, whether from being a vampire, being a thrall, or even being a human, screamed at me.

*Danger.*

"You're going to try and take my territory, aren't you?" Lasren said. "Take my food for your own. I won't let you."

The time to lie was over. He was right. I snarled, my plans bursting into impossibility in the face of a fight that had just come to me. And I had one major advantage, one he would never guess.

*He* couldn't kill *me*. *I* could kill *him*.

And now . . . now I had the knowledge I needed. I didn't have to fear his magic.

"Maybe in a few decades we'll talk again," he said.

I leapt toward his voice, but my fangs met only air. Then the silence in the room grew profound. He had sealed the stone.

The same sense of emptiness, lack of scent and sound and sight, that I'd experienced in the empty temple was rampant here too. I grit my teeth. Nothingness. Emptiness.

This was like death.

No. I didn't have anything to fear in here. I had the same magic Lasren did.

I placed my hand on the stone, molding it away.

But this time, it was thicker. I ground my teeth, my fangs pricking my lip. He was adding to the stone.

I kept melding, fighting his progress, until a pang of hunger, of weakness, forced me to stop. The opening I had made vanished.

I had the knowledge. But without blood, my strength wasn't enough for this.

I had made a grave mistake.

"My food is mine," Lasren hissed, his voice faint on the other side. "The castle, and the stones, are mine. Laurel has chosen *me*, not you." His voice grew fainter as the stones, the earth, filled in the passageway. My hand on the stone no longer rang hollow when I punched it.

Lasren couldn't kill me. But in here, I had no food, no way to replenish my strength or my magic. And even now, he was adding to the stone, sealing my prison.

I was trapped.

# Chapter Twenty-nine

For a moment, alone in the dark and silent stones, I pondered the true meaning of immortality. Unable to die, living forever as the world moved on above and around me, only able to suffer as the hunger grew worse and worse. I would truly become a monster beneath the ground.

I didn't want that. I didn't want immortality. I didn't want to die, but I didn't want to live like that either.

I had to escape. And with my hunger growing, now would be my best chance.

Lasren didn't want to give up his territory. He claimed he was chosen. I may not have been chosen by a dead god, but I'd won my power with my sire's blood. I didn't have a city at my command, but I did have one thing.

Well, two things.

I had Maravin, and I had Johann.

I could easily focus here, no sounds or scents to distract me. I didn't even have to close my eyes to take them. Maravin's scent was fresh in my mind, and Johann . . . Johann was dear to me.

*Come to me,* I willed them. *And bring your weapons.*

No matter how tired or weak I became in escaping this stone prison, Johann would be there for me. I wasn't alone.

I didn't let myself think about the blood I would need. I stayed focused on Johann.

*Johann, his shoulders bare, leaned over a workbench. A solar flare in pieces was strewn on the table, next to two that were intact. The brooch gleamed in lamplight.*

*He stood, grabbing the two that functioned. A melted slab that had once been a statue of Laurel lay next to the table leg, but he ignored it, obeying my orders.*

*Maravin was already outside. He waited until Johann passed by and took one of the two solar flares. The two men began to head toward the castle.*

*No. I willed them more directly as I formed the plan. Go to the crypt.* I willed them, turning them, toward a place they'd never been.

As they kept walking, I pulled my focus back. Now was the time to truly claim Brusque.

Lasren thought he could wall me here and that he would have all the blood he needed. I would see to it that he didn't.

The weapons weren't ready, but if it came to it, I didn't need solar flares. I knew how well fire worked on the statues of Laurel made from the stone Johann had taught me about. And Lasren's castle was filled with them.

A person here, another there, people I'd seen in Brusque that first night. Ruby. Another woman, a serving maid at the bar. The drunk I had seen the night before.

They all began heading toward the castle, under my control, bringing with them torches that would bring long-forgotten light to the statues of Laurel.

Lasren would likely try and stop them. But stopping them meant he wouldn't be stopping me.

*Vampires are cursed to have no humanity.* The memory of Susana's words gave me pause. I was calling humans to fight for me, to distract my enemy. They might die. They likely would.

I grit my teeth, my fangs close to scoring my lip. Then I withdrew my mind. Johann and Maravin would have to be enough. I wasn't like Lasren.

But first, I needed to get out.

I ignored the stone door, the one he'd blocked with more and more stone, and instead began to mold the far wall. That took time, and more energy than I would have liked. But soon the stone gave way to packed, frozen earth.

And this I hacked at with just my claws and brute strength. This struggle would take a while, far longer than magic would have. But not all vampires relied on magic the way Lasren did. And given how slowly humans traveled, I would have plenty of time to make progress.

Earth fell away at the strength of my reaching hands, the scent of dirt filling the once-empty room. I fell into a mindless state of work, creating a tunnel that would arc back toward the town—and the crypt where Lasren had taught me to harness my magic, like a true vampire.

All the while, Johann came closer. Snow had begun to fall. He and Maravin walked in sync, no torches lighting their way.

Lasren had said hypnosis was one of the most difficult magics, and hunger began to grow as I clawed at the stone. But I had to keep focused. I had to keep them safe.

My concentration almost broke as my claws met something that wasn't earth or roots or chips of ice beneath the ground. My fingers hooked through something hard, something that neither root norr dirt. At the same time, something tumbled at my feet.

I didn't want to spare the magic, but instinctively I called up flame on the ends of the roots that jutted from the tunnel I had created. The light illuminated a skull.

A fanged skull. Not human. Vampire.

The empty sockets that I'd accidentally hooked my fingers through were enormous and dark, and the bottom jaw had fallen off onto the floor. More bones were wedged into the dirt, and frayed bits of fabric marked what had once been a shroud.

The firelight glinted off something by the jawbone—a golden brooch, engraved with a picture of a dove.

The image flashed in my mind—a man in fancy robes, a

golden brooch decorating his clothes, and all of Brusque behind him. The painting that had been moved from the front hall, one of the lords of the empire.

The first lord of Brusque. It must be. And the fangs . . .

This was the vampire lord Lucien had killed and buried. This had to be him.

I let the fire die, my mind racing as the tunnel was plunged into darkness. Lucien had killed his sire and become a vampire lord. But he had . . . what had the stories said? What had Johann told me?

He had killed his sire to become a vampire and buried him. He'd taken blood from willing people. He had ruled Brusque. And he had given up his life, letting the sun take him and given Brusque back to the people.

If this was his sire, all those stories were true. I had believed them before, of course, but more as faith, as hope that I could be more than a thrall. Then I had simply trusted Johann. I had never thought about what it could mean for me.

What *did* it mean for me? I could sense the skull in the darkness, see the hollow sockets and the enormous fangs of the vampire who'd probably fought hard to avoid being killed by what had once been a mere thrall.

Lucien had taken Brusque and then given it to the people. I was just like Lucien. And that meant . . .

I didn't need to hypnotize people, to take their minds. If Brusque would be my territory, the best way to claim it was easy.

Lasren hadn't shown me how to do it, but he'd shown me enough. I was a vampire lord, and I could trust my instincts. If Lucien had done it, I could too.

I reached out with my will, with my magic, no longer caring about the strength I would lose, the hunger it might cause. Brusque wouldn't be mine, but it wouldn't be Lasren's either.

I sensed the magic, the bones in the earth that anchored the spell, the bones of Lasren's first victims. Johann and Maravin hadn't made it across the barrier yet.

"By my blood," I said to the darkness, letting instinct guide me. "Remove the magic on the bones of the fallen. Remove and burn the magic of my subject!"

My teeth gnashed, my fangs cutting my tongue on the words, the tinge of blood spicing the air. The magic that I had only barely been aware of, Lasren's fear aura, vanished.

Now the humans—Johann—could truly fight.

I drew my will back from Johann and Maravin. I wouldn't force them. I could only hope they would come to help me. I at least trusted Johann would.

And even if I failed, if I was stuck in here for eternity, or escaped and fell to Lasren, Johann would have a chance. All of Brusque would.

My mouth watered, and familiar craving filled me. With the use of magic, I grew even weaker, hungrier. I understood better now that it came upon me as a result of using the magic. The craving and weakness was more than hunger, more than a craving for simply blood or sex or even both.

Part of it was hunger for power. The control the magic gave me, now that I had felt it and experienced it and understood what it could do, was intoxicating. Even more so than the alcohol had been in life, the snatches I could remember. But the power the magic gave was real.

And like blood, I wanted it. But I didn't want to want it. I knew what the price would be.

I stood in darkness, alone except for the bones of an old vampire by my feet. I *wanted* magic. But I didn't *need* it.

I kept digging. If Lucien's old master was buried here, there must be nothing but earth above me. In time, I would get out.

Like a burrowing groundhog, not at all like a vampire lord, I scraped handfuls of frozen earth out of my path, relying on unnatural strength. It was hard to tell if I was making progress — winter had frozen the living things that should be in the ground, and roots and chilled insect carcasses were scraped away. It was only when one of the roots resisted my clawing, the wood springy instead of brittle, did I know for certain I had a chance of getting out.

I only hoped Johann and Maravin were safe. This was taking too long.

Worry for Johann spurred me further. Soon I had to climb to keep digging into the ceiling, clinging with bare feet to the walls to gain leverage in order to keep moving up. If Lucien had buried his sire here . . . I had to remember. How deep did people usually bury their dead?

A glimpse of memory, of Matilda's grave, mingled with another. A deep hole, the edges ragged, and a shroud. My mother couldn't afford a coffin.

Six feet. I blinked dirt out of my eyes. I was over halfway there. Assuming Lucien had cared enough to bury his sire the proper depth.

I kept digging, thoughts fading in the repetitive action. Something alive fell down my arm, a wriggling worm. The scent of earth grew tinged with the cold crispness of winter and living bark.

I scraped my claws against icy earth, and then cold air rushed in. The rushing hiss of wind and creak of branches filled my ears.

Soon I emerged from the ground, having defeated the trap Lasren had tried to set for me. I stood over the site where Lucien had buried his sire.

The castle loomed over me to my left, and rolling hills that sloped down and then up toward mountains stretched to my right. Brusque lay straight ahead.

Dirt covered my feet and hands, and the pants and shirt I wore, borrowed from Johann, frayed at the cuffs. I looked more wretched than a thrall. And hunger cramped my stomach, robbing me of the power I wanted.

But nothing slowed me as I headed toward the crypt — and toward Johann.

# CHAPTER THIRTY

The forest blurred as I ran. The air was cold, colder than before, and the moon was low in the sky even though the night was young. Winter had settled in earnest. I leaped over patches of ice and snow marked only by the tread of fox and deer.

I didn't know what I would find there. I had learned much about magic, but not everything. Would Lasren sense what I'd done? Would he go after Johann and Maravin? Would he conceal himself in his castle, in the tunnels beneath the ground . . . or did he think he'd already won?

Lasren was mad, but still dangerous. This didn't feel the same as hunting Dimresh, a lone vampire driven into a corner. Lasren was different. I wasn't hunting prey — I was taking a castle.

Less a hunt and more like war.

As I neared the crypt, the unmistakable sound of human voices met my ears. I slowed. Johann, as talented as he was, hushed whoever was with him.

Of course I knew who it was. Maravin. I scented them both, Johann's pine and intoxicating maleness and the acridity of Maravin's fear.

A surge of hunger went through me, a deep craving for blood and power and *Johann*.

"Use the flare!" Maravin hissed, a quiet whisper that was loud in my ears.

"Kaiden?" Johann said. Worry colored the sound of my name, even though I couldn't smell it on him. "Are you there?"

"I'm here." Maravin whirled as I made my presence known. I leaped back, behind the curve of the tunnel, before Johann grabbed Maravin's wrist.

"He's on our side!" Johann hissed. His grip kept Maravin from lighting the wick on the solar flare he held aloft—held toward me.

I bared my fangs, though I doubt he saw it in the dark.

"He mind-controlled us here, took your blood, and . . ."

"Kaiden," Johann said, talking over Maravin. "It's good to see you. What's happening?"

I ached to go near him, to smell him more closely, to feel his nearness and warmth. But Maravin stood between us, his weak human muscles straining against Johann's grip.

There was so much to say. The plans I'd tried to make hadn't worked, were half in progress, with Johann and Maravin here and others called briefly before I had released them. Lasren may know where I was, or may not, or he may recreate the fear aura . . .

I had to focus. I let Johann's scent wash over me, calm mixing with my desire. "Lasren no longer trusts me," I said. "He knows I'm trying to take his territory."

Johann blinked.

"What does that mean for us?" Maravin hissed. He wrenched out of Johann's grip, but he didn't light the flare. He still held the lantern he could use to do it. "Is that why you came here—to take over Brusque and use us just like he is?"

"No," I said, at the same time as Johann. Johann fell silent and let me finish. "I came here to kill him. Just as Johann did."

"You're a *vampire*." Maravin spat. "Why would you . . . why do you trust him?" He turned his back to me, talking to Johann. "You hated Lasren, hated vampires. That's why you left. So what is this?" He thrust the solar flare at me again. "I wasn't bitten last night, but now I'm being mind-controlled again and . . . what is this?"

216

"This is how we kill Lasren," Johann said. "Right, Kaiden? We can kill Lasren without putting others at risk."

I blinked.

"And then what, we give blood to him instead of Lasren? How does that fix anything?" Maravin demanded.

"Before Lasren, Lucien only took blood from those who gave it willingly," Johann said. He met my eyes, and I swallowed hard. No. That wasn't why they were here. "I don't want—"

"You've told me that tripe before." Maravin spat again. "But even if it were true, this vampire isn't Lucien. He's mind-controlled me, dragged us here now before we could prepare for whatever half-baked scheme you said he had planned, and for what?" He turned back to me. "Why did you bring us here? If you want Lasren's territory, what possible use could we be?"

"If you don't want to help, then leave," I said, my fangs thick in my mouth. I was so hungry, and we had no time to deal with this. "I don't need you. I need a real hunter."

My ears pricked at a sound behind me, heading toward the tunnel. Soft footsteps. Not Lasren, but not animal. The sound almost made me miss Johann's words.

"Maravin, trust me. You said you wanted to learn to be a hunter, to show me that you're more than just cattle in Brusque, right? Kaiden didn't bite you last night. He's on our side. We made the weapons, and others want to end this too, remember? We talked to people, Kaiden. They support you. It's just happening sooner than we thought. We can do this. Trust me. And Maravin, please trust Kaiden."

The footsteps came closer. Maravin was being so loud even another human could find us. The human—a woman, I could tell from the sound of her gait and her breathing—stopped in the tunnel. I wondered if she knew I could hear her.

"If you expect us to trust you then tell us why you brought

us here," Maravin said. I grit my teeth. How dare he use the word us, as though he spoke for Johann. "What exactly is your plan?"

My plan. That was the problem. My plans so far had failed, or were only halfway complete. People, at least according to Johann, wanted to fight. The fear aura was gone. But Lasren was still learned and powerful, could even now be using his magic to replace the fear aura I had destroyed. This was happening too early. I had only two humans on my side.

Well, maybe three.

"The best way to kill him will be a solar flare," I said. "He can use his magic to heal through most of the weaknesses vampires usually have."

"We only have the two for now," Johann said. "And we can't charge them. The rest of the statue is back at the town. Others might be working on it, but . . ." He shook his head. "We can't use stakes? Herbs?"

"They won't work. There are other statues in the castle. One of the rooms in the top floor is filled with them. If you could get there, you'd have all the weapons you need."

"What about you?" Johann asked.

I grit my teeth. "If it's just him and me, I'm not strong enough, unless . . ."

I wouldn't have enough power unless I had more blood. I didn't want to say it.

Of course Johann understood. His eyes narrowed as they bore into mine. His pulse beat hard in his neck, the promise there obvious. I knew he would do whatever it took to defeat Lasren.

I couldn't. Not if it meant becoming what I was trying to kill.

"His castle has more than just a fear aura as defense," I continued. "Even if you did find the statues, to even get to him, you need magic . . . magic that I have."

"Of course you'd say that," Maravin snapped. Johann put a hand up, silencing him. My upper lip curled.

"I can give you blood, Kaiden," he said. "You need it. I can tell."

"Johann!" Disgust dripped from Maravin's voice.

This was always what it came to. Blood. If I had blood . . . the magic was in me, waiting to be powered, to be called.

*Vampires are cursed to have no humanity.*

"No," I said. Johann frowned, and I kept talking before he could. "I don't need that from you. There are tunnels in the castle, blocked off by stone. He may be there. He may also be looking for me, so as long as I—"

"He's calling more bitten," the woman said, emerging from the shadows.

Maravin jumped and whirled, the lantern in his hand sending light dancing all over the crypt. I shrank back, but Johann kept him in check, putting one hand on his shoulder. My jaw tensed. I didn't have much more patience for Maravin.

"It's only me," Ruby said. I recognized her red hair as she turned to me. "You called me, didn't you? And two others, Tania and Zekiel. I came here when your control . . . stopped, but they headed toward the castle instead. He's never called two at once before."

I had sent them to their doom. I swallowed.

"Why did you decide to come here?" Johann asked.

"Because of what you said this afternoon," Ruby said. Now she spoke to Johann. "About how everyone needs to fight Lasren, to resist him. If we all had weapons, we could make a difference. Well . . . I believed you. Others did too. But Kaiden called me and those two others, and Lasren didn't call me, so I'm here." She blinked as the lantern light flickered along the walls. "My mother used to tell me I was descended from priestesses. Perhaps I'm meant to help win back my city. We should help the other two, also, before Lasren gets them."

Johann smiled. "We could use your help," he said. "Every

little bit helps."

Unless she died. Unless they all died because of me. I never should have called anyone but Johann. But I didn't voice my concern.

Ruby peered at the crypt walls and then back down the tunnel. "My mother also used to speak of a place like this one," she said. "Deep in the heart of Lasren's territory. Something about a holy place of Laurel, and how the sun should shine into it in the heart of winter. I wonder if this is it."

Fear thudded through me. I didn't think this was that place. But the underground room where Lasren had tried to trap me . . . that seemed much more likely.

"So you're a vampire too?" Ruby said. "I thought there was something strange about you. Are you going to take over if we kill Lasren?"

"No—"

"Why would you ask that as if he's not just as much of a monster?" Maravin shouted. "We're standing here with a vampire, one who has already taken your blood"—he pointed at Johann—"apparently mind controlled you"—he pointed to Ruby "—and is only going to either get us killed or kill us himself once he gets what he wants!"

"Maravin—" Johann began.

My patience snapped. "Enough!" I shouted, my voice echoing in the crypt. Maravin flinched. Hunter material he might be according to Johann, but in my eyes he was even more fearful and timid than Thomas. "If I'd *wanted* it, I would have drained your blood last night. I could do it right now, and believe me, *you* couldn't stop me if you tried." My eyes flashed, my words thick around my fangs. I was so hungry. "If you want to help me, stay. Otherwise, give the flare to Ruby and go."

How could Johann be at all attracted to this coward of a human?

"I'll kill Lasren," Maravin said. "And then I'll kill you the moment you show your true self."

I growled.

Johann stepped between us. "Maravin, we'll discuss this later." He emphasized the word, making a fist. "But to do it, we need Kaiden's help."

He turned to me and I despaired. I wanted to help. But I didn't know how.

"If he's calling bitten to him, he will wait for them in the castle, won't he?" Ruby said. "So if we're fast, we can save them, and . . ."

Of course. He would be out in the open. Where the flares would work. I was thinking too much, when what we needed was action. Speed. The bitten would lead us straight to him.

"She's right," I said. "We should get to him now. With the weapons. The solar flare is the only thing that will work. Once he gets blood, he may hide. Or put up the fear aura again. We have to move now."

"As if we'd trust—"

"Then let's go," Johann said, silencing Maravin. "We'll catch him by surprise. Lead the way, Kaiden."

Lead the way. I licked my lips, uncertainty stopping me until I met Johann's eyes.

"Kaiden, tell me if you need blood," he said. "I trust you." He waited. Trusting, patient.

My mouth watered, my fangs pricking my lower lip. For a moment it was just me and Johann, Maravin's disgust and Ruby's shock fading into the background.

"I don't need it," I said. I turned away. Johann sighed.

I had been in Lasren's castle, in the tunnels. This was the reason I had done all that, had suffered and learned all I could. It would be better if we had a surer plan, but even our plan against Dimresh hadn't worked in the end. No plan would be perfect anyway.

"Let's go," I said. "We'll travel above ground. Be quick."

Johann nodded. I led them out of the crypt, the winter air filling my nose. I had to move slowly.

The humans—and part of me thought *my humans*—followed.

# CHAPTER THIRTY-ONE

The bitten were easy to track. Their scent was obvious, and soon we were on their trail.

"One of them tripped here." Johann pointed to the ground as he stepped over a snarling root. He knelt for a moment. "Their footsteps are narrow. They're not running. We should be able to catch up."

"I could run ahead," I said. "I could get to him before they do."

"Not yet." Johann peered into the night, and I wondered what he could see with his weak eyes. "Let's catch up further. I don't want to risk losing you, Kaiden."

I wished his words meant more than they probably did. But this wasn't about me, or his feelings for me. This was for Johann, for his slaughtered family. For Brusque. I could see his conviction in the way he glared at the darkness, in his purposeful walk, his heavy but careful breathing. He was hunting, and his quarry was close.

I was just as much a weapon as the flare he carried.

Ruby breathed harder, falling behind but still with us. I didn't know why she came. I never should have called her, or any of them, even for an instant. But I was impressed that she'd come when I had let her go.

Maravin kept his grip tight on his flare, and his gaze flicked to me often when he thought I couldn't see him. He shouldn't be here.

And then there was me. A vampire hunting another vampire. Taking his territory.

Is that what I wanted? I wanted him dead for Johann. Because I cared for Johann, and I would present him Lasren's head if that would make him happy.

Did I want more than that? To be the next Lucien and rule a city with blood taken from willing humans?

If one of those humans was Johann . . . a flash of hunger and lust clouded my thoughts. Yes. That would be so good. He would come to me every few days, his neck marked by my fangs. He would tell me about the world, and then he would bare himself to me, my fangs sinking into his familiar veins, his body warm against mine as —

I blinked at the scent, cursing my own distraction, my weakness.

"Blood," I said. "Ahead." I licked my lips.

Maravin huffed in disgust.

"How far?"

I scented the air. "Half a mile." Half a mile through thick brush and trees. We were close, but not so close that the humans would get there in time.

Johann knew it too. "Go," he said. He started to run. "We'll be right behind you."

He passed me for a moment. Then I ran and the forest was a blur.

The scent was new, a trickle of blood from a bitten vein, a flash before it was gone. Lasren wasn't wasting blood.

I should have been faster. He was getting new blood, and I hadn't had anything. This was a mistake. I was weak.

But I kept running, leaving the tree line.

And there he was.

He was bent over a sagging woman, his fangs in her neck. A man stood nearby, motionless, waiting his turn. The man I'd seen in the streets of Brusque, the drunk I had called, who I'd thought would distract him.

The blood was distracting. The helpless man was

distracting. Lasren was biting him, distracted. I had gotten the man killed.

But more than anything, more than my guilt, I wanted to kill Lasren.

Not for me. Not for Brusque. For Johann. That was always what this had been about.

I pounced, with the same ferocity and instinct I had honed as a thrall, coupled with the strength and power and speed of a vampire.

Lasren lifted his head and then turned to mist.

I struck the woman he'd bitten, my claws lacerating her dead, drained flesh as she was knocked to the ground from the force. I skidded on icy dirt, my teeth firmly clenched.

In the distance, Johann and Maravin's steps thudded on the forest floor, Ruby behind them.

The woman on the ground was dead. No blood leaked from where my claws had sliced her. The man who waited blinked, his heart beating steady, the scent of alcohol clinging to his skin. Lasren hadn't taken his blood yet, but he was mindless, controlled.

I should take his blood and not waste it. I could get the power I needed.

*No.*

The earth rumbled beneath my feet, and then a thorn of earth spiked upward. I turned to mist almost too late.

My hunger was costing me. And worse was the weakness.

Vines snaked from the ground. I leapt away, slashing at nothing. Lasren was mist, invisible, and he was still using his magic. The magic of Laurel, of the old empire, at a vampire's command. That magic should be mine.

The force was in me, in my body, but weak. I needed blood. I needed human blood. Thrall blood. *Anything.*

The ground shook again, spiking toward me as I leapt away from more snaking vines. I twisted in midair, relying on instinct more than anything else, like a cat escaping a hawk. I landed roughly, my leg buckling.

I was Johann's best weapon, but nowhere near as effective as I could be.

I leapt again, back toward the man who stood dumbly, not seeing the death that was coming for him. Behind me the ground opened, dirt and ice splitting with a deafening crack.

I bared my fangs, moving toward the man. The bitten. I wanted the blood. For this, I needed it.

No, I couldn't.

But I needed it!

"No," Lasren hissed, his voice loud in my mind. He re-formed next to me, his claws sinking into the man.

At the same moment, someone burst from the tree line. Light from the wick of his lantern caught my eye.

Maravin had arrived first. The rest of my plan — the distraction.

The lit lantern in his hand moved toward the flare. He wasn't going to discriminate. I never should have called him. I shouldn't have called any of them except Johann.

My upper lip curled. I hadn't died this way as a thrall. I wouldn't do it as a vampire.

I tensed to jump, to flee.

Lasren was faster.

Thorned vines sprouted from the earth, wrapping Maravin, the scent of his blood staining the night.

My mouth watered.

The flare fell, the sound of breaking glass mimicking the sharp sound of metal hitting the icy ground.

Lasren leapt away, the man in his grip still. "You can't kill me, you have no power and no blood, and the hunter you fear is chasing you," he hissed. "Die here."

The ground opened up again. This time I wasn't fast enough. The thorn of earth pierced my leg, pinning me in place.

Lasren grabbed the drunken man, his claws drawing blood. Then he was gone.

The pain was mind-numbing, driving weakness and deeper hunger. I sagged against my pinned leg, my fangs sharp as I huffed out gasps of agony.

But Lasren had made a mistake.

Johann wouldn't kill me. And Maravin couldn't.

Maravin's heart beat weakly. Too weak. His blood was everywhere, perfuming the air. Too many cuts, and too much blood.

He would die.

"Maravin!" Johann's shout carried through the night, to me and certainly to Lasren. Pain arced through me as I wrenched against the earth that locked me down, but I needn't have bothered. Lasren was gone. I didn't need to fight him now.

"Maravin, no." Johann's breath clouded the air. He paused by Maravin, readying the lantern and the flare. The firelight from his lantern washed over me, making me blink. "Kaiden," Johann said. "What happened?"

Ruby's footsteps were lighter and slower, and she knelt by Maravin as I spoke. "I was too weak."

Johann knelt by him too, leaving me to claw at the earth with my fingers, breaking and crumbling the icy packed earth until I pulled my leg out. I had to use magic, a bit of my will to make the earth soften and reform, to leave me. Skin and blood was ripped and torn, a hole punched through my thigh, and the healing itched and burned as I stepped away. For a moment, my leg buckled. My mouth watered.

The scent of Maravin's blood was everywhere.

His gaze was glassy and unfocused, the thorns still stabbing into every part of his skin. He didn't even grimace when Johann pulled at them. He was too far gone.

His heart beat fast now, his scent changing, tinged with blood and something deeper, a scent I knew from my time as a thrall drinking the blood of animals. Organs shutting down, trying to spare the body and give energy to the heart as blood left it. A subtle sign of impending death.

"Maravin, please." Johann's hands gripped at the thorns, some plant I'd never seen before, twisted with Lasren's magic. Blood trickled as they were pulled out, thousands of tiny cuts, bleeding the man dry. The blood vanished into the earth. "Maravin, please. Dammit! I told him not to run ahead, I told him to wait . . . Maravin!"

"He's gone, Johann," Ruby said. She put her hand to Maravin's neck, blocking the fluttering pulse, but I could still hear it. "I've seen this before."

He was dying like one of the bitten. But his blood was being wasted.

I needed to fight. But he was human.

He would never have given me permission.

I didn't need it.

This was wrong. I wasn't like Lasren. Not like Dimresh. Not like all of the rest of them.

But with the blood, I could prevent this from happening again.

"Kaiden," Johann said.

I didn't know what his tone meant. His voice dripped of sadness. I could smell his anger and fear, hear the frustration in his voice and the beat of his heart, in the tension in his muscles.

I didn't have time to think anymore. Maravin's heart fluttered. Half his blood stained the earth.

I knelt, grabbing him from Johann's touch and Ruby's outstretched hand. More thorns tore at his skin, so I didn't pull him far. Lasren's words echoed in my mind.

*Do not let them die from loss of blood while your fangs are in their neck, and if you do, drain them completely.*

My fangs sank into his neck.

Part of me expected something impactful, a change or a

feeling. Maybe the loss of my soul, the last of my emotion and compassion vanishing along with the blood down my throat. This wasn't an animal, wasn't a thrall, and it wasn't freely given blood sipped from a flask. This was blood taken from the neck of a dying man, a human, who others had cared for. Someone who had fought for Johann.

But all I truly felt was pleasure.

The blood spurted down my throat, washed through my mouth in gulps, filling me with its warmth. Shivers went through me even though I didn't move, tiny reminders of life in my muscles and my skin, singing in my blood. And there was the power, the strength, the healing as aches and pains and weakness that had come from hunger vanished.

Human blood was so much better than thrall. It was the fulfillment of craving, just as I'd had alcohol in life, but so much better because this wasn't a meager attempt to fill a hole that could never be filled. Right now, sucking the last bits even as his heart stopped beating, his blood was easing my hunger and adding more. More magic, more power. I was more than I had ever been.

My soul wasn't gone. But for a moment, for this moment, I understood.

Power filled me as the last of the blood went down my throat. There was nothing left.

He was gone.

Maravin was gone.

I let him drop, the thorns no longer drawing any blood as he fell. His skin was white and taut, the pallor of death. He wouldn't turn — I had drained every drop, just as Lasren said. Nothing remained — not even the blush of recent life.

I had taken that life. Just as I had called the drunk man from Brusque, and the woman. She had lost her life, and soon that man would too.

I stared, swallowing hard.

"Kaiden," Johann said again.

I couldn't face him. Not after this.

With a push of my will, the magic I now had thanks to Maravin, the vines shrank away from Maravin's body. The dead thorns twisted, dried bits of dirt and petrified plant matter. They'd likely been dead a long time.

Just like Lasren. Just as I was, and would be, forever.

The castle stretched ahead of us, the moon now as high as could be in the sky just above the top spire, the moon a smoky gleam through thickening clouds. The statues of Laurel were there on the top floor. If I failed, Johann could use those.

Maybe he could use them on me, if he had to.

"I'm sorry," I said.

"Kaiden!" Johann shouted, but his voice barely reached my ears. I was already running, heading toward the castle.

If I was a monster, I may as well not let my power go to waste.

# CHAPTER THIRTY-TWO

I had wanted to fight against Lasren together with Johann. I had believed that my plan to have the people of Brusque fight back, distract Lasren while I killed him, would work. Humans weren't cattle. They were more alive, more driven, than I was.

But now I was alone again, racing toward Lasren to kill him. To take his territory.

I had killed Dimresh with Johann's help—I, a lowly thrall, relying on the help of a human. But now, human blood in my stomach and filling me with power, I knew.

I didn't need Johann's help. I didn't need anyone's. All I needed was blood, and then I could do things myself.

Lasren had taken the man with him. His scent, the blood mixed with sweat and fear and alcohol, made him easy to track. I slipped into the castle, the opulent carpeting soft beneath my feet silencing my footsteps.

I scented the air, animal-like instinct working with intelligent cunning. Human cunning, I wanted to think, but maybe not.

I headed down the hall, the paintings of the previous lords and ladies of the empire staring down at me. I hadn't expected Lasren's secret room, the one I had been looking for, to be here. But the empty space between Lord Lamoth and Lady Tieria reeked of Lasren's prey.

I smelled of blood too, the taste of Maravin's blood fresh in my mouth. What I had done was wrong. I never should have bitten him. But that gave me the strength to effortlessly will the stone out of my way.

This long stone hallway wasn't like the one before. The floor was bare but paved with magic, so smooth that a cart could wheel down it without a sound. No light illuminated my path, but I didn't need any, not even when the light from the far hallway faded as I turned a corner. The blood trail in the air was obvious.

Change in the air let me know that the hallway opened up on either side, to rooms that contained scents of wood, paper, and dust. A library, most likely. Another was filled with scents of stinging herbs, and I hurried past that one.

The place Lasren lived was a small castle within a castle. And sure enough, the scent grew stronger. The faint sound of teeth snapping together met my ears, and then feet on stone. If I could use a solar flare, that would sear every wall, killing Lasren instantly. My plan might have worked, if things had gone differently. If I had been strong enough.

"So you killed the hunter, then?" Lasren asked.

For a moment I thought of Dimresh, my once-master, asking me if I had killed the hunter I'd been ordered to kill. That felt like a lifetime ago.

The moment passed. Lasren had been foolish to speak. I sent out my will, twisting the rock around where he must be.

The entire castle shuddered around me.

Maybe it was Maravin's blood, or maybe it was the knowledge that my prey was right there, trapped, but my senses were more heightened than they'd ever been. Lasren moved, a brush of air and the sound of his light feet on stone alerting me to his movement.

I sent a spike of stone, just as he had done to me, and the wet thunk told me the blow had struck true.

I didn't need Johann. I didn't need anyone else. I was a vampire with blood, with power, and Lasren was mine now. The answer to killing him had been in front of me the entire time. And now that I had drunk human blood, I could finish my mission.

Earth rumbled beneath my feet. I squashed it, sending my will to the stone of the castle, quelling whatever Lasren had tried to do.

"Fine then," Lasren growled, pain thickening his voice. "Take my territory.

"It's not your territory I want," I growled. I sent more thorns into him, thorns of earth sharper and more vicious than the ones he'd sent into Maravin. Bleed him enough and he *would* weaken. Then I could take the rest of his blood. My mouth watered. More blood meant more power.

Lasren cried out as thorns made of stone pinned him, and the scent of his blood now added to the bouquet present in the stale air of the isolated castle. His power didn't matter. He had drunk human blood too, more than I had, but he was weaker. I was stronger.

*Why?*

"Stop!" Lasren screamed, his voice ringing in my ears. "I beg you! What do you want?"

I blinked in darkness, but I could sense him—not life, but not true death. Twisted, weak. Fear spiked the air.

*Why was I so strong?*

"You killed hundreds," I said. "Thousands." Lasren's teeth gnashed together, a squeaking sound like a rat or mouse. "You'll die for that."

My fangs were sharp, and I ached to bite him. I sent more thorns into him, pinning him down, and growled in frustration when he turned to mist.

I knew exactly where he would go. His place of safety, where he could hide from hunters during the day, was now his prison.

He fled down the tunnel. I pounced even as I twisted the stone near the paintings to block his escape. He didn't get far.

My claws raked across his face, my strength sending him

careening into the side of the tunnel with a resounding smack.

Lasren reminded me of Dimresh when he had fought me, stronger and faster than I ever was as a thrall. But now, it was me. I had the power.

This was enough. I wasn't here to torture him. It was time to end this.

I growled, preparing to bite.

"You're one of the bastards, aren't you?" Lasren choked out through a broken jaw. "I should have known."

Saliva dripped down my chin, my fangs aching. It wasn't hunger, just craving—for power, to finish him once and for all, for Johann. But his words stopped me.

"What do you mean?"

Bone cracked as his jaw healed, but he didn't move. "Was any of what you told me true?"

I growled. "I'm the one asking questions. What did you mean!"

"The bastards. The blood. You're like him—Lucien Laurel."

Laurel. Lucien Laurel. The image of the laurel tree on the silver brooch. "Tell me!" I shouted.

"You were a lowly thrall, weren't you? But with the blood of the emperor. That's what you are—a bastard given the gift." The scent of fear faded, his voice growing softer, taking on the familiar edge of madness. This time, I concentrated harder on his words than I ever had before. "The blood of the emperor flows, hidden, passed down through bastards forgotten to the empire. Laurel is a bastard's last name. But if one is bitten . . . ah, that must be why you came to me. Chosen. Laurel advised me true." I could sense his stare, his gaze piercing even in darkness. "My lord. I will give you Brusque, my territory, freely. It is your right. *The empire* is your right." His voice wavered. "Please, let me live and I will serve you."

I froze, unable to respond, my craving for his blood

vanishing.

Was this what it all meant?

Was that what I was?

A descendant of a fallen emperor, my blood twisted twice?

"Tell me," I said. "Tell me what that means."

"You have the power, and the right, to take any territory you'd like," Lasren said. "You are a descendant of the emperor, bitten by a chosen, blessed by both sides of Laurel. A true vampire lord."

If I was a lord, some sort of descendant from a bastard of the Empire, then that meant . . . Lucien must have been too. Lasren knew that. He must have. He knew of the possibility, and that's why he never kept thralls. For all his sudden loyalty, he never would have wanted this.

"I can train you," he continued, the madness taking on an edge of desperation, his voice shaking once more. "I can teach you the extent of your power. Leave me . . . leave me my territory, and I can show you everything I know. You can take whatever you want—any territory. There are many far better than mine. Tarek is the largest. In Dremasque, there are many people. Wollasque—I can give you Wollasque. Please, my lord.

My lord. *His* lord. I wondered how many humans had begged him for their lives. How many would have, if he had allowed them to and not controlled their minds.

"Please, my lord," he repeated. "I can give you territory, knowledge, loyalty. *Anything*. What do you want?"

That was always the question. What did I want?

I wanted to know. I wanted to know what I should want.

But right now . . . all I wanted was to keep my promise to Johann. To make Maravin's sacrifice worth the price. To fulfill the mission I'd come here to complete.

That was all I could think of.

My upper lip curled and I lunged.

He must have sensed my intent because he ran. But he wasn't fast enough.

This was barely a hunt.

When he turned to mist I waited, predicting where he would go, striking him down with the stones of his own castle turned against him. When he ran, I ran faster. The air rushed along my ears as I sped past him and tackled him again to the floor.

I bled him for every step he took, every time he tried to escape. The magic he used against me failed every time. And of course, it was never truly a fight due to the most important thing.

*I* could kill *him*. *He* couldn't kill *me*. He couldn't kill me because I was a true vampire lord, descended from a bastard of the once emperor of Leoren. Dimresh had given me the gift, the blood, that gave me the power, but I'd always had it, waiting to be turned further by whatever had made lords like Lasren fall.

I had more blood, more birthright. And I was untouchable.

Maybe he was too tired. Maybe he gave up. But, finally, my fangs reached Lasren's neck.

Vampire blood was always pleasurable, especially compared to foul thrall blood. Lasren's blood was earthy and sweet, even better than Dimresh's had been.

But his blood was nothing compared to Maravin's. Lasren's wasn't human. This life was tinged with death.

And soon it was gone. Lasren lay unmoving, his eyes shut, his priestly robes crumpled.

I had done it for Johann, for Brusque. I had learned what I was. I had gained a victory.

But somehow, as I sat alone in the dark, the taste of vampire blood mixing with human blood in my mouth, it didn't feel like one.

# CHAPTER THIRTY-THREE

The fight was over, but there was a lot to do before night ended. And the most important was seeing Johann.

Fear weighed heavy on my shoulders. I had never felt so distant from him as I did now, knowing what I knew, having learned so much from Lasren. Having killed a vampire without Johann's help at all, knowing I didn't need his help for anything any longer.

All I really needed was blood. Human blood.

I wondered if he'd known that all along, or at least suspected it. If that was why he'd kept offering it.

I would need to search these rooms too, to learn what I could from all the objects Lasren had amassed. But I couldn't stay here any longer right now.

I didn't use flame to light my path, walking steadily out of the darkness of the hidden halls. Soon enough as I turned, the portrait of the emperor of Leoren stared at me.

He had blond hair and ice-blue eyes, the Laurel tree behind him wrought in fine detail. His features were otherworldly and fine, probably a trick of the artist. I didn't see myself in him at all.

Something tapped above my head, but too steadily to be a mouse or rat. Other footsteps thudded from the entranceway, then slowed, almost imperceptible as Johann began what he thought would be a hunt.

I almost left. I didn't know if I could face him. I didn't know why I was so afraid.

"Johann," I called out instead. "I'm here."

"Kaiden!" Light danced along the hall from the lantern he held. The solar flare was still in his hand, but he lowered it as he drew near to me. "What is there to report?"

He talked to me as a fellow hunter, and that shouldn't feel strange but it did. Wasn't he going to react to me biting Maravin? Shouldn't he be upset?

Of course he wouldn't. Johann was a professional. And he didn't know yet.

"Lasren is dead." I licked the tip of one of my fangs as I spoke. "It's . . . done."

Johann blinked. "He's dead? You're sure?" I didn't respond, but he must have seen it on my face. "Lasren is dead. Lasren is . . ." He broke into a smile. "We did it! Brusque is free!"

He turned in a circle, his eyes wide, his lantern sending shadows and light bouncing off the portraits. "All of this . . . I can't believe it, Kaiden." He breathed out, then in, slowly. "It feels unreal. After so long . . . after Maravin gave his life . . ."

I looked away, back to the portrait of the Emperor. He stared over our heads, as if looking into a bright future.

"I'm sorry," I said. "About Maravin."

Johann was quiet for a moment, just breathing. "It didn't have to be him," he finally said. "It could have been me."

I whirled, my upper lip curling. "Don't say that!"

Johann's shoulders slumped, his head bowed under the weight of the coat he wore. "But it was my blood you've always wanted most, wasn't it? You could have had mine. If only . . ."

"I wouldn't take your blood," I snapped.

"But you took Maravin's." Johann lifted his head. "Maravin would never have wanted that." The words were like a slap. They were worse, because a physical blow from Johann would never have hurt me.

"I didn't mean it like that," Johann said. "It's not that,

Kaiden, I'm just . . . After all this, not sleeping for . . . .it's been nearly two days now. I'm so *tired.* And Lasren is dead, but . . . Maravin is gone." He blinked slowly. "I should never have told him anything. I should never have gotten him involved."

"If you hadn't," I began. It was hard to finish the sentence, my jaw tightening. "I might not have had the strength to beat Lasren."

"You could have bitten me," Johann said.

"No, I wouldn't have."

"But you could bite Maravin? Why?"

"He was dying!" I turned to Johann then, trying to hide the snarl in my voice. "He was dying, and if I had wasted his blood—"

"He never would have wanted to die that way," Johann repeated. "*I* did. I've told you, I've shown you, over and over. You could have bitten me, Kaiden. I would *choose* it!" He took a breath. "Just like Lucien only bit those who allowed it. If you would just have taken my blood in the cave, you could have gone and killed Lasren and Maravin would still be alive!" He slumped. "If I had kept Maravin behind instead of thinking we needed the extra manpower, you could have just bitten me and he would still be here. Oh, Maravin . . ."

I hated to see him this way. Shoulders slumped, head hung low, sadness I could almost smell weighing him down.

I had killed Johann's friend, a man he'd known before he had left Brusque. A man—as stupid and foolhardy as he may have been to rush in like that—that Johann cared for.

I had killed Lasren, but somehow, it had all gone wrong.

I wanted to tell Johann what I had learned. What I, and Lucien, truly were. But instead I stood silently in the hall, lantern-light flickering over old portraits. Johann was the only source of life here.

No. There was one other.

Ruby's steps made the stairs creak, so loud even Johann

could hear it.

"Johann?" Ruby called. "I heard . . . shouting. Is Lasren truly dead?"

Johann met my eyes, and I didn't understand what he wanted.

"He's gone, Ruby," Johann called. "Brusque is free."

A sharp intake of breath met my ears. "Truly?"

"It's true," Johann said. "Did you find the statues?"

"Dozens," she said. "Maybe hundreds. Stolen from the city. My mother was right about that too. She was right about so many things. And about Lasren receiving divine retribution. We're free." Her voice became louder as she hurried down the steps. "Thank—"

She stopped, staring at me, her face going slightly pale. A spike of fear-scent greeted my nose.

Johann put a hand on her shoulder and she startled. "It's fine, Ruby," he said. "We should . . . get back. We have news to share. And . . . bodies to bury."

He whispered the last, but I heard it anyway.

"Is Zekiel . . . dead as well?" she asked me.

Zekiel. The man Lasren had called and fed from. His body must be down the hidden hall, where Lasren lay.

"He's gone," I said, and Ruby sighed. "I can show you where—"

"No," Ruby said as I gestured to the hole in the wall. She rubbed her hands over her arms. "I'll just . . . wait outside."

"Here," Johann said. He took off his heavy coat, the wooden stakes clinking. "Wear this. The early morning winter bitter cold is the worst."

Early morning. The nights were long in winter. I didn't sense the morning sun yet.

Ruby turned away, and I couldn't stay here with Johann. I didn't know what to say. I didn't know what to do next. But I hoped I knew what was right.

"I'll fetch the body . . . Zekiel," I said. "I can help you bury him. And the others."

Johann sighed and didn't nod. I knew Zekiel wasn't the burial he had been thinking of. I didn't know if he wanted my help with that one.

Darkness enveloped me in the hidden hallway. Once I turned the corner, where the lantern light didn't penetrate, I called up flame.

The firelight that danced in my hand bounced off blood-covered walls, illuminating Lasren's slumped form. The room I had sensed in the darkness was filled with books, but no shelves—just dusty manuscripts and pages, some without bindings, strewn on the floor.

Another room held a plain cot, like what I would expect to see in the hospital back in Penthorn. Next to it stood a blood-covered vampire.

I blinked. I was the blood-covered vampire, the mirror in the room revealing what I had done. Blood stained my chin and had run down my shirt. I wasn't sure if it was Lasren's or Maravin's.

No wonder Ruby had been afraid.

The last room held the body—Zekiel. Only three rooms and one hallway. Lasren must have been truly confident if he thought he could hide here, in this small place, where hunting him had been so easy.

Zekiel lay facedown, Lasren's fang marks still in his neck. The bite hadn't been clean. Some of his blood had dribbled onto the floor, pooling in a strange shape.

A leaf. A Laurel leaf. I blinked. The blood hadn't pooled at all but flowed through grooves in the stone. If there had been more blood, it would have filled the shape, making a blood-red Laurel tree all along the stone floor.

My vision fuzzed, and for a moment I expected to see another vision of the past, something that would explain what this was. But there was nothing. Just blood on the floor and a dead man drained of it. Even in death, I could scent the alcohol on his clothes.

If I had died in that alley, I might have looked a lot like this.

Of course, I hadn't. I was a descendant of a bastard of the emperor. Bastard or not, I had royal blood. I should tell Johann. He would know better what that meant. According to Lasren, I was a true lord of the empire.

I put out the flames that danced in my hand before I lifted Zekiel's body. I certainly didn't feel like a lord.

# CHAPTER THIRTY-FOUR

I didn't want to face what I had done. I hoped Johann would tell me to stay behind.

When I left the castle, he and Ruby stood in the courtyard, the pale light of the early morning moon shining on the stones. Ruby shivered as I came close.

We stood in silence for a few moments. Maybe I should have covered Zekiel's face and neck. Then again, I doubted Ruby and Johann could see the damage Lasren had done in the dark.

Johann sighed, and it was Ruby who spoke first. "We should take them back to Brusque," she said. "We can bury them there. In the sun. That is traditional."

"I can help bring them back," I said. "If you want me too."

"You would still help us?" Ruby asked. She stared at me in the dark.

"Of course."

"I'll take Maravin," Johann said. "Kaiden, can you take . . ."

"Zekiel," Ruby reminded him. "And Tania was killed too. Can you carry them both?"

"I can. Where should I . . ."

"Bring them to the edge of Brusque," Ruby said. "Johann and I can manage things from there."

"I'll do that."

"When will you need blood again?" Ruby asked, and my thoughts shattered.

"I won't," I said. "Not from anyone in Brusque."

"Kaiden," Johann said with a sigh. He opened and closed his mouth once, then shook his head. "Go on. We'll talk more . . . tomorrow. After I've rested some. And thank you. Truly."

"Thank you," Ruby echoed.

I wavered for a moment, wanting Johann to meet my eyes, wishing I knew what else to say. Brusque was free. I had done what he wanted. I wanted it to feel more like a victory.

The silence stretched on. I wouldn't get that feeling tonight. Instead I carried Zekiel into the forest, leaving them behind, my speed barely affected by the dead man's weight.

The strange thorns Lasren had created still surrounded his body, though my magic before had at least pulled them from his skin. Maravin lay faceup, my fang marks in his neck. They were spaced closer together than Lasren's. People would know.

It was too late to think about that.

The woman — Tania. I had to remember their names, not think of them as just humans — lay some distance away from Maravin, facedown where she had fallen. She was even lighter than he was. Lasren had drained her too.

Mere minutes passed before I was at the edge of Brusque, and that was when I felt it, just as I had in Penthorn.

*My* territory. *My* city.

The wooden houses, the soaring temples in the distance, the winding roads and bars and people . . . all of it was mine.

*No.*

I lay Tania and Zekiel, two people I hadn't known but who had lives and dreams, down along the path to their city. I had called for them to help and only gotten them killed. Old blood or not, I was no lord. Whatever I ultimately decided, whatever came tomorrow night or the night after when I talked to Johann, I was sure of that.

I shrank back into the forest and then headed back to the castle. Trees and reaching branches flashed past me as I darted through brambles and over long-forgotten paths. I didn't want to see Johann carry Maravin. I would give him his privacy, his time with his old friend.

Morning would come soon, but there was one other thing I needed to do.

Burying Dimresh had taken effort, testing my new vampiric strength as I dug clawfuls of autumn earth. My mind had been full of questions, of all the strange statements my old master had made. *Old blood. Fighting as the empire fell.*

Now, as I willed the earth apart to throw Lasren into the room where he had tried to trap me, those questions were answered. The old blood — the blood of the emperor. Fighting as the empire fell — the nobles, turned to vampires, killing those who hadn't been and establishing their territories. Every surviving noble had become a selfish bloodsucker, concerned only with their territory and blood.

But even with those old questions gone, others bloomed in their place. As I closed the earth around Lasren, sealing him away with the noble who had once ruled here and been buried by Lucien, the old memory of my mother teased the edges of my mind.

If I was descended from a bastard of the empire, had she been as well? Would a bite have saved her, turning her to a thrall, and then to a vampire?

Or had it been my father, some nameless man I never knew who had bought my mother's services? Was he still alive somewhere in Penthorn?

The moon fell lower. No more memories came to mind, my past as a human still murky and dim. I would likely never know.

Once Lasren was buried and gone and the sun promised to arrive over the horizon, there was nothing for me to do but sleep and dream.

*Curving roots arced over my head, lit only by the small lantern I held in my hand. A man in robes stood next to me, his hair white with age and his skin wrinkled. He nodded as he gestured to the ceiling.*

*Magical light glowed from his hand, illuminating roots forming spirals, curving in the shape of a crown around the earthen ceiling. The heavy, crisp scent of living wood surrounded me, along with a faint trace of something floral in the back of my nose that was somehow familiar.*

*The man in robes gestured again and the light went out. The glow of my lantern went out as well, leaving me standing in pitch-darkness, the memory of the roots behind my eyelids. It faded as we waited, surrounded by darkness and silence.*

*Then a beam of light entered the chamber, brighter than anything I had ever seen, the light of the lantern and even the priest's magical light paling in comparison. The beam was thin, a stripe along the ceiling, and illuminated the rock wall on the far side of the cavern.*

*A small Laurel tree was carved there.*

*The light grew brighter and redder, and for a moment I thought it was flame, burning the roots above my head. The light showed me more of them, spiraling natural patterns.*

*Then the light spread onto a carved coffin that lay on the floor. The lid was open, the man inside lying peacefully with his arms crossed. He wore a circlet of winding silver that reminded me of the pattern of the roots above my head.*

*The light grew even brighter. I was slow to figure out what this was.*

*Sunlight.*

*The beam of light widened and caught a small statue of Laurel, the stone the same shimmery gray I knew so well from the solar flares. The statue brightened, flaring once, and the coffin caught fire.*

*Chanting entered my mind, echoing all around me, even though the priest's lips didn't move.*

*Light of life to death. Go, go, go.*

*The chanting continued as the flames rose higher and the sun brightened, the light so bright I could no longer see the dead man inside. The statue glowed, and for a moment, terror froze me in place.*

*Solar flare. It would kill me.*

*The light brightened, but I could make out the man now as he rose, the dream fracturing into shards of dark and light. Maravin stood out of the coffin, his skin pale and taut from the blood he had lost.*

*He lifted the statue.*

I woke to darkness, my muscles tense. Instinct told me to run, to fight, and I growled.

The sound of my voice echoed over empty stone. The empty stone of Lasren's . . . no, *my* castle.

I hated the castle.

I leapt out of the spot where I'd chosen to sleep, the same stone enclosure beneath the winding stairs. The lanterns of the castle weren't lit, and for the first time the darkness felt oppressive, even though the faint light of the night outside was all I needed.

I darted out into the courtyard and was met with blustery cold and pinpricks of wetness.

Snow fell in whirling puffs, the cold wind flapping the loose clothes I'd found in the castle. They didn't fit well, but they were better than the bloodstained ones from the night before, and I hadn't looked very hard for others. My clothes were far from the biggest concern I had.

Whiteness stretched ahead of me, the domes of the temples covered. The scent of cold and damp was everywhere, and fresh on the blowing wind. The storm wouldn't stop anytime soon.

Johann wouldn't come here anytime soon either. I would have to go to him.

I wanted to. But I also didn't.

The dream was fresh in my mind, the memory of the fire combating the sensation of cold on my already-cold skin. And with it the memory of Maravin. The first human I had drunk from, whose blood I had tasted as he died.

I hadn't liked him. I had barely known him. He had been close to Johann, winning his respect and attention, while I had been with Lasren learning how to kill a powerful vampire lord, learning who I was. He had been a coward and a fool, running ahead and trying to kill me and Lasren both and only getting himself killed.

But he had been Johann's friend. He had been a human in a world of vampires. Who wouldn't be afraid? Who wouldn't see me as a threat?

And he'd been right in the end.

Human blood was different. Thrall blood was foul, but it had filled me, given me some of the strength I needed. Vampire blood was better. But human blood . . .

I closed my eyes, and I could sense everything in Brusque. The quiet of the temples, abandoned in the snow. Warmth from fires, and the beating hearts of people in their houses, the slow ones marking those who slept. One heart beat oddly, too quickly. Maybe that person was ill.

With the slightest bend of my will, I sensed the castle and lit the torches within it — the darkness and cold of the night in the courtyard suddenly lessened. I could do the same to any of the lanterns in Brusque, I knew. Put out the light, call a human to me, their path hidden in the darkness I created.

I wouldn't. But I could.

Lasren had taught me how to use the magic in my being and blood. But Maravin had finally taught me what it felt like to have full access to it. Human blood was more than food — it was power.

The wind blew harder, snowflakes swirling into the open castle doors.

I didn't *want* to want blood. I didn't know what I truly wanted, what this all meant, what the true importance of my dreams and visions and power truly was. I could go inside, see if Lasren had left any records, but I didn't want that either.

Not right now.

I wanted Johann.

I just hoped he wanted to see me too.

I turned toward the storm and headed toward the city of Brusque.

# CHAPTER THIRTY-FIVE

Snow stung my skin as I ran. It was hard to stay silent as the slush swished beneath my feet. Snowflakes fell in clumps that thickened quickly, a coating of the stuff accumulating even in the short time it took me to arrive at the edge of the city.

Lights glowed in houses in the distance. The beating of human hearts grew louder, my sense of people in my city letting me pick them out — two in the house closest to me, three in the one farther on.

Maravin's house was empty. So was the abandoned building where we'd first stayed.

I closed my eyes, willing myself to see him.

*There — in a quiet, dark room. He slept, covered in a soft quilt.*

I pulled back my magic. I shouldn't waste my power. Not when I wouldn't get it back any time soon.

Maybe ever.

Johann was resting. He likely needed it. I shouldn't be here.

But there was someplace I should be. Close to him, but not to see him.

It took me longer than I liked to find the hospital where the bitten had been treated and where I knew Johann slept. I had to find the scent of blood and death on the snow-laden wind. But once I found it, it was obvious. I still knew Maravin's scent, too.

They'd buried him at the hospital with the other bitten who had died at the fangs of Lasren. What had Sasha said when we first met her? *An honor for their sacrifice.* My time meeting her with Johann, when we'd first arrived in Brusque, felt like a lifetime ago.

The three fresh graves had already been covered in snow, but the hastily made wooden headstones proclaimed their names. Maravin Tensmith. I hadn't known his last name. In the building just next to where he lay, Johann slept, his heartbeat faint but audible through the wood that separated us and the sound of the blowing snow. Someone else slept too, their heartbeat weaker. But at least whoever it was still lived.

Staring at the headstone, I didn't know what to feel. I hadn't liked Maravin. This wasn't the same as being at Matilda's grave, where I'd fought for the memories of the woman who had cared for me, where the sadness had been bitter and deep, even as a thrall. I had mourned then for her, and for the life she had tried to give me that I'd thrown away.

But Maravin's death was still death. And it was the man whose blood even now gave me strength and power. A man I'd helped usher into that death, because of the twisted power of vampires.

Sadness weighed on me, mixed with anger. This was unfair. I shouldn't be mourning like this, because Maravin shouldn't have died. I shouldn't need blood to kill vampires. Vampires like me shouldn't even exist.

The nobles had twisted themselves centuries ago, somehow, and now we were all paying for it.

Someone in the hospital moved, soft steps on wood, and the door swung open. "Come inside," a woman's voice called. Sasha. "Those who fell fighting Lasren wouldn't want you catching your death in the snow the first night of freedom."

I stepped away from the graves. Part of me wanted to dash back into the storm, to hide from those in town. Another part of me ached to be near people. I had been staying in a castle with only Lasren for company night after night and now he was gone. My mission was done. I was tired of being alone.

And Johann was inside.

"Oh, it's . . . you," Sasha said as I came close, her eyes widening. She gripped the doorframe.

Snow had begun to gather on the ill-fitting clothes I'd found in the castle. At least they weren't covered in blood. "Is Johann . . . doing well?" I asked.

"He's been sleeping since this afternoon, after the funeral."

This afternoon. Only a few hours. "That's good then," I said. "I suppose . . . I'll go."

"No. Stay." She let go of the door, pulling her cloak farther around herself as she stepped out of the way of the frame. "We have nothing to fear from you, right? That's what Johann said. That you'd only bite if we gave permission."

My jaw tensed. "I won't bite anyone here, ever," I growled. "You've all suffered enough." Damn Johann. Why would he say such a thing?

"Is it true, then?" she said as I came inside, staying by the door when she shut it and moved toward the desk. The storm was muffled here, a tiny room illuminated with a small candle. The cloying scent of fresh ink wafted from the desk. "That you killed Lasren?"

"It's true." The two heartbeats were louder here, Johann two rooms away, past what must be a hallway, and the other in another room next to his. Another room at the end of the hallway reeked of blood and dirt. The wood in the entire house smelled rotten.

"Yicca hasn't been called. That was what finally convinced me he was gone." Sasha breathed out, her heart slowing as she did. "I was sure she would die if she was called again."

"She's alive?" I looked to the door, in the direction of the weak heartbeat. The woman I'd seen cleaning, the one Lasren had offered me . . . she was here, and safe.

Sasha smiled. "So you truly do care about us, then."

I didn't know how to respond to that. I didn't know them,

not like Johann did.

"What happened here, while I was . . . gone?" I asked. "What did Johann do?"

"Do you mean before, or after?" she asked.

Both, truly. "After. Since last night."

She nodded. "Early this morning, maybe just after the sun rose, he and two others from the village came in carrying Maravin. News spread quickly — that Maravin gave his life fighting Lasren, along with Zekiel and . . . and Tania. Johann went out to talk to others while I prepared the bodies. I've done it enough times." Her gaze went distant. "They were more drained than I was used to, though. No blood left at all. And then, of course, the bites on Maravin's neck." She met my eyes. "I know Lasren's bite marks. These weren't his."

I swallowed. I had expected to talk to Johann about this first, but caught in her gaze, I couldn't just stay silent. "I bit him."

"So you will bite us, then."

"No!" I lowered my voice. "Never again."

"I asked Johann about it. He didn't answer me — he just said what I told you before. You won't bite without permission. But while I didn't know Maravin well, I do know he wouldn't have given permission. He hated vampires, and after that night, he was horrified by having become one of the bitten. Even if he wasn't actually bitten."

"He was dying." I fought to keep the growl from my voice. "He would have died regardless after what Lasren did." As I spoke, I could see the situation again, smell the blood staining the snow, hear his heart beating its last as he bled onto the ground. "I needed the strength, and he would have died. So I drained the last of his blood."

"So he did give his life to kill Lasren," Sasha said. "Just not the way Johann made it sound."

The candle on the table guttered, the light in the room

jumping. "He did try to kill him," I said. "But he was sloppy about it. And then he was badly injured."

"Johann shouldn't have involved anyone else," Sasha said. "I told him that. And that's what's making him suffer the most, I think."

I narrowed my eyes. "What do you mean, making him suffer? Why would you tell him that?"

"You misunderstand," she said, and her heart rate picked up. I made sure I wasn't curling my lip, not exposing my fangs. "It's his own guilt making him suffer, not anything I said. He shouldn't have involved Maravin. He shouldn't have tried to recruit others to fight."

"Why? So you could all be content in being cattle and let him die for you?"

"How dare you." She turned to face me, her face pale. "We're not your cattle. Or did you lie about not taking blood from us?"

I growled low. "If you weren't cattle, why didn't you fight him? Why did you tell Johann to fight for you without anyone to help, if you were so sure he would die?"

"Because I expected him to," she snapped. "For a long time we thought you'd died that first night you disappeared. Every other hunter has. We knew just how powerful Lasren is. Was."

"Not that powerful," I said.

"Not for you, maybe." She took a deep breath. "But we're not vampires. We're not even hunters. Until this morning, I'd never thought I would see Johann and the others again. His crazy plan . . . Maravin returning without marks on his neck that first night . . . it was all unbelievable. I was certain Lasren would slaughter them all . . . or you would."

"You didn't trust me."

"Of course I didn't." Her gaze roved over me, her pulse beating fast in her neck. "You're a vampire. Everyone knows what they're capable of. I don't know why you came here, claiming you won't bite anyone. But if you're going to, get it over with."

Frustration made me grind my teeth together. "I said I won't and I won't. I'm here to see Johann, and . . . pay my respects. That's all."

"Your respects to Maravin?" She glanced at the door, at the direction of his snow-covered grave. "The man you killed?"

The words hurt. I knew I would never escape the memory, the knowledge, the power of that name. The first human whose blood I had drained. Hopefully, the only one. "The man who gave his life to kill Lasren," I said finally.

She sighed. "He never should have gone."

"So you would rather Lasren still be alive?"

"Of course not!" Her voice rang in my ears. "But three people are dead. Why? They weren't hunters. You were successful, and I'm grateful. But why did three people have to die for it needlessly?" She leaned against the desk, staring at the wooden floor. "For years and years now, I've seen people die. They come here exhausted, paler every morning, their knees burned and their hands ruddy with what must be physical labor. I tried everything to keep them healthy. The ones who survived were precious. But so many didn't. Their hearts gave out, they didn't have the strength to breathe. Others didn't return at all. And the worst were the ones who just . . . gave up."

Hearing her talk, I remembered what Lasren had told me. How sometimes, when humans were hypnotized, they would simply . . . die. Having their freedom taken over by a vampire made them lose their will to live entirely.

I had been alone in Lasren's castle, only seeing things from a vampire's perspective. Lessons about how to hypnotize, about the power I had over life and death and humanity . . . Now in the way Sasha stood, the way she spoke, I saw it from the other side. She had fought to assuage the worst of what Lasren had done, all while growing more and more sure that her efforts were pointless.

She knew more about being human, about the experiences in Brusque. I couldn't argue with that. All I had known about being human I had forgotten. But . . ."If they hadn't died last night, then in the next few dozen nights, three others would have died. And it would have been for nothing at all, simply more victims for Lasren's bloodthirsty madness."

Her shoulders shook as she sniffled. "I know. Part of me knows. But . . . Tania was one of my close friends."

Now the situation made sense. I didn't know what to say. The people I'd called, mere afterthoughts as I had used my power to call them, people who Lasren had then taken . . .

They were people with lives and loved ones left behind. That was what life truly meant. A life was marked by who cared when you were gone. Lasren, Dimresh . . . vampires who lived forever had no one left who grieved when they died. Only victims who celebrated freedom from their tyranny.

"I'm sorry," I said finally.

The room was quiet for a time, marked only by the quick beat of her heart and her breathing — sounds of human life I had missed in Lasren's castle.

"I only meant that if Johann cared for Maravin at all, he would regret Maravin dying. There's nothing wrong with fighting for something if you think you have a chance. Johann believed there was a chance. But you also have to be aware that people could lose their lives."

The far door creaked open. "Of course I was aware of that," Johann said.

# CHAPTER THIRTY-SIX

Johann!"

"Making trouble, Kaiden?" Johann said with a wry smile. He wore simple woolens that looked to be too small for him, the sleeping clothes clinging close for warmth and doing little to hide the muscular shape of his body. "I didn't expect to see you tonight."

"I . . . I wanted to see you. But if you're too tired, I can go."

"No, don't do that. We should talk. I'm not going to be able to sleep otherwise, I'm sure." I didn't know if I should be worried by his words or not. "Sasha, I assume Kaiden can stay here? I'll make sure he's on his best behavior."

She didn't smile back at his sleepy grin. "That's fine. But you need rest too, Johann. And don't . . ." She glanced at me then fell silent. I could guess what she'd wanted to say.

I wouldn't bite him. I wasn't even hungry. I just wanted to be close to someone and out of that horrible castle. I had been there, away from humanity, for too long.

The room he slept in smelled a bit like him, maleness and pine, but mostly like rotten wood, washed linens, and the remnants of old medicines. He sat down on the bed with a sigh, and I stayed by the door. The room was pitch dark, only the moon-glowing snow clouds from outside the window offering any light.

"I thought you might be in the castle still, trying to learn what you can from the old artifacts," he said.

"I'd rather do that together."

He smiled. "Heh. Well all right then. I may need a day or

257

two, though. I think I've slept all of three hours in the past two days, and I'm here because . . . well, I couldn't sleep in Maravin's old house." His smile faded.

This was the talk we needed to have first. "I'm sorry about Maravin."

"I know." He let out a shaky breath. "I know you are, Kaiden. And you should know it wasn't your fault."

"I bit him, though. You even said he wouldn't have wanted that."

"He wouldn't have. But he wouldn't have wanted to get bitten by Lasren either in days, months, or years time, and he would have. I heard part of what you told Sasha — that if people hadn't given their lives last night, then more would have died for nothing. Nobody wants to die in war. Nobody wants to lose people they care about. But it happens."

"Did you care about him . . . the same way you care for me?"

He tried to meet my eyes, although his gaze was slightly off-center. He couldn't see me as well in the dark, it seemed. "No. No, Kaiden, it wasn't the same. Not now. But it still hurts. I told you it wasn't your fault. But part of it feels like mine."

All that fear and anger I had, and for nothing. I should have been with him, not in Lasren's castle. I should have talked to him, and listened. "It wasn't your fault. What Sasha said —"

"It's not what Sasha said." He waved a hand. "I should have known better. I wanted Lasren's Brusque to be the Brusque I remembered. A place where people were constantly striving to do better, *be* better. Be the lone place of hope in a world overrun by vampires. I wanted them to *want* to fight back. When we were younger, Maravin was always the one who went with me to explore the temples, talk about the old empire, and help pick out goods for my parents to trade. When we would leave for the six months of traveling and then return, he was always there waiting for me, telling me about what I'd missed in the city. Seeing him again . . . it was like old times."

"He cared for you," I said. "Very deeply."

Johann tilted his head, his mouth turning down. "I know. When we were younger, we'd bonded over the fact that we both liked men. We were . . . close then." I grit my teeth, but let him speak. "It was fun, but nothing serious. We were younger. And now . . . well, he wanted to continue that, too. And I considered it, but ultimately decided not to."

"Why?" I didn't like how close my question was to a growl.

"It's been over a decade since then, since I was a teenager and I thought Brusque would always be a haven. And over a decade since I'd been trained to hunt and kill vampires and he'd lived in fear every night." He sighed. "We became different people. And Brusque became a different place."

"But you remember him . . . and your old life."

"True." He peered at me. "But time still changed things. Just because I have the memories doesn't mean I should let them always dictate what I do. You're missing many of yours, and you do okay. Aren't you, Kaiden?"

I twisted my will, and the candle on the window by Johann's bed lit up. He blinked and his eyebrows went up. "I've learned a lot, I suppose."

"I assumed you had since you beat Lasren so easily."

"The magic is part of me," I said. "But to use it the way I needed to, for the power I needed . . . I needed human blood."

"I don't blame you, Kaiden," Johann said. "Like I said before. I should have known better. I assumed you needed blood. No, more than that—I *knew* you would. I offered it to you. It should have been my blood you took, not Maravin's."

"No," I said.

"I never should have let him come, or put others at risk. I should have let you drink me in the cave."

"No!"

Johann stood, and even without his hunter's gear, he looked strong and powerful—imposing, for all a human could be to a vampire like me. He held up a finger, pointing it at my heart as though it were a stake. "Kaiden, listen to me!"

I fell silent.

"You need human blood to fight powerful vampires. We both know that now. You don't want to drink my blood because you're afraid. You care for me. That's fine. I care for you too. But it's selfish, Kaiden. If you had drunk my blood, if I had trusted my instincts and *made* you drink my blood, Maravin would be alive. For all we know, the other two would be alive also. And dammit Kaiden, I'm sure I would be too. I trust your control. I didn't want to pressure you before. I wanted to believe we could beat him like we beat Dimresh, together. But even then, you used your power. Your vampiric power." He pointed to the candle and then back to me. "You *are* a vampire, but you haven't lost your soul. You *won't*. And from here on, Kaiden, if you're going to fight with me, you will only bite those who agree to it. And that might be me. No more making yourself suffer, making others suffer, because you're afraid of what you are."

"I—"

"I've been thinking this over, Kaiden. Maravin didn't die for nothing. We killed Lasren. But his death meant even more than that—he showed us how to kill other vampires. You're powerful, just like Lucien was. And if you need human blood to give you that power, I'm going to make sure you get it."

He lowered his hand, taking a deep breath.

No. No, this couldn't be. "What if . . . what if I don't agree?"

Johann shook his head, dropping his gaze. "Then you can rule Brusque. Or Penthorn. Or if you want to fight, I'll assign you to a hunter you're not afraid to drink."

My stomach dropped. No. That was worse. "You'd leave me?"

"I'm sorry. But I needed to say that. I can't let your feelings . . . my feelings . . . take away this chance we have. I love you, Kaiden. You've given me more than I can imagine. But I'm afraid that if things keep going like this, people around us will be hurt needlessly." He sighed. "They already have been."

I didn't understand. Emotions flooded me — anger, at my Johann, rejecting me? Sadness. Despair. I didn't want to be alone. I hated that castle, and didn't want to be alone there again. But Penthorn . . . there was nothing left there for me. And another hunter? They would hate me. It wouldn't be Johann. I didn't want that.

But at the heart of it all . . ."Please don't leave me," I said.

"I don't want to," Johann said, and his voice cracked with pain. "But these days apart, and all of this, made me think. I missed you, Kaiden. I want to be with you. But I don't want you to be afraid of yourself, of what you can do, because of me. It hurts me when you push me away all the time. Even if it's over blood, if it's because you care for me, you still push me away, and it hurts. Do you understand?"

No. I didn't know. He was the one who didn't understand. There was so much still to tell him, about what I had learned from Lasren, about the old empire, about my strange memories and visions. I hadn't shared everything with him yet.

Maybe if I had . . . he wouldn't feel like I was pushing him away. Maybe if I showed him what my hunger meant, he would understand.

The last bit of resolve I had crumbled. It couldn't last, not with the fear of losing Johann right in front of me.

I swallowed. "If I show you what I can do," I said. "And . . . bite you." My mouth watered, and the thought made my body heat, even without the hunger. "Will you stay?"

Johann nodded. "I've always trusted you, Kaiden. You're a good man."

"Not tonight," I said. This was too much, too soon. "But . . . tomorrow. If the snow stops. Come to . . ." Not the castle. I hated that place. "The house where we stayed that first day."

"I'll be there," Johann said. "And for now, I should rest. Knowing you agree . . . I'll rest easier, Kaiden."

I nodded. I had expected . . . well, I hadn't known exactly what, after the guilt of getting Maravin killed had hung over me. But it wasn't this.

I was getting what I wanted, and what I didn't want, all at once. Johann trusted me. I was going to bite him, because he wanted me to. Because otherwise he would leave me alone.

Was this what it was like to be a lord?

"Good night," I said. "I'll see you . . . tomorrow."

"Good night, Kaiden."

I left the hospital through the front door, moving silently so as not to alert Sasha. People's voices echoed in the streets and from houses, whispers of uncertainty in some and happiness in others.

I would have to spend one more night alone. I doubted anyone in Brusque wanted to be reminded of vampires the first night in over a decade they were free of one.

But suddenly the long night ahead of me didn't seem so bad.

I had something to prepare for. I didn't know if it was something good or not.

# CHAPTER THIRTY-SEVEN

The painting of the old emperor stared down at me the next night, his blue eyes piercing. Cold air, even colder than the snow-filled air of the night before, blew down the hall. The lamps were unlit, shadows hanging at every corner.

I would come back. I would have to show Johann all of this soon, and explain what Lasren had told me about history — about myself. I would tell him everything.

But first, I would bite him. He was going to let me bite him. Not even that. He was *demanding* I bite him. I had to, or I would lose him.

But what if I lost him anyway?

I tugged at the neck of the new clothing I wore, black cloth pants and a silk shirt I had found in one of the rooms that had been filled with random stuff Lasren had likely stolen. There had been robes there too, along with silk dresses, but everything reeked of dust and age. Nothing smelled like Lasren, or anyone else, and I didn't mind wearing them. They were far better than the clothes I'd found the night before.

I hoped Johann would like the way I looked. I wondered if he would change his mind. I wanted this, but more than that, I craved it, and my craving frightened me. I could still remember the taste of his blood, in the cup he'd given me after Ana's attack . . .

My mouth watered. The craving was there, would always be there. Biting him would make it worse, like the first drink of the day would lead to many more.

But he trusted me. If I couldn't even try to control this

craving, he would leave me. This was something I had to face. I wished I knew what to expect, I wished I had some dreams or visions that would tell me what to do. But the day had been dreamless. And it was time to go.

The doors to the castle were still open, but the snow outside was unmarked except for the tiny prints from a squirrel that I would have thought should be hibernating. The storm had kept people close to Brusque. Or maybe they were still afraid.

Lights met my eyes from the city as I drew closer, and more lights stretched out beyond that. I had to think for a moment to remember what they were — the lanterns on the road Johann had told me about when we first arrived. They were lit again.

But the light that called me most was the one that glowed in a familiar house. Johann was there. Waiting for me.

I paused outside, swallowing hard. The night air smelled of pine from the forest, smoke from the lanterns, and humanity from the city. But laced beneath it was the scent of Johann, the familiar, tantalizing scent of the man I wanted. The man I would bite.

This didn't feel real. It was a dream, a fantasy. I couldn't do this.

The curtains on the window shifted and the door opened. "Kaiden," Johann called. "Come inside."

The scent of dust met my nose as I approached the house, but along with it was well-cooked meat and the spicy, cloying scent of wine.

I half-hoped he'd changed his mind. But that uncertainty vanished when he opened the door, greeting me with no shirt and his tight leather hunter's pants. Without the coat, they were . . . obscene. Tantalizing.

"I'm glad you came." The door clicked behind us. The house was empty, the table bare. I couldn't find the source of the wine and meat scent. But I wasn't thinking much about that.

Johann smelled delicious. He had washed, soap enhancing his maleness, his natural, luscious scent. His heart beat strong in his chest, in his neck, and he stood with one hand on his hip.

"I'm ready for this, Kaiden," he said. "I've been ready for a long time. Are you?"

"I . . ." My mouth watered. I wasn't hungry, not after what I had done to Maravin, but I still craved the taste and power in his blood. Johann's blood. The taste and closeness of the man I wanted, the man I'd missed as I'd stayed alone in that horrible castle.

"I want you," I said finally. "You know I do."

"Then let's celebrate our victory," Johann said. He moved toward me, taking my hand and interlacing his fingers with mine. His hand was so warm. "Come with me."

I was a powerful vampire lord, if Lasren was right. But right now I just wanted to do what Johann told me. I let him lead me through the house, into the back room, where soft woolen blankets covered a straw sleeping pallet.

And next to it on a wooden side table was a basin of water and a cloth like the ones I'd seen in the hospital. My stomach flipped, and I wasn't sure if it was fear or anticipation.

What was I doing? This was wrong. I couldn't bite him. I had killed Maravin, I was—

"Kaiden," Johann said. He turned to face me, taking my other hand as well, our held hands forming a circle between us. His warmth and closeness eased my racing mind. "It's going to be fine. I trust you. I need you to trust yourself. Trust your strength."

"I'm not strong without you," I said.

Johann smiled. "I'm here, Kaiden," he said. "I'm not going anywhere tonight. Now. How would you like to start? We can discuss what you learned from Lasren. We can plan our next mission after setting Brusque free. Or"—he leaned closer to me, his warmth a furnace—"I can show you how much I missed you. And you can prove to me how strong of a vampire you are. Planning should come after that, don't you think?"

His heart beat steadily. He was calm, ready. He wanted this. He wasn't afraid because he trusted me.

I trusted him. I trusted him to trust me. I had to. I had let him down before. I wouldn't do that again.

I let myself want. And I wanted him badly.

He was warm and muscular against me, his breath coming out in a gasp as I hugged him closer. I sniffed his hair, his chin, his neck. His heart began to beat faster, but along with it came the lightning scent of excitement, like the sky before a storm.

He turned his head and his lips met mine. Light at first, softness and warmth, his breath sweet. Testing, tasting.

Then his mouth opened, his lips molding to mine. His tongue flicked into my mouth and I tasted him truly, *my* Johann.

He was careful and I was careful. Our tongues met, his warm and wet, giving me life of a different sort, not blood but still the energy I craved. He kissed me hard and I kissed him back, relishing the contact. My body heated, my passion answering his. I pulled him closer, and his hand wrapped around my back, weak but still there, still holding me.

His tongue flicked against my fangs and then away, teasing me. A desire to bite flowed through me, but I didn't. Not yet. Not like this. There was more I wanted, and if I bit him, I was sure I wouldn't last.

He broke the kiss then, his breathing languid, his eyes sparkling. "Come on, Kaiden." He stroked his hand down my shoulder, along my arm, and took my hand. I loved the contact—I never wanted it to end. I let him pull me toward the bed.

The blankets were soft, masking the old straw that made up the sleeping pallet. Straw-scented dust met my nose, drowned out by Johann's scent, his nearness a constant distraction.

I sat next to Johann, resting my head on his shoulder. He was strong, for a human. The muscle there was taut, hewn from long practice training to fight things like me.

"Why?" I asked. Goosebumps formed on his neck as my words met his skin. My breath must lack the warmth of his. "After everything . . . why do you want to be with me . . . like this?"

He stroked my back, his fingers trailing up and down over my shoulders. "I admire you, Kaiden," he began. "I told you that before, all that time ago in Penthorn. I admire your strength. I admire your determination, your constant struggle to be a good person. In a world that for a long time I thought was dying, to see a thrall, and now a vampire, fight to be good, to fight for humanity is a dream. It's *my* dream. And you've made it come true." His eyes bored into mine. "The legend of Lucien in the flesh. Even greater, because it's real. It's right in front of me, all around me. You defeated Lasren. You freed Brusque. You're amazing, Kaiden."

"All of that . . . I don't deserve it," I said.

"How could you not?" His hand stopped moving.

The words tumbled out. "It's not strength that gave me my mind as a thrall," I said. Lasren's words echoed. "It's not determination, or anything like that. It's . . . blood."

Johann tilted his head. "How do you mean?"

"Lasren told me. The reason I'm like this, a thrall with a mind, a vampire with the power I have . . ." This felt like more of Lasren's madness, but his story made too much sense. "I have the blood of the old emperor. Descended from a bastard, he said. I was turned, but with the blood, with my . . . lineage, I have more power. It's not that I'm like the other vampires, it's more that I'm more of a vampire than they are. I have more of the . . . what Lasren called the gift." I hadn't thought like that until the words came to me. "Whatever noble blood they had that turned them, I have it naturally. So I have the power to take any territory. I'm stronger than Lasren, than any vampire. At least, I am if he was right."

Johann blinked. "So that's what the secret was. Why Dimresh . . . you said he called you old blood?"

"Yes." I could still remember my old master's ethereal beauty, something I didn't have, old blood or not. "The vampires now were once the nobility of the realm. Lasren said I was some sort of descendant of a bastard of the emperor. That's why I have the power I do." Why Lasren had begged for his life, begged to serve rather than be killed. "I'm not special. It's just . . . blood."

"No, Kaiden," Johann said. He put his hands on my shoulders, and I looked up. "That makes you more special. More of a good person." Excitement tinged his words. "You're even more of a dream than I thought."

"How?"

"Because even with all that power, power to take any territory you want, you chose humanity. With you . . ." He pulled me closer, into a hug, his heart beating against my chest. "If I can show you how to embrace your power, we can truly save the empire. I believe in that."

I let him hug me, hold me. I thought of Maravin, of the sound and sensation of his heart fluttering, then stopping, with my fangs in his neck. I thought of the black eyes of the thrall I had been, and the horror if that should happen to Johann. "I'm afraid," I said finally.

"Don't be." Johann took my hand, his grip warm and full of life. His scent surrounded me, soothing my fears with heat and desire. I ached for him. My cock swelled, and my fangs lengthened. Hunger and lust mingled.

"I don't want to hurt you," I said. "I don't want to . . . to control you. To kill you."

"You won't," Johann said. He put a hand on my chest, where my heart had once beat. "I believe in your strength, Kaiden."

He smelled so good. His blood surged through his body, giving his hands on me warmth, warmth that would fill my mouth and slake my hunger. "Why?" I asked.

"It's not just your strength," he continued. I shuddered as he drew a hand down to my hips, and then I gasped, hissing, as he drew down the fabric, exposing me to the air. "I believe in *you*. Completely." He drew back, his eyes shining. "I know you can control yourself. Now show me. Show me what you can do."

His excitement mingled with the spicy scent of arousal, heating the air between us. My mouth watered and craving filled me, a new kind of craving. This wasn't the hunger that came with not having blood, the hunger that had plagued me before. This was anticipation, excitement, a hunger closer to lust . . . and something deeper.

I wanted Johann. I wanted to prove him right. I wanted him to keep wanting me, to give him pleasure, even as I took my own.

"Yes, Kaiden," Johann said. He put his arm on my shoulder, drawing me closer once more, his breath washing over me. "Yes."

I kissed him then, and the kisses turned into licks, my tongue trailing over his lips, his chin, and then down his neck. He groped at my body, tugging at the shirt I had carefully picked out, and chill air met my skin. I hissed again as his hot hands teased my swollen length, Johann drawing my pants the rest of the way off. I hadn't pleasured myself since that time in the woods, alone with the taste of Johann's blood in my mouth. Now I would have that . . . *with* him.

This was it. All my dreams, my fantasies, my desires and fears mingling in this moment.

His breathing was deep and fast, his eyes half-lidded. He put a hand on his belt loop. I followed his guidance, expertly removing it. When I tugged down his pants, the scent of him grew stronger, pine and maleness and unmistakable lust. My cock throbbed and my mouth watered, my fangs scraping my tongue. His body was intoxicating, beautiful, and full of promise.

For a moment, we stared at each other. He was taut and muscular, radiating heat and living strength. I wanted to take it from him, to feel it in me. His erection was full and thick, fueled by the blood I would taste, sex and life I would consume. I licked my lips, leaving my mouth open to help me scent him. My fangs were obvious, and I knew Johann could see them.

"You can take me," he said.

I shook my head. "I . . ." I wanted to ask if he was truly all right with this, with what was going to happen. I licked my lips again, closing my mouth over my fangs. But I didn't say it. I knew his answer. It was clear in his dripping cock, his pounding heart and the scent of his desire. He wanted me, no matter what I was. What I could do to him.

I knew what I wanted, what my aching cock and ravenous hunger longed for.

I leaned over Johann, and he let me push him down, the soft blankets masking the sound of the hay-filled pallet compressed beneath our weight. This time when we kissed, our bodies molded together, his warm body against mine, his thick cock hot against my stomach. He was a furnace, a sparkling fount of warmth and life, promise in his body and his blood.

When I moved against him, lust flowed through me, and for the first time since I could remember, I felt almost alive.

Johann's heartbeat was loud in my ears, the thrumming of his blood through him echoing into me. It was wonderful, too much.

And when he reached for oil, slicking me with his hand, I gasped as though I needed t air, the sensation overwhelming. Pleasure surged as he stroked me, rising to a crest that made me grit my teeth against it, fighting the urge to spill and to take the blood I needed to do it. I had to hold on. I needed control. I wouldn't take what I needed, not yet, not until . . . Until . . .

"Please, Kaiden," Johann begged, his eyes searing with the same need I felt.

My body burned for him, with him. I moved toward him again, against him, on top of him. He moved with me, yielding to my grasping hands and strength, presenting his hips and entrance. Then he was all around me, his heat and pressure sending life and pleasure arcing deep into my body as he groaned. His cock swelled against my stomach, his body shuddering beneath mine. It was too much. Too good.

I moaned, my mouth watering, my fangs pricking my tongue. "Johann," I said aloud. I gripped the blankets, my fingernails curling into claws and shredding them.

Johann moaned beneath me, his body hot and tight. His arms wrapped around my back, his heels dug into my thighs, driving me in deeper, as though his strength mattered. He was weak, compared to me, but I still felt his strength in his fiery grip, in his living muscles, in the frantic heart that pounded his delicious blood through his body. I could feel it in my cock as I thrust into him, could feel his breathing wash over me.

For a moment, I knew this was what I had always wanted. Nothing more.

His body grew hotter, his heart beating faster. He shuddered and gasped out. "Kaiden, please."

His cock was hot and thick between us, the blood in it calling to me. His body called to me, every part of it, a drumbeat of sensation and life that told me he would come. He was going to come, and if I didn't bite him now, he would do it alone.

I wanted to come. I wanted *him*. I swiped my tongue at my lips, my fangs threatening to pierce my gums. He was going to come. I thrust harder. I couldn't come yet. Not unless I bit him. The pleasure he was giving me was life. Blood would complete it. I wanted it, wanted it desperately.

He moaned and shuddered beneath me, his eyes meeting mine, heavy-lidded and filled with desire. "Now, Kaiden," he gasped. "Please, I need you. Just . . . take me."

I opened my mouth, taking in the scent of him. He tilted his head and closed his eyes, the vein in his neck throbbing in time with his heart, with the pleasure surging in my cock.

I lowered my head, scenting his neck, and then tasted him, my tongue flicking over the soft skin. He trembled. Then my fangs broke the skin, drawing rivulets of blood.

He moaned and came, his body shaking and his hot seed coating my stomach in living heat. His pulse beat, fainter than the one in his chest, but still powerful, as he shuddered through his pleasure. The blood dripping from his neck tinged my tongue, mingled with my own need to come.

I closed my eyes, biting down hard. My fangs sank deep the rest of the way into his neck. He jolted against me.

This wasn't like biting Maravin at all. And it wasn't like taking blood from a cup.

Ecstasy washed over me. Johann's blood spurted into my mouth like his cock spurted against me, the blood of someone alive and active. Johann groaned, his hands gripping my shoulders. I gripped him back, pinning him down, Johann powerless beneath my hands and my cock and my fangs.

It was overwhelming, beautiful, and too much. I shuddered, my own climax looming. I bit down harder. Johann's heartbeat flowed into me, through my fangs, the pleasure from my cock in him and my fangs in him washing through me. He was mine. I had his life, the pleasure he felt, mixed together in something that was beyond mere taste. I took power and I gave pleasure, which was given back to me. This was better than anything I had experienced. Better than any fantasy I could have had.

My fangs tore skin, drawing more blood that filled my mouth. Then I was coming too, shaking against him. His grip slackened, his moans mingling with mine. My eyes shut, and for a moment, I did nothing but feel.

For a moment, I was alive again.

Mouthful after mouthful. More than the cup he had given me, much more. And then his heart skipped. I felt it stutter. I knew that feeling. I had felt it when I killed Maravin.

I would kill Johann if I didn't stop.

I didn't have to stop. The pleasure didn't have to end. My fangs were in him. He was mine. All I had to do was drink. He had wanted this. He had given himself to me.

I could keep going. Human hearts skipped beats all the time. He wasn't dying, not yet. I bit down harder, another mouthful. Another. I could take what I wanted, make this last as long as I could. Adrenaline spiked the taste, adding to the spicy scent of sex and making everything better.

His hands were on me, my cock softening inside him, but the pleasure, the life, would last longer. He was just so good.

He sighed against me, his breath warm. His heart fluttered again. He could give more. His arms still wrapped around me, and his hands on my back, pulling me close, felt weak.

I loved this. I loved him. I never wanted it to end.

But if it didn't end now, I'd never have it again.

My body screamed at me to keep biting, keep drinking.

But instead I opened my mouth, my fangs leaving his vein. Blood trickled down his neck, and I lapped it up, faint sparks of pleasure and pain reminding me of what I had just had. What I had just given up.

Johann sighed again, and without my fangs in his neck, I could meet his eyes. His skin was paler than I'd ever seen it. Blood still dripped from his neck, and my fang marks were red and wet. The smell was tantalizing.

"You see, Kaiden?" he said. He breathed deep, in and out, weak but alive. "You can control your hunger."

I had done it. I had bitten him but I had stopped. I reached for him, stopping just short of touching the bloody marks on his neck.

"Was the pain . . . bad?"

"No." Johann grinned. "Well, in a way, but . . . I don't mind pain. It made it . . . intense." He reached for me, his hand on my arm. "We'll have to do it again sometime."

Do it again. I wanted to, but . . ."You need time," I said. Being with Johann was too good to risk losing forever. Whether forever meant me never biting him . . . or not stopping.

"We'll have time," Johann said. He smiled at me.

I rested my head on his shoulder, and he put his hand on my back.

"That means . . . you won't go?" I said.

"Never."

# Chapter Thirty-eight

Johann slept on the pallet where we had made love. His neck was healing already, but my fang marks would always be there.

A smile curved his face, even in sleep. His breathing was slow and deep, the breathing of someone without a care in the world. Very few people slept like that anymore.

But he had won a victory. Two victories, really. And so had I.

I didn't need sleep, not at night. But I was content to sit and be near him, enjoying the sensation of him near me, knowing he was safe. And most likely safer here, where Lasren was dead and no vampires or thralls roamed for miles and miles, than anywhere else in the world.

And finally, for the first time, I knew he was safe with me. The taste of his blood still stained my tongue, and the desire for more would always be there. But I didn't need it. It was under my control, at least for now. When the hunger returned, or I needed more power . . . no.

I let myself be content with the way things were. Johann wouldn't leave me. I could be with him. That was enough.

For a few hours as the moon drifted overhead and the candle on the nightstand burned down, I let myself relax.

The moon had begun its descent when Johann woke, blinking. I called my power, willing the flame on the candle to burn brighter.

"Kaiden." He yawned. "I must have fallen asleep. Still here, huh?"

"Of course." I moved back to the bed, and he took my hand.

"I thought you might get bored just watching me sleep. Or want to stay somewhere a bit nicer, like that fancy castle."

My upper lip curled at the thought. "I hate that castle," I said.

Johann tilted his head. "Why? You didn't hate Dimresh's castle, did you?"

"I . . . don't know." I didn't know quite where this strong emotion came from. The thought of Lasren's madness, the place where I had killed Maravin, the rooms and rooms maintained by humans and filled with stolen objects . . . all combined to make it a distasteful place. "It's full of death," I said finally.

"That's true." Johann sat up, the blankets falling off his warm, bare chest. "But we will need to go back. All the information we could want is likely there. Not to mention materials for weapons, like all those statues you mentioned."

Of course. Relaxation never lasted. Brusque may be safe, but the world wasn't, and hunters were still needed.

I was still needed.

"You know, Kaiden," Johann said. "If Lasren was telling the truth, and you have so much power . . . with me, you could kill other vampires like Lasren with ease. With your power, you could take back every city. Maybe even the capital. If you're truly a bastard prince, it could be your right, couldn't it?" His eyes sparkled.

He sounded almost like Lasren. *My right.*

"I do want to help you," I said. "I want to be with you."

"And do you want more?" Johann asked. "With you . . . my dream can come true, Kaiden. No, more than my dream. The merchant road will be safe to travel, but even more, we truly can take back the empire from the vampires. It won't just be Brusque returned to its former glory. The entire world could be!"

I loved how sure he sounded, how happiness dripped from his words. But deep down, familiar fear grew.

"We can kill them," I said. "Carefully. But . . . there may be more to it than just killing the vampires. The old nobles."

Johann nodded, his eyes narrowing. "How do you mean?"

"I mean . . ." It was hard to put into words, how I understood my power and the tie between life and death. The visions and memories, probably important, that I still didn't understand. "I think there is more to it than just the nobles. They are vampires, but . . . what made them become that way?"

Johann breathed out, nodding in slow realization. "That's a good point. I assume . . . Lasren didn't leave any clues?"

"No." Maybe. He had been mad, hadn't he? Maybe I should have paid more attention to his ramblings. "If there's anything more to learn . . ."

"It will be at the castle." Johann nodded. "I know you don't want to, Kaiden. But we'll have to go back, to learn what we can. And . . ." He stood up from the bed, the blankets revealing his nakedness, his well-muscled stomach and thighs that elicited heat in me even after the satisfaction from earlier. "I think we should invite other hunters here. The barracks are near Penthorn, but now that we have Brusque . . . you don't want to rule here, right?"

"No. I want to stay with you. To help you."

"I know you do." The muscles beneath the freshly-healing bite on his neck twitched when he nodded, and I wondered if it hurt. "So we make Brusque a new location for the Order. We expand the order and train new recruits here and in Penthorn. We make sure the city is never taken again. It might take all winter, but we can turn it into the safe haven it was before Lasren."

I nodded. That was a good plan.

"And then . . . you and I will keep our momentum going.

In spring, when the days get long again, we can set out to expand humanity's freedom. We take back other cities, one by one. Telmet, Tarek, Dremasque, and even the capital." He moved to his bag, taking out a sheaf of paper and digging for a quill and a jar of ink. "I'll send a note now. This is fantastic, Kaiden."

I had to smile, a thin-lipped one that hid my fangs. Johann was happy. We had freed Brusque. We were going to change the world.

But it wouldn't be nearly as easy as he made it sound. I knew that. I was sure he knew it too as he slapped the paper down onto a desk, sending dust pluming as he began to write. But killing Dimresh hadn't been easy. Killing Lasren hadn't been done without sacrifice. And yet we had done both, and learned from the experiences. I didn't believe in my right as a bastard of the emperor, and I didn't know what to make of my visions and dreams. But together . . .

Voices came from outside. I turned. Even Johann heard them after a few seconds. He quickly threw on his pants and coat.

Snow still blanketed the streets, but it hadn't stopped people from gathering outside, torches flickering from what must be . . . it took me a moment to remember. Bendy Street.

"It sounds like . . ." Johann said as we left the house.

"Merchant arrived!" a reedy voice called through the night. "Merchant!"

Johann narrowed his eyes, and I repeated it for him. He broke into a smile.

"A merchant! They must have seen the lights." He pulled his cloak around him, and after a moment, grabbed a scarf from his bag and wound it around his neck. "C'mon, Kaiden."

I followed him into the streets of Brusque, half following the sounds of humanity and half trusting Johann's knowledge of the winding avenues. As we came closer, more and more light spilled onto the streets, mixtures of lanterns overhead and lantern-light burning in windows and open doorways.

"Is it really a merchant?" We joined a growing group of humanity, a mother and her son, judging by their similar scents, falling into step with us. "They never come."

"The vampire is really gone," the mother said, wonder in her voice. "It will be like the old days that my mother told me about."

I kept silent. They didn't recognize what I was. Johann met my eyes, smiling, and kept quiet too.

The wagon had stopped on Bendy Street, and the merchant was talking to a man I didn't recognize but who smelled of hops. "There are plenty of empty houses," he was saying. "But I suppose I should restart the inn business, shouldn't I?"

"I wasn't planning to trade here, but the snows were bad, my axle is run down, and I saw the lights. I'd heard tales of a crazy vampire who hunted others and thought maybe I'd take the risk. Lights on the Brusque road always meant hospitality. Always was impulsive."

It took me a moment to recognize the voice, but Johann got it first. "Aldrose!" he called.

"I'll be. Johann? You really did it, didn't you?" Aldrose stepped forward, others parting while even more began to gather, coming from houses or from the inn itself. Children came too, staring at the wagon, some of them whispering about the treats that must be inside that their mothers had told them about.

"And you." Aldrose nodded at me. A few others around me took second glances. But no one ran. "So, guess I should tell the other merchants, eh?

"Brusque is free," Johann said. "Please do tell them. And . . . I don't know what you've brought, but . . ."

"We could use it," the innkeeper said. "We have all sort of things, and we need to open up Brusque again. Without the vampire . . ." A rustle went through the crowd, and then the innkeeper raised his voice. "Without that damn vampire, we can finally live again!"

A cheer went up, one that sounded as though it had erupted before, but this was the first time I'd heard it. Johann cheered too.

Maybe it was the scent of all the excitement around me, or the knowledge that the world was so ready to recover after the vampires were killed. Or maybe it was just Johann's blood. But suddenly, Johann's plans of freeing the world felt real. "We could really do this, couldn't we?" I said aloud. "We could put an end to the vampires. All of them."

"That's the dream, Kaiden," Johann said. "Something you made possible."

"Not just me," I said. He smiled. "You. Because you believed in me." Even when I hadn't believed in myself.

This was a small thing, a merchant arriving in a once-dead, isolated city. But it meant a lot more.

There was more to do. There always was. But I finally felt a sense of true victory. And even more than that, even better, with Johann beside me and people around us cheering as the merchant began to unload the wagon, I felt almost human.

# YOU MAY ALSO ENJOY THE FOLLOWING FROM eXTASY BOOKS INC:

*Thrall*
Ravon Silvius

Excerpt

The man my master had commanded us to kill stood on the other side of the river. His wagon creaked as the wooden wheels rolled over the bridge. The man was a mere shadow, even to my enhanced eyesight, silhouetted against the rising moon.

To my left, another of us chattered her teeth, her fangs emerging from her lips. My own stomach growled at the thought of the warm blood that would gush from the man's veins and feed us. Until now, Master had forbidden us human blood. This would be the ultimate prize. So much better than the deer and other forest creatures I'd been feeding from.

The wagon moved slowly, the horses straining to pull it across the arched bridge. There were two, both with dark-colored coats. One wore a frayed blanket across its back, and the other limped as though its shoes fitted improperly. This man was clearly no wealthy merchant.

One of us hissed, a sibilant, high-pitched sound that only those like us could hear. An answering hiss came from the bushes near the river. Our master had given us the plan, and we would follow it.

The lead horse flicked an ear. The man in the wagon seat shifted his weight.

As soon as the first horse set hoof on the grassy bank, the one to my left attacked. Four others joined her, dark shapes against the light of the moon, swarming toward the animals and their pumping, flowing blood.

I cursed in my mind. I had been turned too recently, and compared to them I was slow. I swallowed saliva, my fangs pricking my lower lip, and leaped forward, dashing through the forest.

Then light flooded the trees.

The four who'd run ahead screamed, their hissing drowned out by the sizzling of bodies exposed to solar light. I ducked behind a tree, screwing my eyes shut. Heat from the light prickled on my skin.

This was no weak man the master had sent us to eat, a gift to us. This was a vampire hunter.

And I was just a thrall.

The light died, fading to a dull orange glow over the horizon. A solar flare would work only once. I knew that from . . . somewhere. My life before, I supposed.

My muscles tensed when the man spoke—a word to his horses, or perhaps just a comment to himself. The man was mine. The other servants were dead. I would kill the hunter, take all his blood for myself. Me, the newest, weakest servant, able to take human blood. The command tightened my muscles further and pounded in my head. My master's order—Kill.

I peered out from the edge of the trees, my vision sharpening with bloodlust. The man's heart beat in a slow, steady rhythm. The light from the wagon made my eyes water, even used up as it was, but it couldn't hurt me. Not any longer.

The hunter sat in the wagon seat, a weapon of some sort across his lap. He wore tight leather trousers, and my gaze lingered over his muscular thighs. For a moment I imagined taking more than just blood.

The thought died quickly. Since my master had turned me, any lust but that for blood never lasted.

The man had light brown hair, though it appeared red in the fading light of the solar flare. Dark eyes scanned the forest and then settled on me.

I froze, my own thoughts tangled, my body screaming for me to take his blood. His scent—human and sweat mixed with woodsmoke and the bouquet from the village over the river—filled my nostrils.

He raised the weapon. I now saw it was a crossbow outfitted with a wooden stake. His heartbeat was steady. In that moment, I knew I would die.

My master's orders still screamed in my brain, in my very being—Kill. I was a servant. I obeyed. I was a weak vampire servant, nothing more. But I knew I would die if I attacked.

I didn't want to die.

His horse snorted. The hunter held his crossbow trained on my heart. The sharp wooden stake that it would fire jutted from the barrel. A servant like me would never survive that.

I could attack. I wanted to leap, to try to sink my teeth into his veins, to obey the orders of the one who'd made me what I was. My teeth ground against each other, and my fangs drew blood from my lower lip.

Instead I turned and fled without truly knowing why. No shot came from the forest.

The unusual silence in the forest as I ran back distracted me from my hunger, and it took me a moment to remember that every other servant was dead. I was truly alone.

I hadn't known them. It shouldn't matter. We hadn't even spoken, only interacting when we fought during our nightly hunts for deer or other animal blood. Without them, there would be more for me. I should be glad.

But happiness, like anything else, faded quickly. I fought

to keep running, to ignore the command in my mind that told me to turn back and kill the man I'd been ordered to kill. Doing so would be suicide. He was a hunter. He killed things like me for a living.

It was only when I entered the castle grounds that I wondered if my master would be angry with me.

The gates soared over my head, carvings of wolves seated atop iron bars. The castle blocked the view of the mountain that both overlooked it and kept it hidden from curious onlookers. Gray stone and old rotted wood melded against dead trees.

I took my usual path, through dusty hallways on the fringes of the main keep. Inside, thousands of scents mingled, mold mixing with cold stone and dead leaves and the sharp scents of the other thralls. Their scents would fade. The scent of blood wound through it all, and saliva filled my mouth.

I followed the scent, my bare feet silent on the cold stones, and found my master where the stone became plush rugs. A shiver of fear went down my spine but faded quickly, just like every other emotion or feeling I had.

"What are you doing here?" My master's voice chased away everything else. "I still sense that man on my territory."

The vampire who had made me strode closer. His blond hair was tied back with a blue ribbon, and deep blue eyes met mine. He frowned, and I ducked my head, curling in on myself like a cur. I should have attacked the hunter and been done with it.

"Where are the others?" my master said, his voice fainter, the presence of his power decreased on my shoulders and chest.

"Dead," I managed. "The man was a hunter."

"Hm." My master turned on his heel, striding down the hallway. With a whisper of his power, I was compelled to follow. He always paced when he thought.

My master's shoes clicked on the stone floors, the sound loud and echoing down the halls. I heard tiny hearts beating from creatures racing along the floor and outside the open windows, the blazing fast pulse of mice, and once the slower beat of a cat that must be hunting them.

"Why did you return?" my master asked. I tore my gaze away from the bare stone walls.

"I . . . I could not kill him."

"I ordered you to kill him." My master stopped walking, pivoting on his heel like a dancer. He was far more graceful than a human dancer would be, though. "I'm surprised you returned. Why?"

I blinked, mind racing. My master stared at me, blue eyes steady, his mouth a firm line. His shoulders were thrown back and square.

"I thought you might like to know that he's a hunter," I said, my fangs snapping on the words. "He's likely hunting you."

"I feed only on the unwanted, the criminals and the freaks of the village. I am a boon to those humans. Why did they send a hunter?"

The words brought a strange stabbing pain in my chest that it took me a moment to place. Distant, hazy memories, ones that used to matter, played through my mind.

I had been unwanted. Penniless, homeless, a slave to drink who everyone always taunted. The son of a whore, never amounting to anything. I remembered little of my life, fits and flashes, but I knew that much.

But not anymore. My master had made me strong. Nearly two months ago, he'd given me new life.

"Well?" my master snapped, bringing me back to the present and to the drafty halls of the castle. "Did the hunter speak to you, make demands, or any such thing?"

"No." I had not heard his voice. "He killed the others with a solar weapon. He was going to kill me with a stake, but I ran."

"A solar weapon." My master's words were cold. "A relic of the old Empire. Foolish to waste it on thralls, but he may have more of them. Hunters tend to know more history than I'd like."

I didn't respond. There weren't many things that could kill a vampire lord like my master. I supposed a flare was one of them.

"And now you are my only servant." My master frowned. "A disobedient servant." I ducked my head.

"Go and feed on a deer in the forest. Do not enter the city. And stay very, very far from that hunter. I have nothing to fear from him, but you do." My master waved a hand. "Dismissed."

Before I could move, my master vanished the way he always did when he was done with me. His command thrummed in my brain. I headed toward the end of the hallway, out through a door of rotting wood and mold.

The soft wind rushing and the chirps and chitters from the forest quieted the clamor in my mind that competed with my master's order. I had every intention of following his command—my fangs lengthened, saliva filling my mouth at the thought of a meal, even if it was just animal blood. I had yet to taste a human.

But another part of me wondered, even as I crouched into a hunter's stance and listened for my prey, about the hunter and what my master was going to do. He had used his solar weapon, but he might have more. He might be hunting my master.

Of course, my master wasn't stupid enough to charge a hunter as we had. He was no mindless servant.

Then again, I supposed as I picked up the gamey scent of deer, I wasn't mindless either—I'd survived.

I wondered if my awareness, my mind, would last. The others had been older, had served Master for far longer than I. It had been a mere two months since master had drained my blood and made me what I was now. They had been turned years ago, I think, and the only words they'd ever spoken to me with any routine had been "move, weakling," or "wait your turn." They always took the largest share of any animal kills we made. And they had leaped mindlessly to their deaths.

Once, weeks into my turning, they'd told me about a servant who'd taken a human from the village, who had crossed the river to work on the roads. He hadn't had Master's permission. He had been the oldest, according to the female among us, and finally he'd lost his mind completely. It happened to all of us eventually — we turned into animals.

Master had killed him. I supposed that was fitting. He would kill me, too, if I didn't obey.

A strange fear froze me in place at the thought, and a gust of wind scattered the scent of the deer I'd been tracking. I wondered if all vampire servants feared death the way I did. The others had rushed to their demise without thought. And I'd already died once, in a way, hadn't I?

I remembered very little of that. My master had stood over me, his blond hair a halo in the light of the streetlamps. The cloying scent of alcohol and my own vomit, along with the trash that had littered that alley, still singed my nose in my memory.

"What are you doing here?" he'd asked, his fangs sharp and long. I had thought he was beautiful.

When I'd opened my eyes again, it was to the stone wall of the castle hallways and to a hunger that never left.

The scent of the deer blew with the breeze again, thicker and more pungent. Prey was close. My memories scattered like leaves as I broke into a silent, loping run.

The deer stood out in my enhanced vision, standing like a fool in the light of the stars. I leaped, closing my hands around its neck.

Its hooves drew fiery trails down my sides. A lucky kick caught my knee. Bone popped, but I held on, sharp fingernails digging into the fur of its neck. My jaw clenched, my fangs puncturing the skin of my lip. If I bit now, I would miss the vein and spill precious blood on the leaves.

Vertebrae cracked, and the animal went limp. My vision fuzzed. Drool dripped from my mouth as I leaned down to finally sink my fangs into my prize. It was strange not to have others fighting me for it.

I quickly sucked the animal dry, my mouth filled with the coppery taste of life. It infused my body, filling me with energy and power. My knee cracked once more as the kneecap slid back into place, and the pain of the torn skin faded as it mended itself.

I stood, the dark night a little brighter with the energy of the deer's blood within me.

"Hold there," a voice demanded, and I whirled.

The hunter emerged from the tree line, his stake-loaded crossbow in one hand. In his other he held a lantern, and it took me only a moment to realize it was another solar flare. He'd come prepared.

"You," he said. "Servant. Stop right there."

# About the Author

Ravon Silvius lives in a tiny apartment with two tiny cats in a tiny town in the United States. Despite the cramped living quarters, Ravon enjoys coming up with big ideas for novels, with some plots coming from Ravon's findings as a neuroscience researcher and others coming purely from Ravon's imagination.

www.ingramcontent.com/pod-product-compliance
Lightning Source LLC
Chambersburg PA
CBHW071305170626
46809CB00001B/337